EZEKIEL'S JOURNEY: ONE MAN'S EPIC JOURNEY TOWARD FULFILLMENT

(EZEKIEL'S JOURNEY BOOK I)

JOHNNY GUNN

WOLFPACK
PUBLISHING
— EST 2013 —

Ezekiel's Journey
(Ezekiel's Journey Book I)

Johnny Gunn

Paperback Edition
© Copyright 2018 Johnny Gunn

Wolfpack Publishing
6032 Wheat Penny Avenue
Las Vegas, NV 89122

ISBN: 978-1-62918-723-5

I

BOOK ONE: THE JOURNEY BEGINS

EZEKIEL HAWTHORNE, THIRTY-YEARS-OLD, HAD ONE OF HIS mules, Tobias, packed and ready to go. He set the saddle on Ruth, his other blue mule, took one last look at Elizabeth's grave, set himself deep in the stirrups, and on this first day of March 1850, headed out into the great plains. Hundreds of millions of undulating acres filled with billions of blades of grass moving in grand waves of beauty, grace, and motion were waiting for him. His little plot of ground would blend into the natural landscape within two or three seasons, the log cabin would rot into dust, the grave markers would disappear, and for future travelers, Zeke would be an unknown factor.

Hawthorne stood about six feet tall and weighed in at around two hundred pounds. His head was covered in thick auburn hair that tended to hang in ringlets when he let it get a bit long. His eyes, deep set with bushy eyebrows, were a deep green. As one might expect from a journeyman cabinetmaker and blacksmith, his hands were broad with long strong fingers, his wrists were as wide as his forearms, and his biceps and shoulders were massive.

Despite his huge size and obvious strength, Zeke was as soft as a newborn lamb, with a smile that could be seen half an acre away. His eyes mellowed visibly when around Elizabeth and the children, before the bad times had come. He could sing songs in more than one language, recite poetry in Latin or Greek, and had a sense of humor that caught those around him off-guard on more than one occasion.

He forced himself to only remember Elizabeth as the vibrant wife she had been for the first many years, not the sickly woman now buried in the soft, fragrant loam of the prairie. Two children, Todd and Mary, lay with her, along with every dream the man ever had.

Well educated and wise in the ways of nature; that's how many would characterize Zeke, but not Zeke himself. His dreams included an active farm with ample food for a large family, meat animals enjoying the fruit of the prairie, and hard but good work for him and Elizabeth. Basically, Zeke wanted the simple pleasures of an established farmer with a fine family.

He was a journeyman metal worker, a cabinetmaker, a student of classical literature and, for the last ten years, a farmer. He was twenty years old when he'd married Elizabeth and they had settled on the outskirts of civilization, filled with the splendor of anticipation. He and his lovely bride built a simple cabin from the existing woodlands they homesteaded, and he had his forge and all the tools necessary for metalworking.

In the evening, sitting near a warm fire, Zeke would read aloud from his many books, Elizabeth knitting or sewing, enraptured by his voice and what he was reciting. "Don't ever stop reading to me," she said often. "Imagine, Ezekiel," she never called him Zeke, "our children will know of classical literature and without benefit of a school."

"Yes, and they will be trained in metallurgy and cabinet-making." He paused, chuckling to himself, "and know how to slop hogs and clean stalls."

The edge of civilization; Zeke called their homestead, and the prairie supplied some of their victuals by way of antelope, deer, rabbits and many game birds, with plentiful fish available in nearby waterways.

The farm slowly took shape as the two of them put in more hours than most clocks allowed. A small creek ran through the woodlands and Zeke carved irrigation ditches from the raw ground, plowing enough of the prairie to have grains, potatoes, corn, and beans, aplenty. Elizabeth's vegetable garden flourished, and Zeke arranged to have a small flock of sheep for meat, milk, cheese, and fiber. He brought in some hogs, and a flock of egg-laying chickens to round out the little farm.

For the mules, harness leather was purchased, but single trees, double trees, and all the other wood and metal parts needed to plow the ground, Ezekiel manufactured. His plow was as sturdy as any in the territory, and his cultivators were the envy of his neighbors, the few there were.

All the windows in the cabin were hardwood framed and had thick hardwood shutters that closed and bolted from the inside. He made the iron hinges and clasps for the bolts, and even though there hadn't been any Indian problems for several years, he felt that type of defense was necessary.

Elizabeth's first pregnancy ended with a miscarriage, and it was another two years before she became pregnant with Todd. The boy was born vigorous, but became sickly after his second year and died during a cold and blustery winter that produced five feet of snow on the cabin roof. Zeke was a broken man that winter, and it was only the strength and love of Elizabeth that kept him going. Spring planting, a couple of spring lambs and a calf brought life back to the man's heart, and his dreams didn't die.

Zeke was a strong man but he wore his heart and emotions on the outside. Not having that big family he so desired, hurt deeply. "Have I done something wrong, Elizabeth? Have I angered the gods?" Zeke was not a religious man but had a great belief in nature, or as he was wont to say, "the natural way." He was deeply philosophical in his understanding of this "natural way," and felt if man didn't follow along with it, there would be repercussions.

"I don't believe it is fate that drags us through this life, but I do believe that if we don't live within the bounds of nature, she will fight back. Have I done something wrong in how we work with nature? Is this nature's way of demanding our adherence to her law?"

That was his heart talking, not his mind. He had, as he put it, a long, one-sided conversation with himself and put aside such prattle. The farm continued to flourish under the large man's guidance.

Elizabeth got pregnant for the third time the next year, but the birth of Mary was long and hard. Mary was crippled from the physical affects. Elizabeth never regained her strength, and little Mary slowly ebbed into her death at sixteen months. Elizabeth followed the next year.

Zeke met some people moving through the prairie not long after. They told him there was gold in California, thousands of miles to the west. He didn't believe the stories, but knew that he could no longer live on his farm without Elizabeth; without the possibility of a family, without his dreams.

More travelers through the area brought the same news, gold in California, but there was more. Zeke and his plow mule were working up some ground late in the fall when a small group stopped on their journey westward. "You folks headin' to the gold fields in California? Seems like most of the country is goin' that way."

The man leading the group of five wagons, heavily loaded with people and provisions, not to mention tons of furniture and implements, stepped off his tall horse. "No, sir, not Californy, I'm taking these fine folk to Oregon country. These families are farmers, like you, sir, and I can tell you, you won't find better ground to farm than what's there in Oregon."

The emigrants set up camp in one of Zeke's open pastures for the night, and he listened to stories of good soil, plenty of water, and enough wild game to keep a salt barrel filled year-round. Many of the parties that had either stopped overnight or just stopped to pass the time of day, had discussed the wild Indians out west, and Zeke asked the folks if they weren't worried about having Indian problems on their journey.

"We have our muskets with us," the trail boss said, "so we can fight 'em off if they give us any trouble."

"I only count twelve men in your group, sir," Zeke said.

7

"I don't know if you can fight off very many of those savages. Heard some mighty terrible stories, I have." He shook his head some at the casual way the man had discussed the savages, remembering stories from his youth about Indians in the Ohio Valley. "Have you been to Oregon, yourself, sir?" he asked the wagon master.

"No, but I have excellent maps and letters from several families who have made the great trek across our frontier. Your farm is very nice, sir, and I feel you would do well in Oregon."

When Zeke went out to milk the cow in the morning, the last of the wagons were pulling away and he waved them goodbye. *I don't think those folks know what they're riding into. Don't seem to be properly prepared to travel clear across this here continent.*

Growing up in the 1820s, Zeke had read everything he could get his hands on dealing with the Lewis and Clark expedition, and felt these people were not being led properly.

Visions of a new life in fresh country; finding good soil with lots of water, starting over, maybe even being able to have a family, occupied his mind through the long, cold, early spring, and by the time he should have been getting ready to spring plow and plant, Zeke decided to move on. He knew he needed to leave his broken dreams, to just go somewhere and do something.

He knew a lot about metals and iron and he knew what refined gold looked like but not gold buried in rock or the sand and mud of a river. He quickly remembered, though, that he didn't know the first thing about raising corn and beans when he and Elizabeth had first gotten married. He had to chuckle over that as he lit his pipe, and dreamed good thoughts.

With his back straight and his jaw set, he told himself that night that he was going west. He left the next morning with a sack of corn, a sack of beans, some salted meat, a musket, a scattergun, two pair of overalls, two shirts, and two pair of boots. He also packed knives, flint, powder, lead, and a battered old slouch hat that had the flavor of the prairie written all over it.

He spent two days worrying about his tools. "What will I do about my forge and anvil... my hammers and tongs?" he asked his mules, the walls, and the implements as well. His decision was the most difficult of his life, but he recognized that he could not take hundreds of pounds of iron and wood working tools on this journey.

Unlike most of the westward bound Argonauts, Zeke was educated and carried the wisdom of his father and grandfather. He was more than just a thinker, though. *My dream with Elizabeth is gone, and I must find myself now. Who am I, and why am I here?* He'd never had trouble keeping his mind busy; whether working over a forge, behind a plow, or with hammer and chisel. In his mind, this trip west would be glorious.

It won't be the gold fields of California, though, he decided. It would be Oregon and its favored soil, sweet water, and fair weather.

Finally, his mind settled, he was packed, and it was time to go. He remembered what that wagon master had said. "The Willamette Valley is where you want to go, sir. It's Oregon or bust, for us."

2

GROWING UP IN THE VERY EARLY 1800s IN THE OHIO
Valley, Zeke understood wilderness, was a fine outdoorsman, a crack shot with his musket and shotgun, and
understood some of the ways of the Indians native to that
country. He would come to understand that the natives of
the plains were considerably different.

In his diary, he wrote, "I don't want to follow in the
tracks of the thousands I've seen heading to the western
lands. I plan to venture cross-country on my own track,
letting the sun and stars be my guide." He and his mules,
Ruth and Tobias, left the little farm just as first light
brightened the heavens on a course northwest.

"I have a rough idea of where Oregon is, I've read just
about everything ever published by or about Lewis and
Clark. I have my little compass, I have the stars and the
sun to keep me on line, and most of all, I have this great
desire to know who I am."

He felt the early morning chill, watching clouds dance
through their rainbow colors as the sun splashed the

prairie with life-giving warmth. "I guess you mules better get used to me talking to you, cuz yer the only ones around. Won't be any goodies coming your way after a day's jaunt, either, so let's click them hooves and make for Oregon."

His family were pioneers of a sort, a little bit late in coming to the Ohio Valley. His father's family had arrived in the late 1700s, and there were still stories about Boone and some of the others. Zeke's father, Zachariah Hawthorne, was born in 1795 and was a respected merchant by the time Zeke was born in 1820. Maude Clay was five years Mr. Hawthorne's junior and came from long time pioneer stock. The Hawthorne's had five children, Zeke being number two, and the eldest of the boys.

He was brought up on stories of the great Indian wars, the French-Indian War, the Revolutionary War, and how the savages brutalized their victims. There was no quarter, he remembered hearing from his grandfather. The heavy, thick forests provided all the cover the savages needed to attack the pioneers, the armies, and to kidnap women and children. Zeke was aware that he had a built-in fear of Indians, and yet, as he started on this journey, he felt fearless.

His mind was alive during the first few days on the trek, and he could simply let it delve where it wished. "I think I was about eight-years-old when I heard the story of Lewis and Clark for the first time. Everyone knew about Daniel Boone and what he did, but Lewis and Clark... they conquered this vast continent!" he reminded the mules one day. "Mother insisted I attend school and father forced me to learn a trade. Between the two of them, I can read in several languages and I'm a journeyman cabinetmaker and blacksmith."

Later that afternoon, he was thinking of Indians and some of the Indians Lewis and Clark had met. "I wonder if I'll meet my Sacagawea?" He snickered, but his mind was alive with so many stories. "Lewis and Clark opened up the west," he informed his mules. "The Rocky Mountains and vast stretches of mighty rivers, and the Pacific Ocean. Those mountain men that flocked to the mountains for beaver skins and other furs are the men I want to meet."

THE BLOOM of spring was on the land with grasses almost growing as one watched, and as green as anything Zeke had ever seen. Light breezes in the morning created waves coursing across the plains and by afternoon, those breezes were often much stronger.

The first few days were filled with learning experiences as he moved across the open prairie. "I guess it's just us," he said to the mules. "I'll probably do a lot of talking, and I don't want to hear a lot back," he chuckled. The adventures of Ohio Valley frontiersmen were well known to Zeke, and the wondrous voyages of Lewis and Clark were read eagerly with every publication that came out.

"It'll be a little different out here on the prairie," he told the mules. "Building a small fire in the forest is one thing, but out here, the smoke and flames could be seen for miles. I do not want to make myself a target for Indians, so how will I be able to have hot meals and not have my fires be seen?"

He was pushing more than twenty miles a day, he

thought, without much difficulty, but as the miles piled up behind him, he knew he was moving through territory where very few of his kind had ever been. The wagon trains were on trails worn into the ground, and watched over by the natives. Zeke, however, was going cross-country, and he hoped the savages would not pick on a single traveler. When he came to springs, streams or rivers, he was extremely cautious; often leaving the animals tucked into sparse stands of trees and slowly advancing on the site. He had found signs of Indians, but hadn't seen any, yet.

"I should make a plan," he said one day, "for the time I *do* come face to face with an Indian."

He pondered that thought for many days and, finally, decided that he could not make a real plan. He would simply have to let events play out. *What would they do?* he wondered, *and how will I react? My only thought right now is to be as cautious as possible, not kick up any dust, and have no fires that produce smoke.*

Zeke got in the habit of stopping late in the afternoon and building a small fire with as little smoke as possible, eating a hot meal, and then moving on until almost dark before building a cold camp for the night. His morning meal consisted of left-over corn cakes and water, and he would often pull some smoked jerk to gnaw on during the day. The mules were well fed, as prairie grass were abundant.

Buffalo droppings were available everywhere and burned hot with little smoke. He learned to find small depressions in the prairie. Then he would hobble the mules; gather the dung, find dried grass, which was plentiful, and build his small fire, out of sight of anyone out on the plain.

This worked for the first couple of weeks as he got deeper into open prairie, but soon he knew he would start running out of the supplies he'd brought with him. "This creates our first real problem," he told the mules as they settled in one night. "There's plenty of game out here, but I'm sure a shot from one of my guns will bring some howling savages down on us."

He had seen plenty of Indian sign, but nary a savage, yet. "With so much game," he speculated, "I would think the Indians must be well fed. Maybe I should have learned how to make and shoot a bow and arrow. They are quiet, deadly, and far safer to use than my weapons."

ZEKE WAS ANGLING SLIGHTLY northwest and was well into what would have been Kansas, when he came up on a small creek. While he was rambling along the banks, looking for a good place to ford, he spotted the dimples of fish rising to take bugs from the surface. "Oh, my," he said, stepping off his mule and tying the animals to some willows. He grappled in the pack for a couple of minutes, coming up with a small package.

"Fresh fish for supper," he said, finding the hooks and line he had brought. He dug under some rocks and after pulling some grass, he found the grubs he was looking for. Within minutes, he had two fat fish on the creek bank, cleaned and ready for the fire. "We better move away from the water, boys," he said, just in case a savage or two wants fish for supper as well."

He forded the creek and rode another couple of miles, stopping near some lonely trees and eating his fish supper. "This is the first fresh meat of any kind I've had since we started this little journey," he mumbled, wrapping the second fish, also cooked, for tomorrow or the next day.

"I remember the stories of the red fish that Lewis and Clark found," he continued. " Salmon. Well, they had theirs, I have mine," he smiled, wrapping himself tight in a blanket for the long night ahead.

3

THERE WERE RABBITS, BIRDS, ANTELOPE, AND MOST exciting to see, buffalo, in profusion almost daily, as Zeke trekked toward the northwest. As he put it in his journal, "More west by northwest, I think." The prairie seemed to go on forever, an unbroken horizon filling his eyes everyday. Raging thunderstorms slowed his progress a time or two, rivers and streams that had to be forded interrupted his routine occasionally, but it was the endless vista of open prairie that continued to enthrall him.

"Don't think there'll be many people moving into this country," he mused. "So few trees, it would be difficult to build a home and barn, and hard to heat a home all winter. I'm not so sure old Jefferson made the right decision." He loved the vista, but decided he would not build a home here.

"President Jefferson bought all this," he told his mules one day. "This land was owned by the French, they said. We have crossed some trails, seen many animals, but if the French owned it, why have I been reading about the

Indians wanting to keep it? You mules listen to me; don't ever let me become a damned politician!" He laughed gently to the rocking of the mule's pace.

One day, as he was searching for a shallow dip in the prairie, he saw a massive thunderstorm build to his northwest. "Just look at that lightning," he said to his now skittery mules. "No stopping in a swale today, boys."

Those dips and swales filled with raging water fast during thunderstorms. The big black clouds moved closer, the winds picked up and soon it was raining hard. The cold rain was driven by gale-force wind, lightning was smashing the prairie while thunder was blasting Zeke's ears. Fear slashed through him as he saw a funnel cloud form and dig into the ground, just a mile or two away. *Is it coming this way?* he worried, and if it was, was there anything he could do about it? His body told him to run for his life, but his mind took command. He dismounted and hunkered down between the two mules, watching that black whirling death-storm march across the plains. He had a desperate grip on the lead ropes.

But, the storm slowly abated, bypassing the frightened little group huddling on the open plain. Zeke watched the huge storm move away, mounted Ruth and continued plodding through tall, very wet grass, not stopping for a hot meal. He wrote in his journal that evening about how the hair on the back of his neck felt like it was filled with electricity, how the storm made more noise than he had ever heard, and how he was as frightened as he had ever been. He made camp the best he could and prepared to sleep on the wet ground that night.

Later, Zeke and the mules rode over the top of a rise in the prairie and spotted a band of Indians. Zeke thought it was a hunting party of young men, several miles distant. He scurried to get out of sight and rode toward a small stand of trees. He quickly hobbled his mules, checked the old flintlock for charge, and crept back up on the ridge to see what he could see.

The men had long bows and quivers filled with arrows. Each carried an axe that Zeke recognized as the type used by the French voyageurs or mountain men. Some also had stone-headed clubs on long handles that would be effective against any foe or prey.

They wore only wore breach clouts and moccasins, Zeke noted, and their bodies glistened with perspiration. They sat very tall on their horses and he noted that they didn't use saddles, or what he considered traditional bridles. "They just have a rawhide rope around the horses' lower jaws. Amazing." He wrote later in his journal. He watched the men move as they crossed his path. "They must be following a trail." If they saw his trail, they gave no sign.

After they had passed, he moved quickly away from the area, away from the potential problem. He put the mules in a strong walk, not wanting to trot or lope for fear of raising too much dust. After about an hour or so, he let the animals slow to their preferred pace, but kept a close eye out for more trouble.

As he drew near a small stand of trees, he planned on stopping and possibly cooking some meat to eat and giving his mules a little rest. He loosened the pack and took it off Tobias, and after hobbling the animal, he unsaddled and hobbled Ruth. Zeke gathered some dry grass and dead branches for his fire, scooped loose dirt into a small pit and laid in the grass. When he stood to get his fire striker from the pack he found himself looking straight into the eyes of a fierce-looking Indian man who was threatening him with a large knife.

The Indian had left his horse several yards away. Zeke had never even heard him coming, never heard the horse, never felt there might be company. Zeke's blood froze in the veins, his eyes grew to the size of silver coins, and he all but quit breathing.

Then, gathering his wits, Zeke jumped back two steps and drew his own knife. He and the warrior slowly circled each other. The warrior was fast in thrusting his knife but Zeke sidestepped the attack and just as quickly thrust his own.

The blade sliced through the Indian's arm, laying the muscle back and exposing the bone, opening an artery to the world. The Indian then dropped his knife and Zeke stepped in fast and drove his knife to the hilt in the man's belly, withdrew the blade and thrust again, deep into the chest cavity. The Indian tried to fight back but the blood drained from his system in a great flood, and he slowly sank to the ground, dead.

Zeke, heart pounding like a kettle-drum, saddled Ruth and got the pack on Tobias as fast as he could. He took the Indian's knife and rode out quickly. "If he has friends, they'll be looking for me," he said, and headed for a small ridge several miles ahead of him.

I hope that's a rocky mound of ridge there, He thought. *I can't leave good prints for those boys to follow.* He was trying to plan as far ahead as he could, trying to remember everything he ever read about evading an enemy. *Was it Boone that wrote about hiding your trail? Somebody did, I remember. They cut small branches from a tree and dragged it behind them.*

He found some willows at a creek crossing before reaching the ridge and cut some willow switches, letting Tobias drag them from his pack rigging. *Hell, all I'm doing is leaving a trail of willow switch brushing,* he chuckled nervously, and stopped to untie the branches, tucking them into the ropes of the saddle. *They'll be good for a fire,* he decided and they moved on at a fast walk.

His mind turned around and around in dizzying circles, and he felt slightly sick. *I wonder if I should have taken the time to bury the man? No, I need to put as much distance as I can between us, just in case he has friends. If I had buried him, though, maybe his friends wouldn't find him. Damn, this isn't the time to argue with myself!*

He reached the ridge and slipped his animals from pack and saddle, hobbling them on the far side and below the ridgeline. Then he slipped back to the top and spent the next several hours there, until dark. He saw no movement on the prairie. *We'll have to move hard and fast tomorrow,* he thought, *and put a lot of distance between us and that body.*

It was a cold camp filled with fear and self-loathing. *I've never killed a man, never had any desire to kill another human being, but what was I to do? It was kill or be killed. He was going to kill me simply because I was there, and because of that, I killed him. Does he have a wife? Children? Was he a good man, or otherwise?*

Later that evening, attempting to put his mind at ease, he wrote in his journal; "Those hunters were beautiful in an animal way, graceful of movement, strong and lithe in body and limb, and very intelligent. Although I didn't understand their language, I understood what they were discussing as they outlined what I assumed would be their hunt the next day with drawings in the dirt and sand. One man appeared to be the leader, but all contributed to the conversation and planning. I'm very impressed by what I saw. I would like to get to know these men, but I know I will never be able to.

"That lone Indian was able to sneak right up to me. If I hadn't stood up at that moment, I would be the dead one. His immediate thought was to kill me, and I shake from fright wondering what would have happened if I had spotted him coming and tried to offer friendship."

He put the journal aside and continued worrying about his situation, mumbling his thoughts as they fell into place. "I need to do better on my food, but today proved that I'm right in not trying to shoot game. It would bring every Indian on the plains to my camp. I will ride with my rifle fully-loaded, though. That was a very close call today and I can't let it happen again. I need to spend some time thinking about gathering more food." He slept a fitfully that night.

THE NEXT MORNING, Zeke awoke with new plans. He would set snares for hares, and the meat from one hare would last him at least two days. There were the big prairie birds, as well. He figured he could roast one of the chicken-sized birds and it would keep him in meat for almost a week.

He and the mules had stopped near a creek earlier that day and Zeke caught two fish. Ha also cut a lot of willow switches that he brought along to the camp he'd set up several miles from the creek. He cleaned and cooked the fish and after eating half of one he moved again several miles along the track. He spent several hours that evening weaving the willow switches into a snare trap that he hoped would catch a prairie chicken. "I can almost taste one of those," he wrote that night before wrapping up in his blankets.

None of the prairie animals seemed frightened by his presence. They had probably never seen a human before, or if they had, it hadn't been a threat. He stumbled on fox and coyote regularly and at night, he could hear the wolves singing their sad songs to the stars. To the best of his knowledge, he had never been visited by wolves, but he knew foxes and coyotes had come close.

The next day, he watched for prairie hens as his little group rode along, and spotting some, he set his snare near a bunch of brush with a length of rope attached. Then, he crawled under another bush to watch and wait. "With that crushed corn under there," he muttered, "I might get a pretty good meal tonight."

He watched two hens peck and scratch their way toward his cornmeal, and one went for it, inside the raised snare. He jerked the rope and the snare fell over the bird. Zeke got there quickly, dispatching her before she could raise an alarm. Then, he got the bird ready for roasting, dug a hole, put large rocks in the bottom, put dried wood over the rocks and lit the fire.

When the fire burned out, he laid the carcass over the hot rocks, covered it with green willow branches and filled the hole. In the morning, he dug up the carcass, roasted to perfection. "This is the way a man should eat breakfast," he said with a grin, wiping his well-bearded chin. "I could get used to this." He separated the meat into packages, repacked Ruth, saddled Tobias, and moved back on the trail.

That snare found its way onto the pack right along with the ones he had been using to catch rabbits. He had run out of beans a couple of weeks back and wished that he had packed more. "I could eat a whole pot of beans right now," he muttered.

Between fat hares and big prairie chickens, Zeke had meat every day. "Sure could go for a pot of beans, boys," he'd say often, and then think of corn or squash, and want some of that, too. "I had those two apple trees back on the farm... bet I could eat a dozen apples right now.

"I'm heading for Oregon and a wonderful new life," he continued, "but I have to admit that I'm one very happy man. I've never been this free, ever. The only thing I must do is continue my voyage west and stay safe. Think about that, boys, I've never been more free than I am right now, and I know that every minute of every day my life is in danger. Amazing."

The fear of being spotted by Indians ached through his mind every day, though, and there were times that a single tree far out on the prairie would startle him, or coming up on a little swale on the plain and scaring up a small herd of antelope would send his blood coursing through the veins like the mighty Po he remembered reading about as a child.

"I would like to stop and make a real camp and stay for several days somewhere," he wrote in the journal one evening. "But I know I can't do that. That would generate too much interest from the natives. I'm afraid, and I'm tired, I admit that. I've been moving every day since we left."

He contemplated that last line for a few minutes, wondering why he couldn't remember how many days he has been on the ride. "Amazing," he wrote, "I don't know how long we've been out. Maybe two months? Probably two months," he decided.

ON ONE OCCASION, he followed a small herd of bison for two days until he was interrupted by a band of Indians doing the same thing. He retreated immediately and wasn't seen by them. The Indians didn't seem to be hunting, but were following along. "I wonder if that means the rest of the tribe is following behind them. We've got to get out of here, boys," he said. And they made a big turn away from the herd and the possible danger.

"We've been on this trek for about two months now, boys, and except for a few encounters with Indians, we haven't met or talked with any human beings. Thousands of buffalo and so much other game, maybe I don't want to go to Oregon. Maybe I'll just settle here." He laughed at the thought, and said, "Until I made the first smoke, which would bring the savages to my door."

Zeke wasn't purposefully following a large herd of buffalo, it just seemed that they were going the same way. "It appears that these animals just run and eat, walk and eat, run and eat, their way through life. The grasses of the prairie must be nourished by the droppings of millions of buffalo and the churning of the ground by their hooves. Such a natural thing to see. I'm amazed every day on this trek."

As usual, Zeke crawled out of his bedroll at first light, and shivered in the cold. "Haven't felt the cold like this," he muttered, pulling on a heavy coat. When the sun splashed across the prairie, he stood in silence, seeing high mountain peaks more than a hundred miles away. "That's what they call the Rocky Mountains," he said, awed by the sight. "I've never seen anything like this in my life. Look, boys, mountains so high …" and he just let his comment drift off.

Over the next few weeks, slowly moving up and out of the prairie, Zeke's attitude changed somewhat. He could smell the mountains a little stronger each day, and he began to think of the future and what it might hold for him. "Future, that's an interesting word. Mine could have ended several times since I left our little farm, but it hasn't been until just now that the idea of a future takes shape.

"Oregon, and a new farm, and will I find a family? Elizabeth, I miss you so much. We almost had what we wanted, what I needed. I need a family to work my fingers to the bone for, children dashing about and being taught. Is that why I left the farm, to find again what was so ruthlessly taken from me?"

He came to a boiling stream, splashing its way toward the great plains and was startled when he bent to wash his face. "Hoo, that's cold," he gasped, feeling the water stream from his beard and long hair, and drip inside his shirt.

He didn't let the mules drink their fill, as usual, stopping them after a few drinks, then bringing them back to the stream after a pause. Icy cold water could create cramps, he knew, and found that even he couldn't drink much at a time. *My teeth ache, it's so cold.* That afternoon,

Zeke caught his first mountain trout, about two pounds of the fightingest fish he'd ever hooked. He moved away from the stream and quickly cleaned and cooked the trout.

"That is the sweetest fish I've ever tasted," he said, keeping back enough so he would have fresh roasted trout for his mid-day meal tomorrow. Moving slowly out of the plains, he noticed big differences in the nightly temperatures, in the types of trees he trailed through and around, and found himself trying to stay on what he figured were game trails.

As he continued toward Fort Bridger, still several weeks' trek in front of him, he met more and more people; most headed west as he was, and most filled with thoughts of gold, riches, and easy money.

He had stumbled on what most called the Missouri Trail. The wagons and folks in them had traveled by way of rivers and trails far north of how Zeke had made his pilgrimage. Most, he found, were headed for California and gold, few having the least understanding of how that gold was to be gathered.

II

BOOK TWO: FORT BRIDGER

4

"YOU CAME ALL THIS WAY BY YOURSELF?" THE WAGON master asked when his group came across Zeke and his mules. "My, God man, you're lucky to have your scalp. We've been ravaged several times, our cattle stolen, and people dead."

"I didn't come on the regular emigrant trails," Zeke answered with a smile. "Where would you folks be heading?"

"California, of course. Reports are- there is gold enough for everyone. You're welcome to tag along with us. Name's Rutherford Johnson, and this is my second group. Made this trip last year, so I can tell you for a fact that I know where we're going and I know how to get us there." Johnson swelled up just a bit saying that, and a couple of the men that had gathered near-by seemed to agree with him.

"Johnson's a good wagon master," one of them said. "I'm Sanderson, that's my woman Dorothy in the wagon. Where you headed, mister?"

"I'm working my way toward Oregon. Heard there's fine ground for growing good crops, and plenty of water available. I'd be pleased to follow along with you folks, at least to Fort Bridger. I'm Hawthorne, Ezekiel Hawthorne, recently of Missouri.

"So, you folks are going to California to dig for gold, eh? Don't know much about that, I'm afraid."

"What the reports said when we left, was the gold is just layin' about. Easy pickin's, is the way some put it."

"Well, Mr. Sanderson, there is no such thing as easy money," Zeke said, "only hard work done in a proper manner. That is the true meaning of rich, being able to work hard, do the work right, and be responsible to yourself and those that depend on you." He didn't feel contempt for those seeking easy money, but he had little respect for them. "I think you'll find it will be mighty hard work prying that gold loose from this old earth."

"Let's get these wagons moving, folks," Johnson piped up. "We got many miles to go before sundown. You just drop in anywhere it suits you, Hawthorne. You'll be expected to help with camp chores when we stop. You fixed okay for food?"

"I've got enough for a few more days. Was planning on shooting something after that." Zeke let the Sanderson wagon move past him and moved in behind with his mules. *It's been well over two months since I've had a conversation with a real person. I should have kept track of the days, but this trip has been so fascinating, keeping track of days never entered my mind. Listening to Sanderson makes me realize that I'm making the right decision, heading for Oregon and building a good farm.*

Seeing the people in the wagons and those walking

alongside made him realize just what the journey across the great prairie meant. *I am literally threadbare. My shirts are ripped and my trousers torn. I must be a real sight to these people,* He had to chuckle. He ran his hands through long hair and scratched at a beard that had grown long and thick too. *I wonder what Elizabeth would say if she saw me now?*

About an hour or so before sunset Johnson moved the wagons into a meadow filled with good grass and a stream running through its middle. Zeke unsaddled Ruth and pulled the pack from Tobias. He took the mules to the stream for water, and then hobbled the two in tall grass. When he got back, he found Sanderson unpacking his wagon and making camp before taking care of his animals. His wife, Dorothy, was busy discussing the day's activities with some of the other women.

These people have come all the way across this big continent and need to be told what to do. Look at old Johnson there, taking care of the animals, instead of the man that owns the animals. Must be all city folk, Zeke thought as he busied himself making a small camp.

He kept reflecting on city folk venturing across the country, not taking the time to learn how to care for their animals and expecting to arrive in California and just pick up chunks of gold splayed about on the ground. *My folks would be telling them a thing or two,* he thought, chuckling as he walked across the meadow toward the wagon master.

"Need some help with those animals, Mr. Johnson?" he hollered. "You got yourself a handful there."

"You could give me a hand with the long-line in those trees over there, Hawthorne. I'll hobble the mules. We can long-line the horses, and the oxen and cattle will graze all night with no trouble. Shouldn't have any Indian problem in this area, but we might run into a few before we get to Fort Bridger."

"These people don't help you, none?" Zeke asked, making fast a length of rope to a strong aspen tree.

"I gave up on that many weeks ago. These people are from the east coast and don't seem to know much about how to take care of an animal if they don't have a barn and cut hay to feed them. This gold they seek is all that's on their minds. I'm as much a nurse-maid as I am a fron-tiersman and wagon master, I think," he growled, snorting.

Johnson stood about five feet and ten inches. He was heavy boned and carried considerable weight, most of it strong muscle. His neck was wide and he had a broad face under a full black beard. Johnson's big brown eyes danced with mirth and joy, and Zeke wondered as he watched the man take care of his charges, *I wonder if these people are aware of how lucky they are to have this man as their wagon master?*

"Just look at what's inside those wagons and you'll wonder what might be in their minds," Johnson contin-ued. "They have cast iron stoves, full rooms of furniture, and great trunks filled with silverware. When we hit the desert in a few weeks, those things will be tossed, one at a time until we reach the Sierra Nevada.

"I've told 'em and told 'em, and they scoff. I been there, they ain't, and they scoff at me. Well, they paid me to get them there," he chuckled, "just not everything they ever owned." The man pitied what would happen when the women cried, throwing out their possessions, and the men cussed because the oxen couldn't pull the weight.

"What made you want to come west, if not for the gold?" Johnson asked as they walked back toward the camp area.

"Had a good farm in Missouri, but I lost my family to sickness and just didn't want to stay there anymore. Heard some good stories about Oregon and made up my mind to find out if they be true. I'm a farmer, trained cabinet maker, and know my way around a forge and anvil, so I know I can take care of myself when I get there."

"That's more than most of these jaspers can say," Johnson chortled. "There's two trails lead out of Fort Bridger, one through Salt Lake toward California, and t'other, called the Oregon Road. Leads right into the Willamette Valley." The Oregon Trail didn't go straight into that verdant valley, as Zeke would find out, but it did lead to the Willamette.

"That's the part of Oregon I've heard a lot about." Zeke put an armload of fire wood he was carrying on the ground and scanned the Rocky Mountain ridges, seemingly so close, but still miles away. "Just look," he said, waving his arms as if to gather the peaks in. "Those mountains we're looking at are spectacular. I feel I'll probably have to make the rest of the journey with a group. What do you know about this Fort Bridger?"

"Jim Bridger, they call him Old Gabe for some reason, is a mountain man, a trapper, lived in these mountains for years, and started the place so the fur companies could be restocked. It's pretty basic, but some people are making it more permanent. Emigrant groups like mine can restock and rest their animals before the next long stretch.

"You be feeling like talking, I'd love to hear your story

about coming all this way all by yourself," Johnson said. "I wouldn't have thought it possible. You can throw your pack down near mine, if you have a mind to."

Zeke had wood cut and a fire prepared while Johnson made the rounds of the wagons, making sure everyone had what they needed for the evening. The two men ate some of Johnson's meat from an antelope he had shot the day before, and some of Ezekiel's meat from the last of a prairie chicken, and talked well into the night. "The best part of tonight," Zeke said, "is this pot of beans. First beans I've had since leaving Missouri." The fire was just embers when they finally crawled into their blankets.

"We be several days getting to Fort Bridger, climbing all the way to the top and then dipping back down some. You said you thought those mountains we can see are big, well, Mr. Hawthorne, they will loom as giants by the time we hit the Green River.

"Goodnight to you, and we'll be startin' out early."

Zeke laid on his back, watching billions of stars slowly move through the heavens, heard wolves howling in the distance, and visualized grand pictures of a farm, a wife, children, and a place called Willamette Valley. He was asleep in minutes, lulled by the first conversations he'd had in a long time, and several helpings of good beans.

For the next several days, Zeke moved at the pace of the oxen, slowest of the stock on the wagon train, and marveled as the countryside changed from open prairie to what Johnson kept calling the front-range, the ever-steeper slope of the foothills of the Rocky Mountains. There were more trees, and larger, and he was amazed at the number of creeks they crossed. Every one of those coursing streams held fish, and just as Johnson had said, those massive granite peaks loomed immense as they moved closer.

The going was steep and rocky, and for Ezekiel, it was a continuing adventure of a lifetime. His mules seemed to be bred for the country, picking their way through tumbled trees and brush, working around rocks and boulders the size of his old farmhouse. *I've never known there would be mountains this mighty. Majestic, is the only word that seems to fit.* His only memories of mountains were those leading into and out of the Ohio Valley, and they were rounded, as if weathered more that these Rocky Mountains.

I don't know how high we are, but I do know I've never been this far above sea level. Those mountains must be well over ten thousand feet, he was thinking. The eastern mountain ranges that Zeke was familiar with were much older ranges and had been worn down for thousands more years that the Rockies.

The trail they were following had originally been made by animals, then by the local Indians, later by the trappers and mountain men, and now had been widened over the past several years to make room for wagons. Winters brought fallen and broken trees crashing onto the tracks, and avalanches and falling rocks also tended to block the way. Zeke fretted at what those with wagons were facing on this rough trail, thankful that he had his mules.

"It ain't that rough, Mr. Hawthorne," Johnson said when Zeke said something about the condition of the trail. "Back just a few years, a man couldn't get a wagon through this country. Pack animals and saddle stock only. It were them fur traders busted this trail open, and it gets better every year."

Some of the men in the wagons pushed their mules and horses too hard on the long steady climb and Johnson had to reprimand them more than once. At a rest stop, he called everyone together. "The rest of this part of our journey is going to be much steeper than what we've been coming through. The trail will be narrow, steep, and filled with massive rocks until we drop into the Green River area.

"If you keep abusing your animals, I'll leave you at Fort Bridger. We should be coming to the Fort in the next few days. We'll be there a few days to rest the animals and restock our supplies. The gentleman that runs the place usually has animals for sale, but he don't much care to buy ruined stock. What you have been travelling through is mild compared to what you'll face between here and Bridger, and even more so after we leave Bridger.

"I don't want to have to make this speech again. Now, mount up, and let's go." Johnson nodded to Zeke and motioned for him to follow. "Let's ride out a bit ahead of them, let them think about what I said, and you can get a good look at this country."

They moved higher and higher into the Rocky Mountains, forded streams and gazed at the beauty. Massive trees filled Zeke's vision and he could imagine that just one tree would build a cabin, barn, and sheds for a nice-sized farm. Huge boulders spilled from towering spires of granite littered on the landscape, and he was amazed at the wildlife.

"Never saw a buffalo or an elk until I started this trek,

Johnson," he said, when they took a break to let the wagons catch up. "I've never seen a mountain this high or trees this large. This is heaven, I think. I wonder when it was I died," he chuckled.

"This is mighty big country, Zeke, but you ain't even see'd the best of it. Old man Bridger, some call him Major, built himself a fort on a fork of the Green River, and sometimes I think you can see all the way, thousand miles or more, to the Pacific Ocean."

Johnson held back, motioned Zeke to keep on going and that he'd catch up, then rode back to make sure the wagons were coming along. Zeke continued up the trail, and about half an hour later saw some movement in what looked like a meadow, maybe five hundred yards off. He halted the mules and watched a massive bear amble across the open space.

He tried to judge the distance and using that to size the bear, he determined that it had to be the biggest bear he had ever even heard of. He was so absorbed in watching the animal he hadn't heard Johnson ride up behind him. "That'd be a Grizzly bear, Mr. Hawthorne. You do not want to intimidate that brute. They tell me a Griz can run faster than a horse, and can tear a man's head off with one swat of those huge feet."

"I've never seen anything like that, ever, Mr. Johnson. Amazing."

"You can tell how old and how big a bear is by his ears," Johnson said. "If the ears look large, it's a young one and not too large, but if those ears look mighty small, that's a big animal lookin' for a meal."

It was early in the summer and Zeke realized that he wasn't suffering from the heat, as he did most summers.

"Nice and comfortable up high in these mountains," he said, "but it was almost chilly this morning."

"Tomorrow morning, we should be so high that even though it's summer, we'll be breaking ice to make coffee. You'll need that mackinaw you have in your pack. I'll cover my bed roll with a buffalo robe I won from an Indian on my last trip."

"How'd you win it?" Zeke asked.

"He had a knife, I had a gun. Damn fool picked the wrong fight."

They stopped the wagons near a strong running stream and made camp. Zeke took a walk up the stream half a mile or so and found a quiet stretch of water. "Haven't caught a fish for awhile," he mumbled, tying some line on a hook he brought along on his adventure. He found a branch, broke it from an aspen tree, rolled a couple of rocks over and found the grubs he was looking for, and impaled one on the hook.

Back in the Ohio Valley, I could read a river or stream and tell you exactly where I should put that little hook, he thought, smiling to himself, *but this is a high mountain creek with water so cold it hurts my teeth to drink it. Right there, just next to that rock, and I'll let the current take my grub into that calm water.*

Later, he told Johnson, "I'll tell you, Johnson, that little trout fought like an African lion." They were sitting at a comfortable fire, with a well-fried trout in each plate. "That grub wasn't in the water two seconds and I had my first fish on the hook."

"Let me tell you about the fish you'll find when you get down to the Oregon country, my friend," Johnson smiled. "They be some of them as long as your leg, big hooked jaws and bright red meat. Salmon!" he said. "Sometimes you gotta fight the bears off to keep one, though," and he chuckled along with Zeke.

"Sounds like my kind of country, Mr. Johnson. I remember reading about salmon in the Lewis and Clark stories."

"There she be, Zeke," Johnson said, pointing at smoke coming up through the trees several miles distant. "Fort Bridger, and we'll be there well before sunset. The old place sits almost on an island, between forks in the rivers that meet up with the Green River. Indians spotted us this morning, so they'll be expecting us."

"Indians?" Zeke asked. "I didn't see any Indians. You sure, Johnson?"

"Sure, and you bet, Zeke. Been watching us until about an hour ago. They be friendly, or at least not dangerous. Probably Shoshone. The Major's married to a Shoshone Princess, you know."

Zeke didn't know and was confounded by what Johnson said. *I thought I pretty much knew what we were riding through, and kept my eyes open and vigilant all day. This is magnificent country and I don't want to miss anything, but I guess I missed them Indians.* "I guess I didn't see those Indians at all, Johnson. What exactly should I be looking for? I always spotted the savages out on the plains."

"Well," he pondered, scratching at his out of control beard, "most of the time you just catch a glimpse of some brush quiverin', or a tree limb shaking when there ain't no wind. Don't actually get to see the man, you just know by what you see that there be a man making the brush or tree

41

move some. Not like that encounter you told me about. What was it like, killing an injun?"

Well," Zeke stammered a little. "I wasn't looking to kill an Indian, Johnson. I was looking to kill a man who was doing his best to kill me. He was a man with a big knife and a heart full of hate."

"That's a pretty good attitude, I think," Johnson said.

As they moved onto a broad plain, bisected by fast running, snow melt streams, they encountered other people, a few Indians, and just those being nosey. "Why, that really is a fort," Zeke said when they got close enough. "That's a stockade, and there are small cabins outside the walls!"

Fort Bridger had been built by Jim Bridger several years before, with his partner, Vasquez. Bridger had come west early in the fur trade years, coming from Virginia originally, and made a fine reputation for himself.

"That man can speak right along with the Indians, and talks French to them Canadians, as well," Johnson told him. "His partner, Vasquez is from an old, old family that was settled in the St. Louis area, way before President Thomas Jefferson made the Louisiana Purchase.

"Never have met Vasquez, but Major Bridger, he usually be around here. Hope you get to meet him, Zeke. He knows this country like I know the back of my hand, and when he gets to tellin' stories, well, now, ain't nobody ever walked out on one."

Johnson brought the wagons into an area somewhat away from the semi-permanent cabins and tee pees that were arranged outside the walls of Fort Bridger. People inside the fort came out and watched the wagons move in, some waved a howdy to them.

"We'll be setting up here, folks. You'll find supplies and food inside the fort. Keep in mind that we're guests and they make the rules. There are families living in these tee pees and huts, so please, mind their privacy."

He motioned Ezekiel over next to him. "Do you have a tent or lean-to in that pack of yours?"

"No. I had a small tarp I used on the plains, but during one of those monstrous winds, it took a notion to flee. Would they have something inside I could purchase?"

"Let's settle the animals and we'll take a tour. You still plannin' on winterin' over, are you?"

"Even more so, Johnson, now that I've seen this country. I have to know much more about all this splendor."

5

JOHNSON AND HAWTHORNE WALKED INTO THE FORT compound through large stockade type gates, found corrals and animal areas off to their right and buildings scattered on their left; some structures built right into the stockade walls. The stockade appeared built for defense and safety, but not necessarily kept up.

"We can get information from the suttler's store," Johnson said, leading the way.

"Those stockade walls look pretty strong, Johnson," Zeke said. "Must have been some serious Indian problems a few years ago. I don't see much in the way of defense right now, though."

"Bridger was able to make peace with most of the Indians in this country. The Shoshone and Flathead make up most of the savages, and they're relatively peaceful." Johnson caught a chuckle from Zeke when he continued, "Major Bridger married a Flathead chief's daughter, and when she died, he married a Shoshone Princess. That's how you make peace in this country."

The suttler's store was crammed to the rafters with anything and everything you might want if you were traveling through to California or Oregon. One entire wall was hung with various types and sizes of traps, Zeke figured from beaver to Grizzly. Great bolts of cloth, coils of rope, axes, knives, pistols, rifles, and shovels, took up every square inch of space available.

Off to the side there was a ten or twelve-foot plank set up as a bar, on top of barrels, and behind that were various bottles and glasses. "Might have to chase that barley corn after I get these people settled in," Johnson smiled. "Ran out of my own stuff several weeks ago."

"Evening, Gents," the man behind a heavy wooden counter said. "Don't think I've seen you before. Come in on that last train?" and he jerked his head toward the stockade gates.

"Sure did," Johnson said. "Name's Johnson, and this here is Hawthorne. I'll need to help those pilgrims restock for the rest of the trip, and Hawthorne here is lookin' to winter over."

"Pleased to meet you. Names Jeremiah Travis, helping the Major keep things running here. Ever'body headin' out to them gold fields in California, cain't keep much help. You're not goin' to California, Hawthorne?"

"Want to make it to Oregon, but I want to see some of this country, not just pass through," Zeke said, shaking hands with Travis. "Why don't you pour us a nip or two of your rum, sir, and join us, if you would."

Glasses were set up, drinks were poured, and toasts were offered. "My daddy always said, the best way to meet new people is over the rim of a glass," Zeke chortled, his eyes smiling and crinkled at the edges. After his first sip, he gave Jeremiah Travis a good looking-over and saw one big strong man.

Travis was more than big; he was huge. He all but overwhelmed the little store, already crammed with half the world's needs. He stood about six feet tall and weighed probably close to two hundred fifty pounds, and Zeke noticed there wasn't much fat in all that bulk. Travis wore his blondish hair long, braided and twisted Indian style, and wore a possum skin hat, with the head and snout pointing forward. He wore a buckskin over- shirt, fringed pioneer style, and belted on the outside. A large knife in a buckskin scabbard was at his side.

"Some of my people are going to need iron work done on their wagons before we can resume our little adventure," Johnson said. "Wheels are showing some serious wear, and we're probably gonna need to do some animal trading as well. Damn city people just don't know nothin' 'bout takin' care of their animals," he said, spotting cigars in a bowl and grabbing five or six. "These, I like," he said.

"We keep them by the case, Johnson. Them's two-bit cigars, not the cheap ones you'll find other places. No, sir, them's the best Major Bridges can get. He was a boy in Virginia and swears by their tobacco." He took a gold coin from Johnson and offered a light to the man. "Now, about them wagons of yours. The man what ran the blacksmith shop done run-off last week and I don't know if we can get your wagons fixed up."

"Did he take the tools and equipment when he left?" Zeke asked, perking up to the idea of doing some metal work again. "I'm a journeyman metal worker, Travis, and a journeyman cabinet maker. I can run a forge and then build you the most comfortable chair you've ever sat in."

"Let's get you settled in, then, Mr. Hawthorne. The blacksmith shop comes with its own living area. Johnson, get your people settled in and we can talk supplies and animals tomorrow. Hawthorne, let's take a little walk and see if we can't come to a workable arrangement." He reached in the bowl of cigars, grabbed one for himself and offered one to Zeke, ushering everyone out of the store. Travis was on a mission. "Imagine a way-stop like this one, and no blacksmith. You just might be some kind of angel, Hawthorne. Yup, you might just be the most welcome man at Fort Bridger. Imagine having this place and no blacksmith. Just imagine!

Bridger believes in free enterprise, sir, and the deal he has with those working here at the fort is rather simple. He provides the building for you, and the tools you need, and asks for five percent of what you take in each month." He blew out a great cloud of blue smoke as the two strode over toward where the animals were kept. "Major believes in keeping people here, but that gold, it draws people like molasses to a biscuit."

"Is Major Bridger here? Johnson said he isn't around very much."

"Old Jim Bridger's a travelin' man, Hawthorne. Still does some trappin'. He's married to a beautiful woman, Shoshone, you know, and has kids, but he still wants to live the old way, when the fur trade was still good. He'll be back from St. Louis in a week or so. He'll be glad to meet you, I'll guarantee. He goes to St. Loo for supplies every year. Doesn't have to, could just have everything shipped, but, like I say, he's a travelin' man. Ah, here we are, the new *Hawthorne* Blacksmith and Cabinet Shop."

Zeke was impressed with what he saw in the blacksmith complex. A half open shed with the forge and anvils, tools neatly arrayed, either hung on hooks or spread across a large, stout workbench. "These tools are excellent, some of the best available. It will be a pleasure working with them." There were several work stations based on what was to be done, and enough space that one wouldn't feel cramped.

"This is very nice, Travis, very nice. You said there's a living space, too?"

"Right through those doors, Mr. Hawthorne. Old Bridger was a blacksmith, too. That's why this shop is set up the way it is. He jumped off from St. Loo about twenty or maybe thirty years ago and became one of the best trappers and guides in the mountains. You should be comfortable here."

"Call me, Zeke," he said, walking toward a set of Dutch doors. Inside, he found two large rooms, one with a bed and set of open shelves for clothing and other personal needs, and the other a combination of kitchen and living room. He found a table with three simple wooden chairs, a large, wood-fired cook stove, a rocker, and several kerosene lamps, some hanging, some on tables and shelves. Set in the middle of the longest of the walls was a fireplace that was not in very good condition.

"This is very nice, Travis. I think I'll feel right at home." Zeke was already designing new furniture for the cabin, and had immediate plans for replacing the fireplace with one that would heat the whole cabin.

"I'll bring my kit up. May I keep my mules in the corrals? I have two."

"At the back of the shop area, you'll find a corral with weather stalls, just for the blacksmith. After you get set-

up, come by my store and pick up whatever you might
need. Nice to have you with us, Zeke," Travis said,
sticking a huge paw out.

"I'm just proud to be here, Travis. I'm amazed at what I
see, and I'll have that forge cooking tomorrow, sir."

Zeke watched Travis, looking like a bear, walk across
the open ground between the livestock area and the rest
of the fort. *I have the rest of the summer and all winter to
learn about this magnificent country. Thin, cold air, smells of
spruce and cedar, pines crowding everywhere, and the sky so
high, yet I feel I can touch it. It would be easy to call this
place home.*

He spent several minutes surveying the cabin, and
walked into the bedroom. *This is something I've thought
about many times during these last few months. A bed. A real
bed with a mattress to sleep on.*

He re-packed Tobias and saddled Ruth for the short
trek inside the fort, and spent the next several hours
establishing himself. There was an ample supply of coal
and wood for the forge, the fireplace, and the woodstove,
and he discovered that water came from two wells, one
near the livestock. Two young boys, one about ten, the
other close to eight, took care of the stock inside the
fort, bringing water and feed twice a day. The boys
belonged to one of the trappers and his wife, a Shoshone
woman.

For his first supper, Zeke fried some side-meat he
bought from Travis, along with wild onions and potatoes,
boiled a large pot of beans, cooked on his wood stove, and
sat in front of the fireplace, afterward, sipping a cup of
boiling coffee, watching the night come on. *Spruce, fir,
cedar, and pine,* he mused, watching the fire dance about. *I*

can build anything with that wood. I'll probably find oak and other hard woods around, as well. I'm home.

Thoughts of Elizabeth and his life on the farm danced through his head and mingled with thoughts of what might be in store for him. "I'm not wrong in what I'm doing," he said to the fireplace and walls. "I miss you, Elizabeth, and you'll always be in my heart, but I couldn't stay at that farm." He let visions of the old farm join thoughts of what the Willamette Valley might look like, what his new farm would be. He could visualize fields of corn and wheat, great stands of beans, and mounds of potatoes.

It took some doing to break the reverie, stoke up the fire, and call it a night. *I'm fully undressed and in a nightshirt, ready to crawl under blankets spread on a real bed. Didn't even know I had died,* he snickered, *and here I am in heaven.* The thin, cool mountain air was filled with contented breathing mixed with snores and chortles as sleep crept up on him.

ZEKE FOUND the old trapper's rendezvous fort to his liking. It was the end of the mountain man era, but there were a few of the old hunters and trappers still in the area. Over the next several days, he spent as much time as possible with some of them, learning about the mountains, animals, birds, and Indians. "These men love to tell tall tales, but most of what they tell me is probably the truth," he wrote in his journal. He was still fascinated by the true wild Indians, not those he knew from cities in the east.

The first time he saw several Indian braves ride their horses right into the fort, carrying rifles and bows with quivers full of arrows, he wasn't sure if he was supposed to sound an alarm or not.

Then, Travis, the storekeeper, welcomed them like longtime friends, and Zeke stood, he thought, like an idiot with his mouth hanging open. "Those men were painted and carrying weapons. Savages... Indian warriors, and they were treated like friends. I have a lot to learn," he muttered.

Johnson got his wagon train put together after Zeke mended several of the wagons, forging iron pieces and doing woodwork on many of them. "I'm sorry to see you go, Mr. Johnson. Will you come back this way?"

"I'll get these folks to Sutter's Mill in California before the winter snows hit those high Sierra Nevadas, spend the winter sashaying around the gold country, and head east come spring. Yes, sir, you'll see me come late spring."

"We make a good team, Johnson. Maybe you'll get me to Oregon and we can do business together."

"Mighty fine thinking, Zeke, mighty fine. I'll see you come spring," he said, as the two shook hands and Johnson stepped into a stirrup, got mounted and rode off, hollering at the wagon drivers to "get them wheels churnin' west, boys."

6

ZEKE'S WOOD AND IRON WORKING SKILLS CAUGHT THE attention of many around the fort and its perimeter. He was a perfectionist and it was well accepted by the old trappers who put high marks to a job well done. He fabricated iron hinges and wagon wheels, rebuilt tables and cabinets, and even had time to work of some of his own projects.

One hot afternoon, Zeke was putting the finishing touches to a table he had built to replace the worn and tired kitchen table in his new cabin. It hadn't taken long to replace the old cabin attached to the blacksmith shop. It was falling apart, and lumber, he laughed to himself, was certainly available. He gathered a wagon-load of river rock and built a new fireplace as well.

He was talking with Travis while working on the project. "Tell me about these problems Bridger has been having with the Mormons."

"We have hundreds of pilgrims heading for the California gold fields, Zeke," Travis said, "with more hundreds lining up to travel into Oregon territory. These Mormons are doing everything they can to destroy this outpost. The Major thinks we might survive two, maybe three more seasons, and that's about it."

The fight between the Mormons and Bridger had been building for a couple of years after the "Saints" came west and tried to settle in the Salt Lake Basin, an area that Bridger had helped map out and explore. Bridger's partner, Louis Vasquez had moved into the Salt Lake area and opened a branch of the trader's store and did his best to keep the fort appraised of Mormon activity.

"The way Old Gabe sees it," Travis continued, "Brigham Young just doesn't want anyone in the area but Mormons, and even though he's supposed to be a religious prophet or something, Bridger believes he's also a killer. He's threatened, more than once, to burn down the fort. The fight got started over corn, of all things!" Travis had to laugh when he said it.

"Corn. Old Brigham Young told Bridger he was going to raise great fields of corn down in the Salt Lake Valley, and Bridger told him it wouldn't work, that corn don't grow good in this country. Now, mind you, Zeke, Old Gabe has been in this country since the twenties, and Young, he ain't been here a year, but Young gets all hooty about corn and now he wants to burn the place down."

"Doesn't sound like a very smart man to me. What do you think's gonna happen?" Zeke asked.

"Bridger's fed up with the whole thing. He's either just gonna move out or maybe sell this place to the Mormons. Groups of Mormons have attacked some of the Bridger-backed ferry systems on the Black Fork of the Green River and other streams in the area, and have been known to attack wagon trains leaving Fort Bridger. I'll tell you, Zeke, Bridger has held his temper, but I don't know how much longer he will.

"My family will be pulling out next spring, and if you're as smart as I think you are, you should be on your way to Oregon before the last snow's gone. I don't think it will be safe around here."

"Where will you be going? Back east to the Settlements?" Zeke was amazed at what he was hearing. "This fort of Bridger's seems strong enough to withstand any attack that might be made."

"Fort's strong enough," Travis said, "just ain't enough people and guns. Old Jim has made friends with the Shoshone, and we don't have any Indian trouble, but those Mormons, they be more of them and we wouldn't survive the fight. They ain't no army or anything around these parts. You come to this country, you be on your own, far as self protection goes.

"No, Bridger's determined to give this place up, but if I know that old trapper, he'll give them a fight, probably from a different angle." There was sadness to his commentary, and Zeke wanted to ask a thousand questions, but held off.

Travis, though his eyes were downcast, continued. "My daughter Barbara is in Boston, going to school, and Elaine and Sarah will probably go there. I've told the Major that I'll stay as long as I can, and he'll be here with me, so we'll give 'em some kind of fight."

UNLIKE ZEKE, Travis was uneducated, but filled with common sense, an ability to think in the abstract, and to conceptualize; traits which had allowed him to make a good life for himself. Travis came west as a teenager, that was more than twenty-five years earlier, and immediately saw that a trader had a better life than a trapper, and set up business at first one, then another of the rendezvous locations in the Rocky Mountains. He opened his trader store at Fort Bridger about ten years ago and had been very successful.

As many of the men who came west to trap and hunt during the 1830s and 1840s, Travis took up with a local Indian woman, in his case, a Shoshone woman named Walks So Softly, and who called herself Elaine. After two daughters were born, the two married, legally, and had added a son to the family. Elaine had insisted that the children receive a full education. The eldest daughter, Sarah, taught school at Fort Bridger, and the younger, Barbara, attended college in Boston. Their son, Moose, worked with many of the Indian families at the fort, and operated a wood mill for his father. *This Travis family is well established,* Zeke thought. *The old man will be giving up a lifetime of work if this fort closes.*

Along with the suttler's store, Travis contracted with Bridger to supply wood for fires and building at the fort, and Moose took over that operation, hiring anyone willing to work hard. Many of the local Shoshone men and older boys found work at the mill.

The family was close and Travis was unquestionably the head of the household, but Elaine made many of the decisions that Travis in turn carried out. Elaine worked with French trappers before she met Travis and spoke French, English, and Shoshone, which gave the Travis Trading Post an edge with all visitors and customers.

French Voyageurs traveled the Rocky Mountains even though trapping had slowed down considerably since the discovery of gold in California.

Fall came early in the high country and Travis was working hard to make sure the fort was ready for another hard, Rocky Mountain winter. Wood for heating and cooking was stockpiled, and hunters were going out often to bring in meat to be smoked and cured.

Winter was always on the minds of those that lived in the mountains. "Moose," Travis asked one night at supper, "How are we coming on our wood pile?" Moose was just as big as his namesake, and was the youngest of the Travis children. He tended to be much more traditional Shoshone than his sisters, spending considerable time with tribal friends and being involved in tribal affairs.

"We'll be fine, Papa," he said. "Can we talk about something?" He had a worried look on his face as he glanced at Travis, his mother, and his sister Sarah. "I know Mama and Sarah will be going east in the spring, but I don't want to go. I want to stay with my Indian family. I'm much more comfortable with them than with a bunch of white men that can't start their own fires."

Travis laughed at that, his eyes all crinkled up, and Elaine snickered as well. "You're a grown man, Moose, and some day soon you will find that you're also a natural leader of men. You can do a lot for your tribe, and for yourself. I think it would be good for you to stay with the Snake tribe. They will need help if the Mormons try to push the people out of the territory.

"You know, since the territorial shifts, because of California and everything, all this country, which belonged to Mexico is now part of the United States, and the

Mormons don't like that, either. The Mormons don't want to be part of the United States, and I think your Shoshone family will need you."

"Thank you, Papa," Moose said, quietly, slipping another large slab of fresh Buffalo meat onto his plate. "I like this new fella, Zeke. He sure knows how to make wood and iron look pretty."

"He does, at that," Travis answered. "Have you met Ezekiel yet, Elaine? That newcomer, Zeke Hawthorne is his name, the man that rebuilt the cabin at the blacksmith shop?"

"I've seen him, not met him. Is he educated, Jeremy? I heard him order some supplies last week, and he spoke well."

"He is mannered, courteous, and the work he does with wood and iron, as Moose said, is elegant. I don't believe there's a single iron nail in his cabin; every piece of wood is fitted and snug. I haven't seen that type of work in years, not since last time I visited the east coast."

Daughter Sarah said, "I talked with him yesterday, Papa. He asked me if there were any books available that he could buy or borrow. He lost his family and came west, he said, to try to start over. He is well educated, but is looking to start farming again as soon as possible." She lowered her eyes and her voice when she said, "He's a very nice man." Travis saw Elaine smiling, almost as shyly as Sarah, and decided to keep his mouth shut.

Zeke remembered that morning meeting as an eye-opening experience. He wrote in his journal, "I've always called Indians savages, as most people I know do. Today," he wrote, "I met an amazing half-breed woman who not only was not a savage, she was well educated, and a school teacher, and is very easy on the eyes."

Sarah was tall, like her father, slim, with long black hair that she kept braided and decorated with various items such as flowers, twigs, yarn, or anything she could get her hands on. She was very much the Indian woman in that respect, but she also was a white woman in her dress and her mannerisms. Zeke was captivated by what he had seen and made a vow to get to know the woman better.

ZEKE TOOK a long ride into the forest with his new rifle slung loosely over his shoulder, not held at the ready. He had purchased it from Travis. This wasn't a musket, and he was a fine shot. "You'll like this," Travis said. "It's called a Hawkins, and it's fired with a percussion cap not a flint-lock. Very seldom will you have a mis-fire, but don't let yourself run out of caps, you can't find them on the ground like you do flint," he laughed.

"I'll keep the musket for birds," he told Travis, but also was interested in a nice double barrel shotgun the trader had displayed. "Maybe, later on, that one."

On the farm, or before while growing up in the Ohio Valley, Zeke had never felt it necessary to be armed, but since he left the farm, he has been armed every minute of the day. He bought a beautiful knife from Travis, with an elk horn handle and tooled leather sheath. "By God, Zeke, you could kill a Griz with that hunk of steel," Travis told him when he strapped it on. He didn't give up the old knife, one he had built years ago. The one he killed an Indian with months before.

"I've made some fine knives on my anvil, Travis, but this one is very good. I like to use the steel from wagon springs for my knives. "I've got a patch knife I made with a hickory handle, but this one…" he held it back up," with that elk horn handle is a classic. Gonna have to go shoot a deer for supper just so's I can use it," he laughed.

Zeke wasn't looking for game today, he was in deep thought about what Travis had talked about. "I'll spend the winter preparing to move out in the spring. With my mules, and maybe one or two more pack mules, I can travel fast, sure faster than those wagons," he snickered, nudging the saddle-mule Ruth a bit. *And a darned sight faster than on foot*, he chuckled.

The mountains were in their autumn glory, hardwood trees blazing in bright high mountain sunshine, and grass still growing in places. He came to a small stream and stepped off the mule, looping a lead rope over a branch so she could munch on grass and leaves. "Look at those trout," he said, simply standing at water's edge. He sat down and leaned against a cottonwood tree.

"It would be a hard life here," he mumbled. "I need a home," he said, loud enough to startle the mule. "I do, Ruth. I need a home, and as much as I love these mountains, I need one that can be productive. The Willamette Valley is where I need to be." All this talk brought memories flashing through his mind; of his youth, and his life with Elizabeth.

When he was ten-years-old, his father indentured him to a cabinetmaker for three years where he was submerged in the art of woodworking. At the ripe old age of thirteen, he had been indentured to a blacksmith and had learned the art of metal work and fabrication, particularly ironwork. He would go to school every morning, but at noon was required to report to the iron or wood shops where he worked until sunset, then headed home for a late supper and bed.

. The two arts came together when he married Elizabeth and they moved onto their one hundred sixty-acre homestead, miles from the nearest village. Heading south, along a creek that fed the Mississippi, they had shunned the area around St. Louis. It was still just a village, but the young couple felt there were just too many people, and went deeper into the prairie to establish their home and farm.

Virtually everything they owned he'd built, in some cases, manufactured. Plows, hinges, hoes, rakes, and animal implements he forged; the home, furnishings, and decorations he built, and with all that, Elizabeth was a master potter, creating all their earthenware, a skill Zeke learned immediately.

They had very few encounters with Indians, and the few Indians they had met were not threatening or provocative. Zeke often offered corn or beans, but always saw to it that his animals were well fenced if any Indians were about.

I love these mountains, and the meadows surrounded by towering peaks of solid granite, he thought. *Also, I miss Elizabeth and the farm terribly,* he reminisced. He suddenly felt overwhelmed with sadness about losing his family, and yet felt positive about his future. Melancholy did not sit well with Zeke Hawthorne.

The forests of the Rocky Mountains were thick and filled with a green velvet haze that mesmerized him. Tall red cedar, even taller pines, and the rich hues of blue spruce filled the eyes and the aroma was almost pulsating in strength. "I came riding with my new rifle," he murmured, "and I'm sitting by a stream filled with trout. You'd better wake up, Zeke," he snickered to himself. "Don't ever leave without line and hooks again."

The soil was often red, sometimes black, and, of course, a deep golden brown, with great ferns and bushes, what Travis called- buck brush, growing in between the trees. Most of the pathways through the forest were created originally by animals and adapted by men. Zeke watched a sky so blue, so intense, it almost hurt the eyes, and he knew he would be happy here. "But only through this winter," he decided.

My dream is still Oregon, with a productive farm, and a family. But I am enchanted with this country. He had pictures in his mind of that vast Willamette Valley, split by a large free-flowing river and fields of grain and other foods. At the same time, visions of massive mountains covered in interminable forests of magnificent trees, filled his vision and he found he couldn't keep the smile off his rugged face.

Elizabeth continued to be on his mind as he and Ruth the mule rode along a path through the trees. He mumbled, trying to carry on a conversation with her. "I miss you terribly, Elizabeth. Our farm was very hard to leave, but without you, I couldn't stay. I could not bear the burden of living there without you. I'm so sorry we never were able to fill the void of not having grown children and grandchildren." He wiped tears from his sun burnt cheeks, blew his nose, and relived pictures of her and the farm, deeply etched in his memory.

Zeke rode many miles during his contemplations and

had to hurry back before he would be left in the forest after sunset as he knew they closed the stockade gates after sundown. After supper, Zeke continued to contemplate what his new life would be like, and remembered his old one.

His mother, so insistent that he read, learn, and think creatively, and his father; a taskmaster who believed that only hard, physical work mattered. His mother sending Zeke to school every day and his father demanding that he be indentured to craftsmen, to learn a trade. He could still hear his father demand, "You'll never amount to anything reading a book, only by learning a trade." He never argued with his father, but for many years, he'd resented his father's attitude.

That night, Zeke wrote long thoughts in his journal. "Interesting, that both Ma and Pa were right. I can read English, Latin, and Greek, and I'm also known as a master ironworker, carpenter, and cabinetmaker. I can think and I can create, and they both need to take full credit for that."

His newly built fireplace inside the cabin hadn't fully cured yet, so he ate supper outside. Lighting a fire in a fireplace before the mortar was fully cured and dried would allow steam to build in the mortar and explode. Zeke had seen that more than once in his years. He rose from his log seat near an outside fire, walked into the cabin, and called it a night. "It's been a good day, I think."

7

The first storm of the early fall season came roaring in one night, catching only newcomers to the Rockies unaware, one of those being Ezekiel Hawthorne. He awoke with a start when the front door of his cabin blew open accompanied by bitter cold and huge snowflakes. The Travis family had discussed its possibilities for two days, watching scudding clouds and high wind, but to Zeke the changes were just changes.

He couldn't do much blacksmith or carpentry work, so spent considerable time planning and designing what he would build when he got to Oregon, when he found and established his new farm. His renderings and elevations were finely detailed, even colored and inked. "Oh, this will be a fine farmhouse," he murmured, plotting out various ways he could build what he imagined.

The storm blew itself out in three days leaving about six inches of snow on the ground. Zeke made his way across the parade ground to the trader's store, scuffing the snow and welcoming the new buffalo robe coat he had purchased just the week before. He had a packet of his renderings with him to show Travis and his wife. He found them in a grim mood, huddled near the potbelly stove, cherry red on an icy morning.

"Am I interrupting?" he asked.

"No," Travis said. "Come in, come in. Elaine and I are discussing what we're going to do come spring, and you might be interested as well. Coffee?"

Zeke smiled at Elaine, pulled a chair near the fire and settled down, thanking Travis for the coffee. "Um, a little rum to warm things, eh?" he joked taking that first sip. "I've been doing some thinking on next spring as well. With that storm, I had time to sit and design what I want to build when I get to Oregon."

"Travis wants me and the girls to go back east while he stays here, and I really don't want to," Elaine said. "I've never been comfortable out of the mountains." Elaine Travis was known in her Shoshone Tribe as Walks So Softly, and had been as far east as St. Louis twice. She added, "I know it will be dangerous here. The Mormons have threatened to burn us out, but with Travis and Moose here, I'll be safe," she said, sadness dripping from her words and tears smudging her pretty face.

"Moose will be with the tribe and I'll be ready to ride at a moment of attack by those fools from Salt Lake," Travis said, softly. "You and Sarah must be with Barbara and be safe."

"Instead of east," Zeke said, "have you thought of Oregon or even California? It's still mostly open country, with opportunity for anyone willing to work hard, and I know you and Travis work hard," he smiled at Elaine. "The Cascade Mountains, the Sierra Nevada, those are massive ranges, like the Rockies. You might find yourself right at home." He nabbed another cup of hot coffee, tucked a nip of run into the cup and continued.

"Travis, old man, you and Elaine could set up a business in no time in that country, and the both of you would be happy."

"I like the way you think, Zeke," Elaine said. "Show me those pictures you were talking about. I want to see your Oregon farm." Travis fixed himself another coffee and scooted close to see, as well.

"Never been to Oregon," he said. "Bridger's been there, and talked good talk about that Willamette Valley. Said the Snake River Valley, before you get to the Columbia is mighty nice too. In places," he snickered.

"Elaine, we might have to give this idea of Zeke's some thought. I was planning to get a message to Vasquez in Salt Lake that we would be pulling out next spring, anyway, so it wouldn't matter if you went east and I went to the Yellowstone country, or we both went to Oregon, the main thing is, you would be safe."

"Just look at these pictures, Jeremiah," Elaine said, spreading them out on the table. "My goodness, you do fine work, Zeke.

"This is what one might expect from an architect," Elaine said. "You do beautiful work." Sarah Travis came into the trading post as Elaine was pointing out a feature or two to Travis.

"What have we here?" she asked, joining the table. Zeke stood immediately and offered her his chair. She gave him a big smile, then lowered her eyes and slipped into the chair. Zeke pulled another one up to the table, and sat next to her.

She is one of the most beautiful women I've ever met, and amazingly open and friendly. Half Indian, educated, a teacher, and someone I have got to get to know much better. He let his eyes slowly take in the whole picture of Sarah Travis, and hardly heard a word from any of the others.

She shuffled through Zeke's renderings of a farm-house, barns, even farm fields, looking first at a picture, then looking at Zeke, lowering her eyes once more, but with a smile at each picture.

"You do beautiful work, sir," she said. "You are obviously a master craftsman."

"Thank you," he said, smiling. "I spent many years learning my trades. I'm looking forward to my Oregon farm."

"I have to get back to my little school," Sarah said. "Just wanted to pop in and see how things are going. Zeke, if you get a chance, come by the school later. I have a nice stack of books you might enjoy."

"I will," he said. "Thank you." She stood, as did Travis and Zeke, and Sarah headed out the door and back to her one-room school. "You have a beautiful daughter," Zeke said, sitting back down. To himself, he said there was no doubt in his mind that he would be visiting Sarah's school later that day.

HE SPENT the rest of the morning with visions of Sarah interfering at every step. "What a delightful woman," he muttered many times, finally putting his work aside, slipping into his buffalo coat, and grabbing his new all-beaver flat-top hat and marching to the school house. Travis had a pencil drawing of Jim Bridger wearing that style hat and found, to his consternation that he had to have one just like it. *Sometimes I'm still just a foolish little boy*, he thought, but still, he wore the hat every time he stepped outdoors.

Walking through the fort was like walking through old history. He enjoyed seeing the stockade walls with slits cut for riflemen, even a platform for big guns, and all the buildings within the fort made from logs, not milled lumber. Stone chimneys, most showing smoke after the big storm, were rough in nature. "This must have been what it looked like when my grandparents first settled in the Ohio Valley," he mumbled, walking onto the porch of the log cabin schoolhouse.

"There were still problems with the French and the Indians, and the country was wide open, with plenty of game, and ground ripe for planting crops. I never got to meet those people," he said, letting good thoughts fill his head.

He knocked and Sarah opened the door immediately. "Hello, Mr. Hawthorne. I saw you walking across the old parade ground. Welcome to Fort Bridger Elementary School," she said with a brilliant smile. "Come in, come in," and she stepped back into the large single room. "My, isn't that a nice hat," she smiled, helping him out of his heavy coat.

There were ten or twelve little desks, rough-cut timber and rough wood for the children to write on, spread around the room. Behind the teacher's desk was a large blackboard, and the alphabet and numbers, one to ten, spread across the top. *Very primitive,* splashed through Zeke's mind as the two walked toward Sarah's desk. "How many students are there?" he asked, taking the seat she offered.

She hung the hat and coat on pegs before she settled in behind her desk, prim and proper, he thought. "I have about seven full-time students, and there are four or five that show up once in a while. Education isn't a priority with some of the families that live outside the fort." She stood back up and offered Zeke a cup of tea, the pot of water boiling away on a potbelly stove.

"Thank you," he said. "My mother was a stickler for learning and my father felt having a means of making a living more important. I got both in heavy doses," he laughed. She set his cup on the side of the desk and sat down with hers. "I would say these children are very lucky. I doubt that every frontier outpost has a full-fledged school with an educated and proper teacher." He almost found himself blushing and noticed a rise of color in Sarah's cheeks as well.

"I put together a few books from my cabin that you might be interested in," she said. "We are getting supplies in from St. Louis and other points east a lot more often now, so you can order just about anything you want. Of course, it will be six months or so before you see it," she laughed. "I have some good lists of newly published works, and of course, the classics are always available."

"Where did you go to school, Sarah?" He still found himself amazed that an Indian girl, even though half-white, would be fully educated. He still had that word "savage" in his vocabulary.

"My father has relatives in Boston, and when I was twelve, Mr. Bridger took me east. I lived in Boston for ten years, and studied just about every day of those ten long years," she chuckled. "I love Boston, and I got to travel a lot up through New England. I even visited New York City several times."

Zeke watched the animation in the lady as she described her earlier life and continued to be amazed at what he was seeing and hearing. *She has visited the cradle of our country, and here is pious Ezekiel Hawthorne- judging he-she should be the once questioning my background.* He couldn't take his eyes off the lady, and his thoughts continued. *Her eyes are dancing, and that smile is better than any lamp I've ever seen,* he was thinking, sipping the hot tea.

"Travis and I were talking about this coming spring," Zeke said. "Will you be going back to Boston? I know your mother doesn't want to go, she made that very plain." He watched her face cloud over and wished that he had kept his mouth shut, never asked the question.

"Mama is not happy about what might happen," Sarah whispered, looking down at her desktop. "I know it won't be safe here, and I was comfortable on the East Coast, but I don't want to leave either. I don't know why that man in Salt Lake thinks he has the right to burn us out, to ruin this wonderful Fort Bridger!" She was angry and frightened at the same time as Zeke watched her open and close her fists and saw her shoulders shudder just a bit.

"When you came into the trading post earlier, we were talking about your mother and father possibly moving to Oregon, and they both seemed interested in that," Zeke said. "Maybe you could talk to them about that." He had a bright smile on his face as he continued, "There would always be a need for another fine teacher in that beautiful country."

She returned the smile but didn't take the bait. They spent another hour talking and enjoying each other's company before Zeke finally had to get back to his shop. She filled a wooden box with books for him and said there would be more anytime he wanted them. Zeke didn't want to leave, but didn't know how to prolong their meeting. Worse, didn't know how to ask to see the lady again.

Sarah answered that question. "Did Papa tell you about the little shindig he has planned for Saturday? We're going to roast some venison, and many of the ladies will be making pies and cakes. Mr. Willoughby will have his banjo and harmonica out, so there might even be dancing. I'd like it very much if you would join our family for the occasion."

Zeke stood very still for a moment, sure that his mouth was wide open, and finally stammered, "I would be delighted, Sarah. Saturday… that's day after tomorrow, if I'm keeping my days straight."

"Good," she said, ushering him to the door after helping him into his big coat and handing him his new hat. "I gathered some wild apples and will make us a nice apple pie."

Zeke had a strut to his walk as he made his way across the fort, back to his blacksmith shop. He hummed a little song or two, seeing images of he and Sarah, and was already designing new desks for her students. "I love this country," he said to the world, putting his box of books down on the table in his cabin.

AUTUMN CAME EARLY in the high country, and there were tinges of frost as Zeke prepared his morning meal, still at the outside fire. "That stone fireplace should be ready tomorrow, and the way it feels this morning, it will be just in time." Among the supplies he had purchased from Travis were bucksaws, axes, and wood splitters. *This will be my first winter in the high mountains,* he was thinking. *I wonder just how cold it gets around here?*

Cold has never bothered Zeke, growing up in the Ohio Valley with snow drifts as high as some building's roof lines, and then living in Missouri all those years. *With this air, and being so high up, I imagine we'll have some strong winds and icy temperatures.*

The young boys had been bringing him firewood every day for a week, and the woodpile was looking good. Most of it, but not all, he noticed, had been split but some he would have to split himself. He would need to knock those rounds down to a size that fit his wood stove. *Elizabeth and I had some pretty rough winters at the farm, back in Missouri,* he remembered, *but this is high country. Well, I know I can handle it,* he smiled, swishing a chunk of bread through the side-meat gravy and the last of the egg yolk.

Moose showed up as Zeke was finishing his breakfast. "Morning, Sir. My name is Moose Travis, Jeremiah's son." A large hand was thrust forward from a magnificent buckskin shirt the man was wearing. His black hair was pulled back and tied at the nape of his neck, and he had feathers woven into the long braid that hung down his back. Beads and bones decorated the shirt, and fringes hung from chest, back, and arms.

Although half Irish, Moose was all Shoshone in Zeke's eyes.

"It's a pleasure! Will you join me in a cup of coffee?" he asked, standing up to take the man's hand. "I understand you're a fine hunter and trapper. Please, sit down."

Moose had the size and strength of Travis and the easy personality of his mother and sister. "I understand that you won't be traveling east with your mother come spring," Zeke said.

"No, I've been there before, Zeke, and I don't much care for that kind of life. I'm Shoshone top to bottom, and Jim Bridger is my best friend. I'll stay with my other family."

"Were you educated back east, as Sarah was?"

"Not for as long as she was," he laughed. "I couldn't stand it and had to come home. Mama was upset, but I can read as well as she can, I can do my numbers well, and I'm best at being a good hunter. If it wasn't so cold today, I'd be wearing a breach clout only, and be very happy at that."

"My Mama made me learn everything there was to learn," Zeke chuckled, "and my Papa forced me to learn what I needed to take care of myself and my family. I'm very glad for what they both demanded."

Moose smiled at that, saying, "You sound an awful lot like my father, Zeke, but I understand completely. My sister, Sarah, has beat that into my Shoshone head for fifteen years," he laughed. "But, look, I'm running a lumber mill, and have a crew in the forest bringing me lumber. Are you coming to the feast Saturday? Should be a lot of fun. Some of my friends from the village are going to be dancing to the drums. You'll like that."

"Yes, Moose, I'll be there. Sarah invited me to be with your family. I'm looking forward to that."

Moose's face was shrouded slightly as the two said good-bye and the large man headed out the stockade's gate.

I wonder if I said something wrong? Zeke wondered as he picked his coffee cup for a refill.

8

IT WAS A GAY DAY AT FORT BRIDGER; BUNTING FLYING FROM ramparts, ladies dressed in their finest, men strutting about, and at least three large deer roasting over coals. About twenty-five young Shoshone men, painted as if going to war had been dancing and singing to incessant drums and rattles, and several of the old white trappers had brought out their fiddles and banjos, serenading anyone and everyone that got within ten feet or so of them.

Zeke was enthralled by the pageantry, noise, and excitement. *This must have been what it was like ten or fifteen years ago during the time of the beaver. These are the real mountain people.*

"No," Travis said to Zeke's question. "It isn't Bridger's birthday, as far as I know, and it isn't in celebration of the founding of Fort Bridger, it's just an end of the summer party and feast. We do this every year, along about the end of August."

The two men were standing near one of the pits where

the meat was roasting, and watching the warriors from the Shoshone village dancing and giving off frightful screams of terror.

"These are some of the most savage warriors in the west, Zeke. The Snake or Shoshone are feared from one end of the Rockies to the other, and Jim Bridger loves each and every one of them. The Flathead and Crow respect the Shoshone, and only the arrogant Sioux disdain them.

"They haven't been treated very well by the government back in Washington," Travis said, "but they are adapting. Many people seem to think they have a right to just shove these people aside. I'm not one of them."

He was watching his son Moose, painted, in loin clout and moccasins, wielding a battle-ax, dancing with the group. "Look at that boy."

"He would scare the hell out of me," Zeke said, in all earnestness. "It looks like some of the men are beginning to carve up the venison, Travis. Should we join the ladies?"

Sarah and Elaine had a large table brought out to the festival site, and were loading it up with platters of food, great dishes filled with pies, and an earthen jug that Zeke figured was filled with rum, which seemed to be the preferred drink around the fort. Sarah had dug a small pit and had a fire going with a large kettle of beans cooking, and a coffee pot bubbling away on a rock near the fire.

"There was a rider came in this morning. Jeremiah. Bridger is about a week or so out, and there's even better news... Barbara is with him!"

Elaine was as happy as Zeke had ever seen her at the news that her youngest daughter was coming home. "She sent a note with old man Tanner that she will be with us all winter. Isn't that wonderful?"

"We'll have the whole family here for Christmas," Travis smiled, pouring half a cup of coffee and topping it off with some of the amber liquid from the jug. "I suppose, then, that Sarah and Barb will travel east together, come spring, and we won't see either one for two or more years."

He shook his great shaggy head, wandered around the table looking at all the ladies had prepared. "I'm glad my family is educated. Very glad. But I don't like them having to leave."

"You just shush, now, Mr. Travis," Elaine said, wagging a finger at him. "This is a party and we won't have any of your melancholy interfering with it." She was stern on the one hand, but smiling as she said it, and Travis gave a smile, catching a quick wink of her eye.

"Can you help me bring some chairs out, Zeke?" Sarah asked. "I can carry two if you can get the rest."

They started back toward the trader's store, almost striding in beat with the Indian drums. "This is quite the soiree," Zeke said. "It looks like there's enough food for the fort, the village, and half the people back east. Travis said this happens every year?"

"It's our big party," Sarah said. "We have been doing it ever since I was a little girl. Oh, here comes Walking Bird." She was looking at one of the Indian warriors, painted, and carrying a club with a large stone attached.

"Walking Bird, it's nice to see you. You're all sweaty from dancing. This is my friend Ezekiel Hawthorne. Zeke, say hello to my friend Walking Bird."

"Hello," Zeke said, sticking his hand out.

Walking Bird ignored the greeting and the offered hand. "You eat with me, Sarah, not with the white man," and he reached out and grabbed her hand, turned as if to take her with him.

"No!" she wailed, trying to free her wrist. "No, Walking Bird, I'm with my family." She was fighting to get her arm free, and Walking Bird gripped her arm even harder, jerking her almost off her feet as he tried to walk away.

"That's enough," Zeke stormed. "Let her go, Walking Bird. She was with me and she will stay with me." There was anxiety deep in his stomach, but Zeke showed no fear of the Indian warrior and was ready to defend Sarah. "Let her go now," he said again, as he squared his shoulders, and knotted his fists.

Walking Bird flung Sarah's arm away and swung the heavy club at Zeke's head. Zeke danced aside and drove a fist deep into Walking Bird's groin, doubling the man over. He used both fists as one, drove them across his body and slammed them into the man's head, driving him into the ground.

Zeke jumped on the writhing Indian, wrenched the club from his hand and threw it aside. He was flinging fist after fist into the warrior's face when Travis grabbed him and jerked him to his feet. "He's had enough, Zeke," he said. "Are you alright, Sarah? What happened here?" There was anger and fright in his face and his tone, and he kept an eye on Walking Bird as the warrior tried to get up.

"He tried to force Sarah to go with him," Zeke said. A crowd had gathered, trappers, wives, and warriors, some grumbling, some amazed that Walking Bird was bleeding from his nose, lips, and ears, and Zeke was unmarked. Some of the Indians were making noises as if to attack Zeke, but Moose stepped in at that moment.

"I've told you to stay away from my sister," Moose said to Walking Bird, "and now look what you've done. You've harmed Sarah, you've insulted my father's guest, and you've embarrassed yourself in front of my friends and family.

"Go home, Walking Bird. You don't belong here." There was a lot more to Moose Travis than Zeke had considered, and as he watched this show of leadership, he realized that Moose would be a force to be reckoned with in the future. *That is what leadership is all about.*

Zeke was amazed as he watched the other Indian braves step aside as Walking Bird shuffled from the area. "My sister and family will expect an apology, Walking Bird." Moose stood next to Sarah, holding her hand, as she gently caressed the huge man's shoulders.

Zeke was primed in case someone else decided to take a shot or punch at him, and had an almost quizzical look on his face. *What an amazing scene. Indians painted as for war, dancing as for war, and I get into a fight with one of them. What on earth would Elizabeth say to this?* The danger of the scene and the humor of the scene played out over and over as Zeke stood next to Sarah and her brother.

"He has lost face and will want revenge, Zeke. You must be prepared for that at all times now." Moose, too, knew that he had put himself in line for a revenge attack. Not for standing up for his sister, that was expected of a Shoshone warrior, but for standing with Ezekiel, a white man... a stranger to the tribe. "I'm afraid this will not end well," he said, spinning on his heels and striding back to the Indian dance circle.

The crowd slowly worked their way back to tables and food, but there was a subdued atmosphere over the group. "Let's get those chairs, Zeke," Sarah said, stepping toward the store. They walked side-by-side across the parade ground as Travis and Elaine watched.

"Thank you, Zeke," Sarah said, very quietly. "Walking Bird has always thought I should be his woman, but I have never encouraged him. He must have been drinking," she continued, talking from fear and fright, and thrilled that Zeke did what he did. She reached down and took his hand in hers for the last ten feet or so before entering the store.

The fracas was soon out of the minds of the Fort Bridger populace. There were more interesting things to attend to, Travis said, as he piled slabs of roasted venison on his platter, covering about half with beans well boiled with plenty of hot chilies. The feast continued well into the night, with Indian drums and rattles playing at one end of the partiers, and banjos and fiddles snarling traffic at the other end.

Travis and Elaine called it quits and went back to their cabin behind the trader's store, and Zeke and Sarah danced and talked for another hour. "This has been a wonderful day and evening, Sarah. You're a fine dancer, and I apologize for the bruises I'm sure will show up on your pretty ankles in the morning. I'm a stomper, not a dancer," he chuckled, escorting her back to the table.

He poured each of them a cup of coffee, and he laced his with a taste of rum, while she dished two more slices of apple pie. "That's the best apple pie I've ever eaten," he smiled, not bothering with a fork.

She giggled watching him take half a slice in his mouth. "It's the altitude, I think," she said. "Apples taste different up here, where the trees grow in the clouds. I think I'd better get back to my cabin, Zeke. It's getting late."

They were holding hands as they walked across the parade grounds toward her cabin. "I don't think Walking Bird will be foolish enough to come after you, Zeke," she said as they stood at her front door, "but you should be aware that he can be very dangerous when he's drinking. Thank you for a wonderful day, and for protecting my honor." She wanted this wonderful man to take her in his arms, kiss her a thousand times, make love to her all night, but knew she would not let that happen.

Zeke brought her hand to his lips, kissed her fingers lightly, and held the hand as long as he dared. "Thank you for allowing me to spend a wonderful day with you and your family. Sleep warm and stay well, Sarah," he said.

She went into her cabin and he strolled across the fort to the blacksmith shop and home. Those nearby heard a couple of tunes hummed along the way, and watched his booted feet dance just a bit.

ZEKE SPENT the next several days working at the forge, repairing wagon pieces and parts for Travis, and building school desks for Sarah's children, as she called them. Moose was at the shop regularly and teased the man about his sister. "She has a terrible temper, Zeke, and is a fine shot with that flintlock pistol Papa gave her. Why," he smiled, "I've seen her use an axe on a piece of wood when she's angry, and she could fell a spruce in no time."

Zeke snickered at these comments, and continued working. "She's a delightful lady, Moose," he said, pouring some coffee, or making marks on a piece of wood, but down deep, he wanted to know as much about Sarah Travis as he could. "You're quite a bit younger than Sarah, Moose. Did she help your mother when you were growing up?" Zeke had fun teasing back, as well.

Moose let the remarks flow as did Zeke and they continued making their plans for the spring, each knowing the other would not be seen again in all probability. "Papa and I are going hunting in the morning, Zeke. Papa needs some meat for the winter, and so do you. Will you join us? There will be five of us all together. You'll need both your mules, and we'll be gone for several days."

"Wonderful," Zeke said, understanding he was just given some high praise and honor by being invited. "I'll be ready."

ZEKE WAS AMAZED as he and Travis rode out of Fort Bridger just after sunrise, joining Moose and what looked like half the Shoshone Nation waiting for them. "I thought you said there would be five of us," he said as Moose rode up on his beautiful bay stud.

"Oh, yes," he said. "Five of us hunting, but we need the women and all the pack animals to take care of the meat and get it back." There were at least fifteen women and each one was mounted and had a pack animal as well. "We will eat well this winter," he said, motioning everyone to ride north.

They followed the Green River north through fabulously beautiful country, had fresh trout and large Arctic hare for supper the first night, and gathered around a large fire. The hunters were in one camp and the women, who were separated, had their own fire, and their own food, which they'd brought with them.

"I was never able to enjoy an evening fire like this coming across the country," Zeke said to Travis as he put another log onto the flames. "Too dangerous."

"As we move farther north, we won't either," Moose said. "We'll be moving into Crow and Blackfoot country, so we will be wary and defensive." Moose and his two Shoshone companions talked about the next day's hunt while Travis continued to eat and Zeke piled into his bedroll, a heavy buffalo robe over the top.

Each of the hunters had brought a pack animal and light camp provisions. They had only some beans and coffee, and bedrolls, planning on letting Mother Nature provide the rest, needing space for meat to bring home on the packs. Morning found bright sunshine and bitter cold, but no wind as the five spread out across the broad valley, hanging toward the foothills on the east side.

"Should find elk and deer," Moose said when they had morning coffee. One of his companions, a big fellow named Sings With Wolves, seemed to disagree.

"You take elk, Moose, I want buffalo. Two buffalo for Pretty Bird and my son."

Travis was laughing as he said, "We don't have enough pack animals for two buffalo, Sings With Wolves. Maybe you could pack one out."

Sings With Wolves sniffed at that, and simply said, "Mebbee so," and poured more coffee.

The women held back more than a mile behind the hunters, moving as quietly as possible. Sure enough, about mid-morning as the hunters rode across a low bench in the hills, Moose spotted a small herd of buffalo, less than half a mile away. "I see at least twenty big animals, and they don't see us."

He tested the wind with a feather from his hat. "They won't smell us either. Let's go in low and slow," he said, dismounting and slipping his lead rope around a scrub Piñon pine, fastening it tight. The rest followed suit and moved at a low crouch toward the herd. As they got closer, they got all the way down into a crawl through rocks and brush.

Zeke's heart was pounding so loud he was sure it would spook the buffalo. The enormity of the situation was almost more than the man could handle. *I'm with the Fort Bridger trader and three Shoshone Indian Warriors, hunting buffalo. My God! I'm about to shoot my first buffalo, and we may be in enemy Indian country. What on earth would Elizabeth say about this?*

He was also aware that he would be shooting his new rifle at something other than a target. It was a fine piece of engineering, this Hawkins of his, but he had never fired it at anything alive. *It shoots as true as anything I've ever shot before, so calm down, Mr. Hawthorne,* he chided.

They moved slowly, sagebrush-to-sagebrush, scrub tree to scrub tree, with Moose directing traffic. He had them in a broad line, and as the group got to within about eighty yards or so, Moose motioned to lay flat and take long, slow aim. Zeke's knees and elbows were scuffed and sore from the rocks, and his heart sounded like elephants raging through the jungle. He brought the new rifle to his shoulder.

The buffalo were spread out in front of the hunters, grazing on deep early autumn grass, unaware of visitors. *Those heads and shoulders are massive,* Zeke was completely in awe. *I can't imagine how much weight we're looking at.* Travis fired first, Moose and the two Warriors fired almost together, and Zeke finally drew down on a very large bull, squeezed, felt the shock of the shot, and as the smoke cleared, he saw his animal slowly sink to its knees, and roll off to the side. It kicked twice and didn't move again.

There had been five shots, there were five animals down. Within a short time, the women came on the scene and Moose had all the men move so they surrounded the women. It took only moments for everyone to reload, just in case. "Those shots could bring Crow or Blackfoot warriors. We must be prepared to fight," he said.

Zeke was amazed at how fast the women were able skin, clean, and make the animals ready for packing. Men and women hefted and hauled, and every ounce of useable buffalo was set on packs or travois, and they moved off to the south, at what Zeke thought was a brisk pace.

While neither the Crows nor the Shoshone liked the Sioux; they also disliked each other and were at constant war. *We're on Crow hunting ground, and I'm a white man hunting with a Shoshone party. This is for real,* Zeke was thinking, watching the back trail as much as the front. *For Travis and Moose, this is how life is lived, and for all my years I have never been as excited, or scared, as I've been this morning.*

Moose had his two companions spread well to each

side, keeping close watch as well, when the group saw several mounted Indians advancing on the party. The women huddled with their animals and meat, and the five men started forward toward the visitors, rifles in hand, ready for a fight.

"It's okay," Moose said. "That's Slow To Fight. He came to give us protection." The groups joined within minutes, getting some good comments about how much meat was in the packs. One of those with Slow To Fight was Walking Bird.

"Moose," Walking Bird said, scowling at Zeke, "Crow warriors in the hills to the east. Maybe twenty," he said. Then, in the Shoshone language he made several other comments. Moose bristled, didn't say anything back to the angry man, instead, spoke quickly to his father.

"Dad, you and Zeke get the women and meat back to the fort. Slow To Fight, let's go." He and the Indian braves turned and put their horses in a long trot to the east. Most from the village had the new rifles provided by Bridger and the men were looking forward to new scalps on their lances.

Travis motioned for Zeke to follow and rode directly to the women, motioned them to move fast toward the fort. "Zeke, you trail behind, I'll lead. Keep your eyes as open as they've ever been and be ready for a fight." The horses were well trained to haul heavy loads or drag filled travois, and moved out at a strong walk, staying in a close-knit group moving through the bottom land near the Green River.

Zeke fell in behind the group and spent more time looking back over his shoulder than he did forward. There was meat for several families involved in this retreat to the fort, and the women were careful as they rode, looking toward the eastern hills constantly. Zeke could see Moose and the men start to spread out, now a couple of miles into the foothills of the nearby range. Finally, they dipped below a ridge and he lost sight of them. That's when he saw the dust of riders coming up on his rear, probably two to three miles distant.

With his heart pounding, Zeke howled for Travis. "We have company!" Travis wheeled, said something to the women and rode hard back to where Zeke was pointing out the dust. "Looks like maybe five riders, and they are coming fast." Zeke's heart was in his throat, every nerve in his body primed for whatever was going to happen.

"Stay with the women for another half mile, Zeke, then get off your horse and find good cover to shoot from. Hurry," Travis said, jumping off his horse and making his way through the sagebrush. He dove behind a slight rise in the surrounding ground and held his rifle cocked and ready.

Zeke moved forward another several hundred yards, bailed off his mule and found a dip where he could get as low as possible. Then he brought his new rifle to the ready. *I've never shot a man before,* he thought, watching the riders come toward him at a lope. *Easy, Zeke, take it eas...*, *nice and slow. Don't panic,* he continued to tell himself, watching the riders. As they closed on Travis, Zeke could see they were painted and wore breach clouts and moccasins only. *They must have heard our shots. Magnificent,* he murmured, watching the men advance.

When they got close enough, Travis fired his rifle, knocking one rider off his horse. Zeke saw a second man jump from his horse toward Travis.

The other three riders broke into a full charge and rode wide of where Travis was. They were intent on capturing or killing the women and getting the meat. Travis had reloaded fast and shot one more time before they were out of range, dropping another rider. At least one of the men on the ground was not shot dead, and Travis had to put all his attention on what that man might do.

The last two riders came hard toward the women, not knowing that Zeke was there, and he fired, knocking the lead rider off his horse. He didn't have time to reload before one of the Indians dove right on top of Zeke, screaming his war cry, looking to bury a heavy iron hatchet in Zeke's skull.

Zeke rolled with the impact of the heavy body and slammed his fist into the man's face with one hand, grabbing the man's wrist that held the deadly steel. Zeke's knife flashed in the fall sunshine as he drove it into the Indian's heart, once, twice, and rolled off the man in time to see the other Indian, the one he shot, about to spring on him.

He jumped to his feet, and met the attack head on. The man was seriously wounded from the rifle shot, and Zeke drove the heavy knife into warm and yielding flesh. The Crow warrior was weak but heavy, and despite the mortal wound he took Zeke to the ground. Zeke thrust the knife deep into the man's body two more times before the fight ended.

Jumping to his feet, he grabbed his rifle, and got it reloaded. He looked for a target, his eyes as big as saucers, his mouth as grim as it had ever been, and his body taught with anticipation. He saw the women continuing to move forward, with no one trying to attack them. Then, he found his mule quietly munching on some stubble, mounted and rode hard toward the women.

As he got close he heard gunfire well off to the east. *Sounds like Moose has found the rest of the Crow party,* he thought, looking around for Travis. He wasn't with the women, and Zeke almost panicked. He stood tall in the stirrups looking back up the trail, saw Travis's horse, but not the man, and put his mule in a hard charge.

He got there in time to find Travis in a hand-to-hand fight with one of the Crow warriors and jumped off his mule, driving his body into the fray. All three hit the ground hard, and Zeke had that knife into the Crow's back, pulled the blade out, grabbed the man's long hair, pulling his head back, and ripped his throat out with one slash.

Travis was injured, moaning when Zeke pulled the dead brave off him. He was covered in blood, but Zeke figured right away, most of that came from the Indian's throat. "Let's see what's wrong with you," he said, pulling Travis's heavy buffalo coat to the side. "He gave you a pretty good smack, my friend," Zeke said, looking at a serious gash in Travis's arm.

"Looks like he hit you with his hatchet, Travis. I'll get this bound up, get the bleeding stopped, and then we'd better get back with the women. It sounds like Moose found the war party. Let's hurry now."

They caught up with the fast-moving women quickly and determined that none had been hurt and no meat was lost. They continued to move fast toward the fort, still several hours away. Zeke kept a close eye on Travis who had lost enough blood that he wasn't too solid in the saddle, and watched for other possible attacks.

They were almost in sight of Black Fork and Fort Bridger when Zeke spotted riders coming hard, once again from behind them. He motioned the women to keep going, moving fast, and slapped Travis hard on the back to catch his attention. "Riders," is all he said, jumping off the mule and bringing the rifle to bear on those coming up the trail.

He had pulled down on the lead rider when he recognized Moose and took his finger off the trigger. Travis had dismounted and found some scrub brush to hide in, and stood to welcome his son and the Snake warriors. "Crow war party coming hard behind us, Papa. Let's make a good stand," and the others were off their mounts and looking for good cover right away.

One of the Indians grabbed the lead ropes of the animals and took them away from where the fight would be, tied them off and rejoined the group. The Crow war party could then be seen and heard, coming on hard. The Crow could see the women well ahead of them, not aware of Travis, Zeke, and the Shoshone warriors hiding in the scrub brush.

As soon as the riders were in range of those rifles, the barrage was deafening, dropping most of the war party. Zeke and Travis were reloading when they saw the Shoshone braves drop their rifles and continue the fight with bows and arrows. The Shoshone braves, led by Moose, immediately advanced on the downed riders, and Travis yelled at Zeke to mount up and get the women and meat into the fort.

As the two re-joined the Shoshone women they could

hear scattered screaming behind them, but kept riding. "Moose has good odds now," Travis said, nursing his injured arm.

"The men dropped their rifles, Travis. I wonder why?"

"Very simple, my friend, and something the U.S. Army will learn the hard way, I'm afraid, if they try to fight the Indians. A brave with a quiver full of arrows can shoot as many as eight or ten in the time it takes to reload a rifle. They will use the rifle to shoot once, the first shot, then go for their bows.

"It would have been the same with the buffalo if the first shot hadn't taken the big animal down. The kill shot would then have been an arrow." They rode in silence the rest of the way into Fort Bridger.

9

ELAINE, SARAH AND MOST OF THE SHOSHONE WOMEN SPENT several days taking care of the meat and skins. Every part of the animal was used in some way, and then it came time for distribution. The men that took part in the hunt would normally take their pick first, then those that rode to protect the hunters, and what was left would be shared among the village.

"Sarah," Zeke said as everyone gathered. "I don't want to take very much, just enough for a few meals. You pick for me, please. It's more important for the village to have as much as possible."

Travis heard and came over to where Zeke and Sarah were standing. "Moose and I have decided to take just one animal for the family, Zeke. There would be more than enough from that one animal to include you, if you would like to give your animal to the village."

"Yes, I would, Travis, that's a wonderful idea," Zeke said. He looked at Sarah and said, "I would very much like to have a buffalo robe of my own, though." He got a smile back and a nod, before Sarah lowered her eyes, and Travis slapped him on the back saying something about rapidly becoming a mountain man.

"I was very content with my farm back in Missouri," Zeke said, "but I admit, I've learned more about what a man's life should be since I came west. Me a mountain man, like Jim Bridger? No, I'm not that kind of man, but the clothing and accessories make more sense than anything they wear back east. I have my big coat, but I want a real buffalo robe."

Gentle laughter from Travis and his family all but proved his point.

"Besides," he continued, "I think I'd look pretty good wrapped in a buffalo robe." Sarah quickly dropped her eyes to her work as a smile spread across her face and the thought that, yes, Zeke, you certainly would, flooded her mind. She didn't say it, but she also remembered how good he looked in his buffalo coat and new hat.

The distribution went well with many families getting considerable amounts of meat, sinew, and skins. Sarah said she would see to it that one of the skins would be made into a fine robe for Zeke, and he could dip into the salt barrel anytime he wanted for a hefty chunk of buffalo meat for the stew pot.

THE MORNING FOLLOWING THE DISTRIBUTION, Zeke had a large fire going in his new fireplace, some sidemeat sizzling in a cast iron pan and a pot of coffee boiling on the hearth, when he saw Moose come to the front door. "Come in, Moose. Good morning to you."

Instead of his usual smile, Moose was wearing a scowl

as he stood by the fire warming his hands. "I don't have good news to bring you this morning, I'm afraid," he said, taking a cup of coffee from Zeke. "Walking Bird is making threats, Zeke. He says he will kill you and take Sarah for his wife, and no one can talk him out of it. He's a very dangerous man, and I think it might be best if you move out of the fort, maybe to Salt Lake." His face was clouded in anger as he said this, and probably fear for his sister's safety.

"I've never run from a threat, Moose, and I certainly won't run from this one, particularly since it also involves Sarah's safety. No, I won't run. Thank you for the warning, though." He poured the two of them coffee and offered some of the fried meat to Moose.

"No, thank you, Zeke," he said. "I'd better get back to the woodcutters. We have lots of work to do. Protect yourself, my friend, and be aware at all times. You stood with us against our enemy, the Crow, you hunted with us and provided meat to the village, so know also, you have friends in the Shoshone tribe." Moose was tall, strong, proud, and one worried man as he shook hands with Zeke and headed out into the fall sunshine.

In just a few minutes, Zeke found himself opening his door to Travis. "Busy morning at the blacksmith shop today," he said with a smile, offering coffee and a chair to the trader. "You just missed Moose. Hope you have better news than he did."

"I know you've been looking forward to Bridger's arrival, but I'm afraid I don't have good news. Bridger sent word that the supply train should be here in a day or two, but he is heading north and into the Yellowstone country instead of spending the winter here."

"That's bad," Travis, "just too bad. I really wanted to get to know that man. Well, damn, is all I can say." He saw Travis ease his wounded arm a little by resting it on the table and asked if it was still bothering him.

"It's sore as hell, Zeke, but Elaine keeps it cleaned out and bandaged. Good thing I had that heavy coat on or that ax would have cut my arm right off. Elaine has a splint on it just in case the bone was fractured. Glad you got there when you did, too, or I'd be without hair and buried deep. I sure want you backing me up if I get in any more fights with Indians," he smiled, reaching for the coffee pot. "What kind of bad news did Moose bring?"

Zeke threw some more wood on the fire, poured himself another cup of boiling coffee and sat down across the table from Travis, worry spread across his face. "He said Walking Bird wants to kill me and kidnap Sarah. He wants me to leave the fort."

"I sure as hell hope you said no. Walking Bird's a fool, but ain't nobody gonna kill you, and I sure as hell won't let no damn drunken fool Indian kidnap my daughter!" Travis's anger flowed across the room as he thumped his coffee cup on the table, and waved his wounded arm in the air, ready for war.

"Run away?" Travis continued. "You? After what I saw in our pitched battle, I don't think I could imagine you running away from a fight." Travis, besides being angry at Moose for even thinking that Zeke might be willing to run from a fight, was also worried about his daughter, Sarah.

"Sarah seems to have good feelings for you, Zeke," he added. "Why don't you and Sarah have supper with us

98

tonight? We have much to talk about. Go see her and tell her what I just said, and we'll see you this evening."

He was a little cryptic there, I think, but I relish the thought of spending an evening with that lovely lady, Zeke thought. He spent some time pondering what to do about the threat from Walking Bird and decided there simply wasn't much he *could* do. "My knife is sharp, my rifle is loaded. I must simply maintain a high level of awareness," he murmured, doing his chores and firing up his forge for the day's work.

At mid-morning, he walked to the schoolhouse to visit with Sarah Travis and bumped into Slow To Fight coming across the parade ground. "Good morning, Zeke," he said with a smile. "Many families have said thank you for providing your meat from the hunt. Travis tells me you saved his life. It was a good fight."

Zeke stuck out his big right hand and said good morning back. "I'm glad I could help, and glad no one was hurt bad in the fight. Moose tells me you're a fine leader for your people."

"Moose will be a fine leader, too, and very soon, I believe. There are some that worry because he is half white, but his heart is all with the people. Moose will always work to keep us at peace and well fed."

They shook and Zeke continued to the school. *He's a fine leader teaching another to follow. Just a few months ago I always referred to the Indians as savages, and I have learned so much. These are fine people, and it's simply a case of differing cultures that we aren't as close as we should be.* He could hear singing inside the school as he stepped onto the porch. "They're singing the alphabet," he murmured, and caught himself humming right along. He waited for that final xyz before slipping inside.

"So, children," Sarah said, "this is Mr. Hawthorne, the man who made those nice new desks you're enjoying." Almost in unison, the seven children in the room said "Hello, Mr. Hawthorne. Thank you for the desks."

Zeke blushed a bit as he doffed his hat and shirked out of his heavy coat. "Hello, children. I'm glad you like the desks. I listened while you sang the alphabet song and it brought some wonderful memories back from when I went to school." He smiled as he walked up to Sarah's desk. "Good day, Miss Travis."

"Children," she said. "It's time for lunch now. Be back for afternoon study in one hour, please." The kids scattered like wildcats out the door and across the parade ground, except for one little girl, about six-years-old. "What is it, Apple Blossom? Is something wrong?"

"Mr. Hawthorne gave my mother buffalo meat from the hunt last week and I was supposed to go by the blacksmith shop and say thank you, but I was afraid to."

"Why were you afraid?" Zeke asked, taken aback by such a statement. "Please don't be afraid of me."

"My uncle Walking Bird says you are a bad man and you would hurt me."

Zeke was horrified that something like that would be said to a child, even if the two men did not like or understand each other. Zeke stood mute, not knowing how to respond to the little girl.

"Zeke, I'll see you in Papa's store in ten minutes. I need to have a talk with Apple Blossom," Sarah said, taking the girl's hand and walking toward the schoolroom door. Zeke got back into that big buffalo coat and followed them out the door, turning toward the trader's store.

"I'm sorry you had to hear that," Sarah said when they sat down at a table before the fire inside the store. "Walking Bird was very wrong to say something like that to a child."

"There's more to it than that, Sarah. Moose told me this morning that Walking Bird has threatened to kill me and kidnap you. Travis and Elaine would like us to have supper with them this evening to discuss this and other things. I would like that very much." He poured each of them a cup of hot coffee, added a goodly taste of rum to his, and continued.

"There are a lot of things I want to talk to you about, including this coming spring, our lives," and he caught himself before he made a complete fool of himself. He spent the next few seconds admiring the fire in the large rock fireplace, trying not to look at the beautiful lady.

She must think I'm a mad man, saying something like that. I wonder if I'm just lonely, needing warmth, love. I miss Eliza-beth so much, am I just trying to replace that wonderful woman? Zeke's mind was reeling with thoughts of love and a family, and then doubts about himself; doubts about these feelings. *I could fall in love with this beautiful lady in just moments, but we've only known each other for a few months, haven't spent that much time together. I want to just say it, just say the words, but like a little boy, I'm afraid to.*

Sarah wanted to hear what Zeke was terrified of saying, wanted to say some of the same things, and she also took a few moments to enjoy the warm fire. *Zeke is the kind of man I've wanted, dreamt of, searched for. Not the dandies in Boston, not the swaggering warriors in the village, but a man who simply gets things done, and is honest and fearless. Oh, yes, Ezekiel, Please, say those words.*

The quiet was overwhelming, and she felt she had to say something. "I have known from the moment we met that we would be a couple, Ezekiel Hawthorne, and when you whipped Walking Bird I knew for positive. I also knew your life would be in great danger from that moment." She reached out and took the big man's hand and held it tight, squeezing it hard with both of hers.

"I'll cancel this afternoon's class and we'll take a walk down by the Black Fork River, Zeke. Then we can talk." She brought his hand around her waist and he gathered her into his arms, rocking slowly, back and forth, enjoying the aroma of the lady, feeling the strength in her arms wrapped around his neck, letting their bodies mesh tightly.

She raised her face to his and their lips slowly closed on each other, a passion raging through their bodies and minds. "I too have imagined this from the moment we laid eyes on each other," he whispered. "I want this to be love, I want this to last forever."

"In the white man's world, I understand, you are to go to my father, ask for my hand, allowing as how you can love and support me. In the Indian's world, the woman and man determine that they will be married, and thus it is. Which will it be, Mr. Hawthorne, sir?" she teased, a little giggle just before another long kiss.

"We'll make ourselves known at supper," he said, without actually answering her question, teasing back just a bit.

SOME CALLED IT TRADE WHISKEY, BUT MOST WHO ENJOYED A nip of good whiskey from time to time called it rot gut, not fit for human consumption. The leaders of the Shoshone tribe had banned it from the village but, of course, it found its way in. Walking Bird was burrowed deep in buffalo robes, insanely drunk, babbling nonsense about how unjustly he was being treated by Sarah Travis, and how it was all Ezekiel Hawthorne's fault.

He had not drawn a sober breath from the day Zeke kicked his butt in front of the whole tribe and the whites at Fort Bridger, and his rage had grown with each passing day, until he felt he had to kill both Zeke and Sarah. It was mid-morning before Walking Bird stumbled through the village, mounted his horse, and rode toward the fort, more than an hour away under normal circumstances.

Walking Bird found he had to stop often to vomit, to relieve himself, and once, he fell off his horse, and passed out for a while. When he came to, filthy with vomit and rolling around in the mud, he found his horse and continued toward Fort Bridger, still a full, half hour away.

SARAH WAS in a fine buckskin dress, beaded and fringed, wearing high top mocs with a wool blanket wrapped around her shoulders, very much the Shoshone maiden, as she led Zeke along a well-worn path from the fort to the Black Fork of the Green River. Fort Bridger sat almost on an island, surrounded by rivers, and the two planned to walk along the bank of the Black Fork.

"Your mother is planning to move east with you and your sister while Travis stays for another season at Bridger," Zeke said, holding tightly to Sarah's hand, "but I have a better idea. I would like to have you, your mother, and your sister come to Oregon with me, and Travis can join us when he closes the fort. I would like you to be my wife when we make that journey." Zeke's heart was beating as hard as a Shoshone war drum as he said these things, afraid to even sneak a glance at Sarah.

Sarah caught her breath, squeezed Zeke's hand so tightly it hurt, and stopped dead still in the middle of the pathway. "Oh, Zeke, I want that, so much. You must talk to Papa... you must!" She threw her arms around Zeke's neck and held on tight, tears flowing across her high cheeks. She was breathing hard, finding it hard to control any of her emotions. "Could I have a school in Oregon?"

"So, I'm to do some of this as a white man and talk with your father, eh?" he laughed, and she took a little jab at him, laughing and dancing in the trail. "I'll build you a school, Sarah, and our home, and our furnishings. I'll build us a farm, and we'll have children." They stood, her arms around his neck, his arms around her waist, gazing into each other's eyes, and finally letting their lips come together in a long, wet kiss, breaking off only at the sound of a horse approaching.

"Quick, into the bushes," Sarah said, running off the forest path and hiding behind a large cedar tree. Zeke caught sight of Walking Bird at the same time the drunken Indian spotted him.

"I will kill you, white man!" Walking Bird stammered, having difficulty dismounting his pony.

"You're drunk, Walking Bird. Go home before you get hurt." Zeke had his hand wrapped around the handle of his large knife, watching the big Indian stumble toward him. Walking Bird had his war club raised to attack, but tripped over a rock, and fell toward Zeke.

Zeke stepped back and watched Walking Bird fall on his face. He kicked the war club into the bushes, pulled the warrior to his feet and drove his fist into the man's nose. Not letting him fall, Zeke drove his fist again between the man's eyes, this time letting him fall to the ground, unconscious. "I won't kill a man who can't defend himself," he muttered as Sarah came out from behind the tree, and picked up Walking Bird's war club.

"Just leave him where he is, Zeke. Let's go back, find Papa, and have a nice long talk about Oregon." She handed Zeke the war club, smiled, and said, "I think you earned this, Sharp Knife."

"Sharp Knife?" he asked.

"That's what Slow To Fight calls you, and many in the village. You have quite a reputation, husband." Zeke slipped an arm around the beautiful lady, a wide smile splashed across his broad face, and started back toward Fort Bridger, idly swinging the Shoshone war club.

"Your mother is called Walks So Softly, what do they call you?"

"Hummingbird," she answered, dancing a little bit, and running a few steps ahead. "Catch me if you can!" she sang and sprinted forward. He had her in less than five strides, as she knew he would, and they rolled in the grass for a few minutes. "I've dreamed of having a husband, of being a mother, and you're even more than I dreamed of," she whispered, letting his hands roam as they kissed, gently at first, then savagely.

"I didn't think I could love again, my little Hummingbird," he murmured, "but I was wrong."

It was several hours later that Zeke was in his cabin getting ready for supper with the Travis family. He held Walking Bird's war club in one hand, and the war club from the young Indian he had killed on the plains several months ago. "So different," he muttered, going over how they were put together, the sinew lashing that held the stone in place, the decorations and feathers. "We white people simply call them Indians, or worse, savages. And yet, just like us, they are different from each other. Germans aren't the same as the Scotch, and the Russians don't think the same way as the English, and so- I've found the Shoshone don't think the same as the Crow.

"I wonder," he mused, "just who are the savages?"

It was a full table at supper with Travis and Elaine at each end of the long table, Sarah and Zeke sitting next to each other on one side, and Moose taking up the other side.

Buffalo, roasted with potatoes and corn was the featured menu item, and more of Sarah's apple pie awaited those that had room after supper. "We will abide by Shoshone tradition and accept that Ezekiel Hawthorne and Hummingbird Travis are now married in everyone's eyes," Travis said. Elaine was beaming, and Moose tried his best to remain aloof, but grinned ever so slightly.

"Now, I believe the conversation should be about spring and Oregon." Travis had a platter full of meat and potatoes, Zeke's plate was full, and the ladies did not hold back. Moose's plate seemed to hold more than anyone else's.

"I told Bridger that I would stay through this next season, and I will, based, of course, on what the Mormons decide to do. There are still threats of burning the place down.

Zeke, your idea of taking my family with you to Oregon is a good one. Elaine can start building a mercantile business with Barbara, if that's what she wants, and Sarah can open a school." He laughed gently, as he continued. "That means everything will be in place when I get there, and I'll have little to do."

Lighthearted banter continued for another couple of hours as rough plans were made for the big move to Oregon. "We still have a long winter ahead of us and there is plenty of time to make hard and fast plans," Zeke said, as he enjoyed a last piece of pie washed down with rum-laced coffee. "Mr. Johnson said he would return in the spring to lead the rest of the way on the Oregon Trail. He said he's been over the trail and knows it well."

"I do, too," Moose piped up. "I would like to be the one to lead my family to Oregon. Major Bridger and I have been over that trail many times. He changed it from a single track, when the trappers used it, to where it now will accommodate wagons and teams of oxen.

"There are places, particularly when the trail first meets up with the Snake River, that are very difficult. You will need someone who has been there to lead, and I would like that to be me." He wasn't being arrogant at all, simply telling it like it was, and there were many smiles scattered around the table.

"I would like that," Sarah all but whispered, smiling brightly at her little brother. "I would be so proud." She reached across the table and took hold of one of Moose's huge hands, rubbing her fingers over gnarled knuckles, and feeling his great strength.

"I think it's time to go home now, Sharp Knife," she said, standing up and smiling at her, now, husband.

"Yes, dear," is all Zeke could say, helping her into a great coat and slipping into his own. They were ushered out the door with lots of laughter from Travis, Elaine, and Moose.

They walked across the parade square, watched millions of stars sparkle in the early winter cold, held hands, rubbed shoulders with each step, and tried to understand that in the eyes of the Rocky Mountain west, they were now husband and wife. "I'll never be able to put into words just how happy I am," Zeke whispered as they walked up to his little cabin next to the blacksmith shop.

Sarah stepped across the threshold and stopped, turned to face Zeke, and whispered, "I love you." He stepped across and took her in his arms, slowly rocking back and forth, before he reached behind him and closed the door.

"Our first home," he said, putting some wood on the fire, stirring the coals about and getting a good flame established. "I promise you that I will always have a warm and comfortable home for you, never let you be hungry, and will fight to the death to keep you safe."

Morning came early to the Hawthorne household with hollering, even some sporadic gunfire in the fort. "What on earth?" Zeke said, rousing himself and untangling limbs that were wrapped about Mrs. Hawthorne.

"It's the supply wagons," Sarah said, slowly coming awake. "Barbara's here, and books," and she dressed hurriedly as Zeke got a fire going in the fireplace and one in the cook stove as well. "It's a tradition, Zeke, lots of hurrahs and firing of guns to welcome the supply wagons to the fort. In the old days, the wagons only came once a year, so it was a holiday.

"Oh, it'll be so good to see Barbara again. You'll love my little sister, Zeke. She's so tiny, and ferocious, according to Moose. She terrorizes him. Let's go meet the wagons," she said, urging the big man on.

"I thought the entire Crow Nation was attacking," he chortled getting into his heavy coat, helping Sarah into hers. "Or maybe Walking Bird woke up."

"Don't tease about him," she said. "He's still a very dangerous person, and maybe more so now, since you stole his war club."

"Not me, my lady, you stole that and gave it to me," and they were laughing and walking hand in hand across the parade ground to the large gates, wide open and filled with people.

"How far out are they, Papa?" Sarah asked as the two walked up to the trader. "Oh, I see 'em, I see 'em," she yelled, pointing out a train of six, or maybe more wagons making the ford about a mile away. Each wagon was pulled by four horses or mules and there were at least fifteen outriders spread throughout the group.

"The whole village will be here today," Travis said, and we'll have a feast tonight. Moose and Slow to Fight led a group out to find some elk and deer."

"Looks like they're leading some cattle in, too," Zeke said, watching the large group wend its way to the fort.

"We'll slaughter one," Travis said, "one for some of the trappers near-by, and the rest will go to the village. Bridger does this every year, just in case the hunting is bad. Elaine will tell you, though, buffalo is better for you, tastes better, and the hides are warmer," he chuckled, joined by Elaine and Sarah.

It was a long, slow process getting the wagons all situated so they could be unloaded, the teams un-hitched and corralled, and the cattle settled into pastures outside the fort. "You'll be busy at that forge of yours," Travis said to Zeke. "Those wagons will be busted and torn up some, and you can bet there'll be wood to fix, too."

Sarah spotted Barbara while the wagons were still some distance away and urged Zeke to walk out with her to meet her sister.

"Even from here, I can tell she's tiny," Zeke said. "Is she well?"

"She is now. She was sickly as a youngster. Mama was sure she wouldn't make it through her first winter, but as she grew older, she slowly got better, and stronger. She's full of life today, just very small."

Barbara spotted Sarah and Zeke and jumped off the wagon she was riding in, and raced through the sage and grass toward them, howling like a banshee, or more accurately, as a Shoshone. The women threw their arms around each other, dancing and laughing, hugging and kissing, finally slowing down enough for Sarah to introduce Zeke.

"Barbara, this is so exciting, you're the first person I get to introduce this man to." She settled herself down, squared her shoulders, and very formally said," Zeke, I would like to introduce my sister, Barbara. And Barb, I want you to meet my husband, Zeke Hawthorne."

There was dead silence for about ten seconds, and Barbara Travis exploded in laughter and dancing, threw her arms back around Sarah, whopped Zeke across his broad shoulders, and danced some more. "Big sister is married? Really married? How wonderful. Are you pregnant?"

Again, a period of silence.

"We were married yesterday, Barbara," is all Sarah said, blushing, lowering her eyes, and gripping Zeke's arm with vice-like fingers. "So, no. Not yet."

IT TOOK THE REST OF THE DAY TO GET THAT WAGON TRAIN situated but certainly not fully unloaded, and the party began when Moose and half a dozen Shoshone warriors arrived with two elk and three deer, ready for the roasting pits. As the meats cooked, villagers began showing up, mostly dressed in their finest outfits.

There were more beads, quills, teeth, claws, shells, and bones attached to buckskin than Zeke had ever seen in his life. The women were gorgeous in flowing buckskin dresses, mocs that almost reached their knees, necklaces and bracelets. "I thought I saw pageantry during your summer party," he said to Travis, watching the village come to the fort.

"Wait 'till the men show up, Zeke," was Travis's reply, coupled with a chuckle. "I talked with the wagon master and it looks like he won't have enough merchandise to freight back to St. Louis to fill all the wagons. I'm going to buy what he doesn't take back."

"I hope you got a good price. I can build a fine wagon awfully cheap."

"He knew if I didn't buy them he would have to leave them here to rot, so he almost gave them to me."

There were fifty men in Bridger's supply train and they were as ready as those from the fort and village for the feast and party. Drums started right away, jugs of rum filled flagons and mugs, freshly brewed beer and ale flowed like water, and there were fears late in the evening that the food would run out.

While the Indians danced to the drums, fiddles and banjos appeared across the way, and dancing among those from the fort began. Sarah, Barbara, and Elaine danced with every man from the supply train, apparently also a long-held tradition, and Sarah and Zeke danced often.

It was late when the party finally started breaking up, with promises of trapper and mountain man games set for the next day. There would be horse races, man races, shooting exhibitions, and of course, a few games of chance with cards and dice. The rendezvous atmosphere would last for several days, with the wagons being emptied and goods distributed when it didn't interfere with the games.

The liquor created a few fights and arguments, but nothing of any serious consequence. Nobody ended up with stiches or broken bones, and the squabbles were forgotten within hours. Zeke kept a sharp eye out for his one enemy but never saw the man.

"I feel a storm coming on," Sarah said as she and Zeke made it back to their cabin. "I'm glad the supply train made it in before it hits. If you listen to the old people, they are saying it will be a heavy, cold winter."

"Have they ever been wrong?" Zeke asked with a smile. "Some of the people I grew up with used to try to predict the winter, and they were seldom right."

"When the old ladies skin out an elk or deer late in the fall, they will tell you about the coming winter, and most of the time, you better believe them." She snuggled in Zeke's strong arms as they stood in front of a roaring fire. "I don't care if it snows a hundred feet, if I can be with you."

They woke up to a very quiet Fort Bridger, and when Zeke got the fire going and opened the front door of the cabin to bring in more wood, he discovered why. "Look, Hummingbird, it snowed all night. That's what makes it so quiet." She joined him at the open door, watching great flakes of snow slowly settle onto what appeared to be a base of almost a foot already.

"Looks like your little old ladies know what they're talking about," Zeke chuckled, getting them back inside where it was warm. "This will slow the distribution process, I'm afraid."

"Those muleskinners and freighters will want to get moving as quickly as possible," Sarah said. "Rocky Mountain winters are fierce, and more than one wagon train has been lost in blizzards."

The next few days were spent distributing supplies and getting the wagons loaded with merchandise to take back to St. Louis. Some of the old timers were talking about how few pelts would be going east.

"Back in twenty-five," Travis said, "There wouldn't have been enough wagons to haul the beaver out of here. According to Bridger, the people in Europe bought most of the skins and turned them into hats. Somebody said they're making hats out of silk now.

"Well, the number of beaver left in the creeks and rivers is way down too. Last time Old Gabe was here, we was talking about his scouting for the army instead of running a trap line. The world is changing, Zeke." It snowed for several days, creating a base of almost three feet, according to Travis.

"Don't have the skins we did twenty year ago," one old trapper said. Travis and Zeke were sipping coffee and rum when the old guy came in, covered in ice and snow. "Took me a whole year to get a month's take, and what's there ain't a good grade. 'Bout the end of our way of life, I think." His name was Whiskey Pete and he'd been in the mountains since '28. "Guess it's time to find a warm woman and settle down to raise beans."

The wagon master was howling at the men every day to hurry things along. "We got to get down out of these hills before the heavens decide to keep us around for the winter. Love to talk with you more, Mr. Travis, but we got to get the hell out of here." They were on their way to St. Loo by the end of the week. The mules and oxen would be plowing through deep snow, and breaking ice on the ford.

"It's a shame you didn't get to meet Old Gabe," Travis said, as he and Zeke stood by the stockade gates, watching the mules and oxen trundle their heavy loads along the trail. "That man can tell a story like none I ever heard before. You actually believe some of the things he says," he laughed. "Well, don't be surprised when we get to Oregon that old varmint will show up and tell us some real whoppers."

THE HEAVY COLD snow of the high country came early, but not before a good harvest of potatoes and beans, and a limited corn crop. "Bridger spent a lot of time trying to tell those Mormons that corn just doesn't do well in this country. Well, Zeke, look at what a miserable crop this is, and Jim Bridger would stand right here and say, "I durn well told you so!"

Travis laughed loud. "Why didn't the Mormons believe him? Hell, Travis, he all but called the Salt Lake area home. He certainly would know."

"Oh, he knew, but the Mormons think he's lying to keep them out of the valley. Now, they want to burn this place out so all the wagon trains will be forced to come through their country. Bridger's tired of messin' with 'em. He told me to just let 'em burn it down if it comes to that." Travis scratched his unruly head of hair and said, "I might just go ahead and move out with you and the women come spring. You been workin' on what we'll need to take with us? Elaine's makin' our plans. Shoshone women know how to pack and move, Zeke. They can have a village down and packed in a matter of minutes, I think. Army's sure learned that a time or two," he laughed, passing the rum jug to Zeke to add just a touch of taste to the coffee.

"Army scouts would tell the colonel where the village was" he continued, "and by the time the cavalry came ridin' in, weren't nothin' but simmerin' fire pits."

He got long in the face and contemplative for a minute, before saying. "The Indians ain't never gonna win, though. Those from the east, hundreds of thousands of them in big wagons and mighty teams of horses and mules, will just ride over this country, and it will be the end of the Indian nations, the end of a wonderful way of life."

"Until I came to Fort Bridger the only thing I knew about Indians was what I read in the newspapers and heard from politicians," Zeke said. "Nobody back east even considers them part of the human race, Travis. And, I know you're right, which just bothers the hell out of me and there isn't one thing I can do about it."

The two men kicked some dirt around with their boot toes, poured another mug of coffee each, with some added flavor, and Zeke continued. "Sarah and I will need two small wagons, one for the blacksmith shop and one for our stuff, eight mules to pull, and two saddle animals.

"Moose said the trail can get chock full of large rocks and felled trees, and the smaller wagons are best. He said the country is steep enough in some places that we will need some good pulling mules.

"What does Elaine have in mind for you folks?"

"She and the girls have been talking and Sarah must have told her mama what you two will be doing. Because of the suttler's inventory, we'll need at least two, maybe even three wagons."

"Sounds like I've got my work cut out for the winter, Travis. I've already worked out a couple of good designs for the wagons, and have enough iron laid aside, that I can have them built and fitted with wheels and tongues well before spring. I'll also be making barrels and crates, measured to fit in the wagons."

THE DAYS WERE short and the nights long and cold in the high country. For many, it was a time of contemplation and for some, boredom, which was not the case with the Hawthorne family. Zeke had his forge cooking almost every day, creating all the ironwork he would need for the wagons. He was also building wheels and axels, and the frames needed for thee wagons. It was a long and precise type of work and Zeke loved it, explaining much to Sarah as he worked.

"The wheels are in many parts," he explained. "The center part is the hub which connects to the axel. The spokes come out from the hub and becomes the wheel. Then the iron tire is fitted onto the wooden wheel. We put it on very hot, and when it cools and shrinks, it's really tight on the wheel.

"Now, little lady, you build the next wheel." She whopped him across his big shoulders, and laughed while she danced away from him, back into their cabin.

He often needed help with some of the pieces that weighed more than he did or were so clumsy that one person had a hard time. Putting the iron tires onto the wheels was one of the chores where Sarah was right there. The iron tire had to be fitted when it was red hot, and then it was cooled with water to keep the wood from catching on fire, and as it shrunk, it was an incredibly tight fit on the wooden wheel.

Getting the iron pieces to fit the single trees and double trees often took both of them, and the wagon tongues had to be shaped from single pieces of timber, with the iron fittings put on hot.

"By God, we're a good team, Mrs. Hawthorne," Zeke would say when they either took a break or finished a chore. "I always wanted a young'un to train, and it looks like I got one, for sure… for sure," he'd say and then give a big long laugh.

Sarah continued teaching and holding regular classes, for three days each week. In the evenings, sitting around the blazing fire Zeke read from one of the classics one night, and Sarah would tell Shoshone legend stories the next night. "Next week is Christmas," Sarah said after telling of a young warrior who had saved his tribe by way of his spirit animal.

"We have to get a Christmas tree, Zeke, and put ribbons and sparkles on it, and use candles all over the house to make it pretty. I have a special present for you."

She truly lives in both worlds, he thought, hearing her Shoshone legend coupled with looking forward to Christmas. *I must be the luckiest man in the world.*

"Christmas," Zeke said, almost in wonder. "My God, what a year this has been for me. I must have lost all track of time. Christmas," he said again, so quietly Sarah almost didn't hear.

"What would you like for Christmas, Hummingbird?" He enjoyed calling her by her traditional name, seeing her in that way, sometimes. "Jewels? Furs? Silver and gold?"

"I have my Christmas present," she said. She got up from her chair and walked to Zeke. Climbing into his lap, she rested her head on his large shoulder. "Want to know what your present is?" she teased, nibbling gently on an ear.

"Shouldn't I wait 'till Christmas morning?" His arms were filled with his little Hummingbird, and his face was filled with the joy of a happy man. "But still" he grinned, "I guess it would be okay if you gave me a hint," he teased back.

"I'm almost certain, oh husband of mine, that we will be *three* before we reach Oregon."

THE TRAVIS FAMILY Christmas dinner table groaned with the weight of buffalo steaks, elk roasts, great bowls of mashed potatoes, corn and bean puddings. There was stuffed grouse and minced quail, fresh trout and cornbread, and there wasn't room for the pies.

The day had started early for Zeke and Sarah, with a large breakfast and then gifts offered in front of the tree that Zeke had brought in two days before.

"You can't possibly have another gift for me," Zeke said. The smile hadn't left his face since Sarah's declaration, and he rubbed her tummy gently, saying, "This is the finest gift of all time." He sipped a cup of hot coffee, letting Sarah up to get a little package she had wrapped for him. "What will we name him?" he asked.

"Him? The mighty Sharp Knife expects a son, does he? Ah, but the beautiful Hummingbird might just have a surprise in store for her warrior." She smiled, dancing away from the swat aimed at her bottom, and brought the gift to his chair.

He found a hand tooled, hand laced scabbard for his hunting knife, already attached to a fine belt, also tooled and laced. "Oh, my," is all he could say, standing and slipping the belt on and pulling it up tight. "This is beautiful," he said. "I have a present for you, too, little one."

He walked out to the forge room and carried a small chest in, placing it on the table in front of where Sarah was sitting. It was maple wood and had two drawers that pulled open over the top of a single bottom drawer. Intricate carving on the wood included a beautiful humming-bird across the top.

Sarah stood and grabbed Zeke around the neck and hugged him tighter than she had ever done before. "I think we need a little nap before the day gets any further along," she whispered, and the two slipped quickly into the bedroom.

"FOR SUCH A JOYOUS time of the year, this is a sad supper," Travis said, quietly as everyone watched him carve great slices of buffalo roast. "This will be our last Christmas together at Fort Bridger. On the other hand, we're looking at the possible wonders of a new beginning in Oregon country. Our family has expanded, and from what I understand," he smiled at Sarah, "is expanding more, so we have much to be thankful for, as well. Let's eat,"

Talk around the Christmas table continued for another hour. They discussed the coming move to Oregon and all the possible ventures the Travis and Hawthorne families could become involved with. "I've been working with a couple of people in Boston who have created something that will surely change the way clothing is made," Barbara said, "and I brought one of their machines with me."

"A machine?" Elaine asked, looking first at Barbara, then at Sarah, and finally, back to Barbara. "How would a machine make clothing?"

"It actually sews pieces of fabric together the same as if we were doing it with a needle and thread. I made this dress," she said, standing up, turning around and around, "using the machine. It's wonderful, and it makes it so much easier to sew. I was able to buy the machine because I made many dresses and shirts, and made good money doing it."

"I'd be very interested in seeing that machine of yours," Zeke said. "Would you be able to demonstrate how it works? It sounds fascinating." He was an engineer again, sitting toward the edge of his chair and gazing first at Barbara's dress, looking at the stitching, and letting his mind ponder how a machine could do the work.

"I've watched you sew up my shirts, Sarah," he said. "Can you picture how a machine could do that? I want to see this, Barbara."

"The one I bought is a complete unit and sits on top of a wooden cabinet. It's a little too heavy for me to pick up and take somewhere, Zeke, but I have it set up in my room, so you and Sarah can come over, maybe tomorrow, and I'll show you how it works.

"I know that when we get to Oregon, I will be able to open a clothing store and make dresses and gowns for women and girls, and shirts and pants for men and boys. The machine is strong enough to sew canvas, so I can also make work pants for the men."

"We've certainly learned a lot at our Christmas dinner this year," Travis said, reaching for a cigar with one hand and the jug of rum with the other. "Zeke's abilities with wood and iron, and now, Barbara's abilities with a machine, all I need to do is have Zeke build me a store, and Elaine and I will be in business." Laughter flowed around the table.

"I guess my job will be to guide lots of people to the Oregon country so you'll have lots of customers," Moose piped up, adding to the gayety of the party. "But I don't think that will happen. Slow to Fight has asked me to stay and work with our people. More and more white people are coming into our country and they have no manners, no sense that this is our country, and Slow to Fight feels things could get ugly."

He sighed adding, "The Sioux tribes are very angry at how they are being treated north and east of us, the Crow have been decimated by white people's illnesses, and the Mormons are continually talking about running us out of our own country."

"You'll do a fine job, son," Travis said, quietly. "Slow to Fight knows you will be the leader of the Shoshone one day. Your mother and I are very proud of what you are going to be doing."

It was late when the party began to break up. "This is my first Christmas with my new family," Zeke said, "and I've never been happier in my life. I love you all more than words will let me express." He just sat there for a moment, looked at each person, and finally said, "Merry Christmas," which was answered back all the way around the table.

"I'M REALLY LOOKING FORWARD to seeing this machine of Barbara's," Zeke said as he and Sarah made their way through fresh snow to the Travis compound.

"I don't understand how a machine could possibly sew," Sarah said. "It's an intricate process putting in seams, making two pieces of cloth into one, and sewing it so that it looks nice and holds together."

Barbara was beaming when she opened the door to

her room, part of the cabin structure behind the trader's store. "Come in," she said with a flourish. "Coffee's on, and I made some sweet rolls."

She had her sewing machine set up in the center of the large room and poured coffee for everyone, setting a platter of sweet rolls on a table. "There it is, just like Zack Singer made it. I worked with him for two years, Sarah, that's why I own the thing. Part of my wage went to the purchase price.

"He's in the middle of a big court fight over whether he stole the plans for the machine from someone else, but *this* machine is mine no matter how that turns out."

She sat down at the machine and Zeke watched as she put her feet on a moveable platform under the little table. "He calls this a treadle." Then she fitted two pieces of cloth together, placed them under what he saw was a needle, and started rocking the bottom platform back and forth with her feet, while the needle went up and down and the cloth moved freely forward.

She stopped and opened it up a little. "Watch, now," she said, and slowly moved the needle up and down. Zeke watched the bobbin make its journey around and around, catching the thread when it came down and bringing it around, then letting it go to become the stitch.

"Zack calls this the bobbin, I guess because it kind of bobs about, grabbing the thread and then letting it go." Barbara beamed with pride.

"Amazing," Zeke exclaimed, getting right down on his knees to watch the intricate movement of the treadle, needle, bobbin, and cloth. "This is just wonderful," he repeated. "And you worked with the man that invented this? Oh, Barbara, you're so lucky. He must have a brilliant mind."

"All business," she said, "except when it comes to women. He's a bit of a gad-about, I'm afraid," and she found herself blushing as she said that. She continued sewing the two pieces of cloth together, snipped the thread, and handed the completed piece to Sarah for inspection.

"Just look at that seam," she said, pulling a bit this way and that. "It's as strong as anyone could want."

Barbara pulled a shirt from a dresser drawer and handed it to Sarah. "I made this for Papa, but he doesn't know it yet. Look at the seams, the collar and cuffs, and feel how strong they are. He won't rip the shoulders out of this shirt," she laughed, knowing just how big and strong Travis was.

"I think you'll find yourself very busy as a seamstress when we reach Oregon," Sarah said, handing the shirt to Zeke. "In fact, dear sister, I'll order two shirts for my dear husband right now, if you'd be kind enough to do the measuring."

1 2

"DOES WINTER EVER END?" ZEKE ASKED ONE MORNING IN late February, watching snow pile up deeper and deeper in the fort's parade ground. "We must have ten feet of snow out there, Sarah. We won't be able to move until late April, maybe even the middle of May if this keeps up."

"Papa was saying yesterday that we should plan on leaving about the middle of May. The rivers and streams will be really high and fast, and we'll be working our way through rotted drifts and mud as well." She stood next to Zeke while he sat at their kitchen table, finishing up a platter of corn cakes and coffee. "You've done a beautiful job making those wagons and the packing crates that are fitted in them, but we can't force nature to bend to our will."

"I know the wagon for our personal stuff is plenty big and strong, but I'm not sure about the one to carry my blacksmith and carpentry tools. Maybe I should leave most of it and buy new when we get to Oregon. That stuff is awfully heavy and bulky." Zeke had been fretting over taking everything and still wasn't sure what to do.

"No," she said, "you'll need your tools, Zeke. That's your life."

"I remember Mr. Johnson complaining about all the personal property and belongings those in his wagon train were trying to bring with them. How the animals were having such a hard time because of the weight and bulk. I wish I knew what to do.

"Bridger was a trained blacksmith," he continued, "and these tools and equipment of his are really good. It would be a crime to just leave them to sit and rust away. Well, maybe by the time the snow melts, I'll have made up my mind."

Sarah chuckled, listening to this same conversation for what she thought was the twentieth time. "You sound very much like my father sometimes. Mama said he's been pacing around, first complaining about how much stuff to pack, and then actually went outside and measured the snow. And, Moose, he's driving everyone nuts complaining every minute about the snow."

She was interrupted by a knock on the door, and started to get it when Zeke jumped up and motioned for her to let him get it. He moved quickly and opened the door, keeping one hand close to the handle of his big knife. Thoughts of Walking Bird just showing up some day still bothered him.

"Barbara, good morning. Come in, come in," he said, holding the heavy door open for the small lady. "What a nice surprise."

"I was going through all my trunks and cases again, trying to separate what I need to take with me to Oregon and what I want to take," she laughed, coming into the warm cabin and slipping out of a heavy buffalo robe. "I found some papers that Mr. Singer gave me. I wanted to tell you all about him and how we met, and show you these papers."

They settled in at the dinner table and Zeke spread working diagrams of the sewing machine out across the tabletop. "That man was a fine craftsman," he said, looking over papers that explained exactly how the machine operated. "You said someone thinks he stole these plans?"

"It's very complicated," Barbara said. "A man named Howe says he invented the machine and Singer says he did. I think the two men actually like each other, and one day will work together."

"I hope you have a means of keeping in contact with this Mr. Singer. You might want to think about being his representative in the west. I'm sure no one within a thousand miles of where we're standing has one of these machines."

"He moved to New York because of the trial and all, and a couple of women he may have had relations with, but I have his contact information. He was interested in the west, also. He knows a man who is working to create a machine that would sew harness leather. Now that would be something."

"Something for certain," Zeke said, still going over the mechanical drawings of the Singer machine. "A machine that would sew harness leather. My God," he said. "Well, Barbara, with the machine you have, you'll be busy as a bee in Oregon."

They talked about the machine, and Barbara, using the

diagrams and drawings had Zeke convinced he could manufacture the parts needed to build one. "Of course, that would not be right, since your Mr. Singer has a patent on all this. But, if pieces break or need repair, I know I could do it.

"These will change the way we dress," Zeke continued. "Trousers and shirts fit properly and won't be falling apart at the seams. What will they think of next?" he and Barbara laughed.

THE CALENDAR SAID it was late winter, early spring, but looking out the front door of the cabin, it was still mid-winter at Fort Bridger. "Come on, Zeke, you can make it," Moose laughed, watching Zeke try to haul half an elk up the slope from the Black Fork of the Green River to the fort. Moose was hauling the other half and both men were wearing Shoshone snowshoes, made with willow boughs laced with buffalo sinew.

"These drifts are at least a hundred feet deep," Zeke panted, trying to get back on his feet after tumbling into a drift. "And this elk weighs a thousand pounds."

"Just think about how good supper will be tonight," Moose laughed, "with half an apple pie for dessert."

The struggle finally ended and the meat was cut into proper sizes, some to be stripped and hung in the smoker, some to be put in the salt barrel, and some to be eaten within a day or two. Those pieces were simply hung outside in the freezing temperatures.

"It's March, and that means it really is spring," Zeke said, shrugging himself out of the heavy buffalo coat and getting as close to the fireplace as he could. "I spent most of today floundering about in snow drifts deeper than I am tall. Moose dances around on those snowshoes like a New York ballerina while I flop around like a beached whale."

Sarah was laughing along with Zeke as she put a platter of fried sidemeat and corn cakes down in front of him, and covered them with beans cooked with lots of dried chilies. "Here, oh mighty hunter of the Rocky Mountains, get your strength back," she laughed.

"We need to talk, Zeke," she said, getting serious. "Our trip to Oregon will begin just about the time we will be having our baby. And as time goes by, I'm more and more sure that we will have two babies, not one." She sat down, across from him, and stretched her arm out to hold his hand. "Mama is a fine mid-wife, has helped many women deliver their babies, but we will be on the open trail."

"Is there something about being on the trail, other than the obvious, that bothers you?" he asked, seeing worry and fear in Sarah's eyes. "We'll make our wagon as comfortable as possible, I've included a full bed for you, so you and the baby will be warm and not thrown about if we're moving."

"Hold me, Zeke," she said, getting up. He jumped to his feet and put his arms around her, holding her to him, and moving slowly to the fire. "I've never had a baby, I've never been on a really primitive trail, and I've never been this much in love," she whispered, letting his hands run up and down her back, massaging, scratching, loving hands.

"When the time comes, we will simply stop our wagon train and we will have our babies. We won't move on the trail until our babies are warm and safe, snuggled with their mama," he said, ever so softly. He nudged her gently down the hallway and they spent the rest of the day in their bedroom.

"These little buggers really do kick," he said, rubbing her extended tummy, feeling the sharp nudges from within. "What an amazing thing, creating life." The fire was down to bare coals when they emerged.

"I am not as worried as you, Sarah," he said, "but I too have never been on the kind of journey we'll be taking. I've never been a part of a wagon train except for those last few weeks getting here.

"I'll make our wagons as strong and safe as possible, my little Hummingbird, and as we move along the trail, if you feel we need to stop, we will. That's a promise."

MARCH SLOWLY TURNED into April and with it came spring thaw, with rivers cascading over their banks, mud clinging to every boot and moccasin, and green leaves and the buds of flowers showing up in bursts of color and aroma. "I'm so fat," Sarah wailed, holding her belly with two hands, Zeke chuckling as he rubbed his hand gently over her tummy.

"You're the most beautiful woman in the world," he said, and put some more wood on the fire. "You must be right, though, we probably are going to have at least two babies. I have something to show you," and he took her hand and they walked out of the cabin and into the carpenter's shop.

"Will you look at that!" she exclaimed, dashing across the open floor to a twin set of cradles on rockers. "Zeke, what a wonderful idea. Oh, my, but what if it's just one big baby?"

The little shop rocked with their laughter, and Sarah spent extra minutes making sure the rocker worked just right, that the sides were good and strong, and the cradles were long and wide. "It's beautiful."

"Something else, little one," he said, walking her out to where he had been building the wagons for their Oregon adventure. He had a ladder that allowed easy access to the family wagon and asked Sarah to get inside. He joined her.

"My goodness," she said, walking toward the front of the wagon, where she found an oversized armchair, fully upholstered and well padded. "For me?"

"Just for you," he said. "I put it in sideways so you can be comfortable, even stretch your legs out, and there will be plenty of light for you to read as we move down the trail. It's bolted in so it won't tip over in rough terrain or move about. Moose wants us to take one of the older boys from the fort as our wagon driver and camp boy.

"What it means, I guess, is that we will start our trip with a built-in family. He wants the boy, Hiram- Little Eagle- Pierson, to stay with us when we settle. We seem now to have a twelve-year-old son, Sarah."

"This chair rocks," she laughed. "I hadn't noticed before I sat down. Little Eagle is a good boy. His mother belongs to the tribe and his father is a trapper. They're having a hard time, and this is good for Little Eagle. Pierson is a good man, but totally uneducated. All he knows is trapping and hunting. He has no other skills."

"Moose thinks it would be a good idea for Hiram to join our family right away, rather than waiting until it's time to leave."

"Why don't we invite the Pierson's to have supper one

night soon and we can make all the necessary arrangements?" Sarah smiled as Zeke helped her out of the wagon. "I'll fix a big buffalo roast and maybe even make a pie or two."

"Twelve-year-old boys eat pies by the half-dozen," Zeke laughed back. "If this thaw continues, we should be able to move out during the first week or two of May, I think, so the sooner we get to know our new son, the better. Moose says he's a good worker. We'll need that on the trail."

He sat very still, smiling at his wife, watching her try to get comfortable. "This is a big change for both of us. Are you sure you'll be okay being a stepmother to a twelve-year-old? We can make other arrangements if you're not."

"Zeke, this is really just right. You'll have help, I'll have help, and the Pierson's will have help. I'm very okay with the idea."

BENJAMIN PIERSON WAS ABOUT FIFTY, he thought, and had come to the Rockies as a youngster, following in the footsteps of some of the original mountain men. They used him as a camp boy for a couple of years until he grew big and strong. He married White Flower of the Shoshone tribe, and she bore him three children, a daughter who died at birth, Hiram, now twelve, and a son who didn't make it through his first year.

"Nice cabin you got, Zeke. You do fine work." Pierson was called White Beard by most in the area, and he and his wife, White Bird, and their son, Little Eagle were all jammed into the front doorway of the cabin with Zeke and Sarah standing close on the other side. "Thankee for the invite, and for askin' to care for young Hiram. Mighty good of ya. Brought a taste of Barbados rum, if ya be kindly to it? Old Bridger sent it to me on that last rendezvous."

"Come in, White Beard, come in," Zeke said, getting the door as wide open as possible. He and Sarah had the fire roaring on this spring evening, and the house reeked of the good aromas of roasting buffalo and apple pie. "I'd be pleased to share a cup with you."

"Don't know nothin' but trappin' and fightin' injuns, Zeke. That's all I done since I be Hiram's age, and I been watchin' you build things so easy like, and hammerin' iron and tin like it was clay or sumpin', and I got to rattlin' that round an round in my old headbone, ya know, and well, it be sumpin' a man could be proud of." White Beard had settled into one of the large overstuffed chairs Zeke had made, sipped heartily on his rum, and continued.

"Yes, sir, I think it would be wonderful if young Hiram could learn to do some of the things that you seem to conjure out of the air. I know in the east this is how a boy learns to be a tradesman, knows how to work with his hands and tools, how to be sumpin' other than a trapper and fighter."

Zeke motioned to Hiram to come over and join them, offering him a seat on a divan next to him. "What do you like to be called, Hiram or Little Eagle?" he asked, leaning out and stirring the fire some.

The boy was tall for twelve, and skinny as a lodge pole pine tree, with coal black hair, brown lively eyes, and what Sarah had called, a devastatingly beautiful smile. He was well mannered, had shaken hands with a strong grip on arriving, called Zeke sir and Sarah ma'am, and offered to bring in wood first thing.

"My friends call me Pine Tree," he laughed, "but I think I would rather be called Hiram. Mama will always call me Little Eagle, and that's fine, too. Did you really make all this furniture? And, I know you built the cabin because I watched you do it."

"Yes, I did, Pine Tree," Zeke joked, catching a big smile from the boy. "You're well spoken, son, did you learn all that at Miss Sarah's school?"

"Yes, sir," he said, "and I know my numbers good too." Hiram looked over to where Sarah and his mother were working in the kitchen, probably hoping to get a nod or affirmation from his teacher. Sarah wasn't paying any attention to the men, and Hiram put his attention back on Zeke and his father.

"You'll need that, Hiram. Have you ever done any work with wood or metal, or maybe I should ask, have you ever thought you might want to work with wood or metal?"

"I told Papa, when I saw what you were doing, that I wished I could do that. I really do want to learn."

Zeke could see history repeating itself right in front of a wonderful fire in a cabin high in the Rocky Mountains. He could see his mother demanding he learn languages and histories, and could see his father demanding he become a finished craftsman.

He smiled as he continued talking to young Hiram Pierson. "Sarah will want you to read all the classics, learn history and geography, and become a wizard with numbers. I'll want you to build the finest cabinetry and make the most attractive iron work possible. That's a big task, Hiram, and it will be hard work."

Hiram's smile spread across his face as he looked at his father first, then Zeke, and stuck out a large hand. "I'm your man, Mr. Hawthorne. I want everything you just said." He started to say more when Sarah and White Flower announced that supper was ready.

After all the pleasantries of supper, White Beard called Zeke aside. "Bridger's gonna let this fort die, Zeke," he said, "and me and the missus won't have nowhere to live around here. I've never been well accepted by the tribe, bein a nasty type of feller when I gets to drinkin' too heavy." He scuffed his feet a bit on the floor, and continued.

"We be headin' south, I think, when the snow's gone. Hear the Spanish got a nice place called Santa Fe, and I know some of the old boys have ventured into that country. Carson and Bent and others. Gotta be warmer than this," he snickered.

"Well, anyways, what it is I want to say is, take care of Hiram. Make him to be your son. I doubt we'll get up this way again, and I'm sure we won't get near Oregon so, Zeke, what I'm trying to say, is, Hiram is now yourn. Raise him to be the man you are and love him, okay?"

Zeke and the one called White Beard stood in front of the fire for a few minutes, quietly looking into each other's eyes. "Your boy will be raised a man, White Beard, and we'll see to it that he will always know who his mother and father are."

"No," White Beard said, so very softly, "I want him to be your son. We probably will get lost in the frontier, and he has the opportunity I could never offer. No, Sharp Knife, he is your son."

Zeke and Sarah lay in bed later that night and Zeke told the story, in words filled with wonder and love. "They gave up their son, Sarah, because of the people we are. I've not been this frightened, nor this proud, ever in my life. Hiram has just been adopted by us, Mr. and Mrs. Ezekiel Hawthorne."

There were soft murmurs, lots of cuddling, and then some sparring for Sarah to get as comfortable as possible "Pierson is a good man, Zeke. Things have never gone right for him, he never learned to read or write, and even after all these years can't speak Shoshone. He and his wife have already lost two children.

"We'll see to it that Hiram has the best life possible, and will never let him forget who his real parents are. God, I love you."

"ACCORDING TO TRAVIS, WE WILL BE LEAVING FORT Bridger in three weeks, Hi, so that doesn't give us much time to get you trained up with these mules." Hiram had become Hi within hours of moving into the Hawthorne household, and his schooling intensified during evening suppers. He spent most of his days with Zeke, helping shape up the wagons, and learning the ropes as far as working with the animals.

"Pa just had that one old saddle horse. Ain't done much with horses, and never with any mules. They're awfully big, and kinda scary."

"They are big, Hi, but shouldn't be scary. Treat 'em right, don't be beatin' on 'em or trying to hurt 'em, and they'll treat you right. Most of the time they want to work and be with you, just like we do with each other. Treat 'em like a friend, Hi, and they'll do just about anything you ask of 'em.

"You'll be doing most of the driving," Zeke said, breaking out harnesses for the two mules. "These animals have pulled plows, pulled wagons, carried saddles, and been pack animals, so they have a fine idea of what's expected of them. We need to bring you up to their level."

Every morning they would harness the mules and take one of the wagons out on the range for a driving lesson. Hi was becoming very good, both as a driver and working with the mules. "Pa has a horse that I rode once in a while, but these mules are beautiful to work with. I like Ruth the best, but don't tell Tobias," he laughed.

"You'll be driving our wagon most of the time, but I will see to it that you and I also have saddle horses. Sarah won't be able to do much driving and certainly won't be riding a saddle animal, so getting us to Oregon will be up to us, Hi, you and me, to get this family to Oregon."

Hi's voice was changing as he slowly entered that period of life known as adolescence, and the gee'n and haw'n with the mules every day wasn't helping things. It was Barbara Travis that kept the young man on his toes regularly. "My heavens, Hiram, you sound just like an old frog I heard once," and the boy would turn scarlet and do some hemming and hawing of his own.

"I cain't help it, Miss Travis," he croaked, blushing and wanting to run off somewhere. Hiram's eyes, huge and dark brown, lit up anytime he was near Barbara, and then her teasing sometimes froze him in place. From tenor to falsetto to baritone in just one sentence would send Barbara into fits of laughter and teasing, and grand moments of foot scraping for Hiram.

As he spent more and more time with the mules, his voice got stronger and deeper and one day, about a week before departure, he was bringing the animals and wagon back into the fort, when a little boy dashed out from the side of the stockade, right in front of the mules. "Look out," Hi howled and pulled the mules to a stop just inches from the boy.

"I swear you could have heard that boy in Nebraska," Barbara said at supper that night. "Here was Hi, sitting up on the wagon seat, just a little boy himself and when he howled, the stockade walls shook. What a voice," she chuckled, "and those mules listen to him like he's old father nature himself talkin' to them."

"I guess you won't tease him quite so much now," Travis said, quietly, getting a nod from Elaine. "Sarah said he idolizes Zeke and asked if it was alright to call her Ma. Last year at this time," he lit a cigar and stared up at the ceiling for just a minute, "we had two daughters and a son, Elaine. Today, we have two daughters, a son-in-law, a grandson, and we're about to have two more grandkids.

"By next week we won't have a home until we reach Oregon. Life is a strange piece of pie, isn't it? How many ways can it be sliced, how many changes can we face, what exactly is in store for us?" He had a big smile on his broad, weathered face, and took a few more puffs on his cigar.

"For the next several weeks, my darling wife, our entire family will be together every day all day. We haven't been able to say that for a long time."

"WE TOOK the wagon across the stream three times today, Ma. Pa let me drive all three times, and then we stopped and had dinner and caught all these fish. Could I have some more potatoes?" The family was seated around the table for supper of fried trout, mashed potatoes, green beans, and biscuits.

Since Hiram had joined the family he became a son in every way, with Zeke and Sarah becoming Ma and Pa, and he, often... Son. Zeke said that Hi was so close he was his shadow, but he also said it with so much love that everyone knew it wasn't a complaint. "That boy has a quick mind, Sarah. He's going to be a fine man."

"You sure can, Son." She spooned another two big helpings of mashed potatoes on the boy's plate, catching a smile from Zeke. "So, you boys were out playing in the creeks and fishing all day while your poor old Ma had to work and slave getting ready for our big trip."

Zeke rocked back with laughter, and reached across to pat Hi on the shoulder. "This young son of ours is one fine wagon master, Mama. He picked the fords, nursed the mules across and out without a hitch, and there was some high and fast water out there. It won't always be that easy on our trip, but I have a lot of confidence in him. We'll be safe."

The wagons were slowly filled to capacity, decisions on what was to come with them and what was to be left behind were difficult, as were the many people that had to be told goodbye. Elaine, Sarah, and Barbara spent considerable time at the Shoshone village, crying and saying goodbye, and Travis made his way through the little enclave of trappers doing the same.

"I'm glad you decided to bring the blacksmith tools and the wood working tools, Zeke. It's heavy, but we have strong animals and strong wagons, and when we get to Oregon, you'll be the first to say you are glad, too." Travis walked into the area where Zeke was loading his wagons.

"Looks like we can pull out of here tomorrow morning, Zeke. I can't cram another thing in either of my wagons. I hired two of the old trappers to drive our extra wagons, and Moose and I will be outriders. How you coming?"

"I wanted to talk to you about that. Hi will drive our main wagon, so now I don't have to worry about the second one. Thank you, and it gives us some extra guns in case we need them."

"George Felix will be driving for you, Zeke. I've known him for many years. He's a Frenchy but his English is pretty good. He knows Indians and he has been a teamster for Bridger for many years. He'll do good by you.

"He's a loner, so don't expect him to be joining you and the family around the fires in the morning and evening. I've actually watched him go three days without saying a word to anyone, but he'll work his knuckles raw."

"I've met him, Travis. I'll get together with him and make sure he knows how I've got things put together for packing and unpacking. It was damned hard packing the Bridger blacksmith shop, but you're right, I'll need it in Oregon. We're packed and ready to shove off. I just wish old Mr. Johnson had gotten here in time to come with us. I think he and Moose would get along just fine."

"Looks like we'll have one more family along," Travis said. Sandy and Mavis Trehane want to come. He has a fine wagon and team of oxen, is a good frontiersman and she isn't a complainer. Like Elaine, she's done some midwifing too, so that will be good when it's Sarah's time."

"I've met Sandy," Zeke said. "I like him fine. Hi is

dancing with anticipation. He's over saying goodbye to Ben and White Flower. The only one of all of us who knows where we're going is Moose," he laughed, putting just a nip of rum in his coffee. "We better be nice to that boy if we want to get there."

THE DAY DAWNED dark and gloomy with heavy spring clouds building to rain and blow on the Travis-Hawthorne parade. And a parade it was, led by Moose, then the two Hawthorne wagons, Trehane's rig, and Travis's two wagons brought up the rear. Moose, Zeke, and Travis were the only ones' saddleback. "Bundle up, Sarah, it's going to be nasty as we get started. Moose is already a couple of miles down the trail, and we'll meet up with him in a few hours."

Sarah didn't sleep very well the night before they were to leave, and spent some time in the morning talking about her worries. She, Hi, and Zeke were having their final breakfast in the blacksmith's cabin, a warm fire was crackling, and the coffee pot was bubbling as she served up slices of side meat with fried potatoes. "Can we have chickens when we get to Oregon? I really like fried eggs with my potatoes," she tried to smile as she said that.

"We'll want chickens, maybe even some geese, and a milk cow. You'll find it a lot different down in a valley where it rarely snows, and the grass grows year 'round. We'll make our own cheese and butter, raise our own meat and, vegetables, and grains."

"I can help," Hi said. "I know how to plant 'taters."

"I know you do," Sarah said. "White Flower has always had a nice garden, but I think what Zeke's saying is a little more than that. Will this storm bother us?" She finally put into words what had kept her awake most of the night. "I'm worried about being out on the trail."

"We'll be fine, Mama," Zeke said, giving her a warm smile, hoping it would be reassuring. "The wagons are very sturdy, the mules are good and strong, and we only have this first ford on the Little Black Creek. There will be many other creeks to cross, but only this one today.

"And," he said, "you have a pretty comfortable over-stuffed chair to sit in. Hi is an excellent teamster, wagon master, and he'll get us to our first camp safe and sound. We better get out there and hitch that team, Hi, and get my new horse saddled. We'll trail your horse behind the wagon today.

"Have you got all your stuff in the wagon? Sarah, how about you, everything in? All my personal gear is on board. Let's get started, shall we?"

It was finally dawning on Sarah that she would be leaving Fort Bridger for the last time. *I've left before, going east to school, traveling to St. Louis, but I always knew I would be coming home. Home. This has always been my home and I'm about to leave it and never be able to come back.* She wanted to cry but the tears wouldn't come, and she had pictures of Oregon, the Willamette valley, a farm as described by Zeke, dancing through her mind.

"I'm packed and ready. Somebody help me get in the wagon. I'm just so fat I can't do it alone," she laughed, walking to the back of the wagon. Hi was there in an instant and helped her in, and watched as she stood at the back of the wagon, giving Fort Bridger a complete look, those tears welled and spilled and she moved forward and into her overstuffed chair.

III

BOOK THREE: THE OREGON
TRAIL

1 4

THEY ONLY MADE ABOUT FIVE MILES THAT FIRST DAY, WHAT with high water, a muddy trail, and howling wind. Travis's teams hadn't been in harness for a long time and threw more than one fit getting underway. He had to tie off his saddle horse and take the reins himself, as the trapper he hired knew almost nothing about handling a team. It turned out that Sandy Trehane's team had never been in harness.

"You ever driven a team, Sandy?" Zeke asked, watching one problem after another take place. "I'm gonna tie my horse off on the back of your wagon, and I'll spend about two hours on the seat up there with you. It's a long way to Oregon, Old Son, so you pay attention to what I'm gonna tell you."

Zeke had the team settled down, let the two horses learn how to work together, gave them just enough head that they were forced to work together, and had a two-hour conversation with them. "These horses are pretty smart, Sandy, so give 'em a chance to learn what to do.

Nudge 'em left, gently with the reins, and then to the right, gently, again, and it won't be long, they'll understand.

"Don't be jerkin' on the reins, that just gets you, and them, upset and don't be whippin' on 'em. It might take another day, maybe even two, and they'll have a good idea of what you want. Just be kind to 'em. Without them, you ain't goin' to Oregon, so remember that, too."

Trehane learned fast, seemed to understand what Zeke was telling him, and by their first rest stop was back to doing the driving himself. "Ain't never spent much time working with animals, Zeke. I had a mule once, but Indians stole it and I didn't try to get it back. Came west some many years ago on the boats and walkin'.

"My woman, Mavis, she always wanted me to get a horse, but to tell you the truth, they kinda scare me."

"Well, Sandy, you treat your animal as a friend, and you'll have a friend. Don't give a horse or mule a reason to be afraid of you, and you'll get along just fine. Just like anything, you can whip a horse into submission, but you won't enjoy what you end up with."

During the short mid-day break, Zeke went over some of the fine points of handling a team, holding the reins, commands to give by voice and by way of the reins, and the rest of the day went well for Sandy Trehane. "Wish you'd have a talk with my horses the way you talked to Trehane," Travis said, trying to maintain a good humor.

"Well, Travis, I do somewhat remember saying something about putting your animals in harness and riding with Hi and me when I was teaching that boy how to drive a team. Seems as how I remember something about you not having the time to just ride about in the woods."

After a gentle jab or two in the ribs and some tussling around in the mud, the two laughing and having fun, Moose said it was time to "get this circus back underway."

"YOU WERE the best mule-skinner out there, Son," Zeke said, leading the mules and horses to good grass for the night. "Now you know why we went to all the trouble to get you and our mules trained. Being trained in what your job is and understanding how to get that job done is what makes for a good life." He and Hi got the animals hobbled and gathered as much dry wood as they could find walking back to camp.

George Felix brought his mules up and joined Zeke and Hiram. "Good day, boss," he said. "Old Travis, he'll never make good mule man," he snickered. "You have good team."

"Thank you, George. We'll be fine after a couple of days. Wagons are doing fine, teams are working hard and now, all we need is some sunshine and less mud." That brought a round of laughter and Zeke watched George take his mules into the grass.

"Ma was scared a couple of times, watching grandpa Travis fighting with those horses. I bet Barbara could do a good job with them. She sure is pretty."

Zeke smiled and walked back to the wagon, remembering the first time he knew what it meant to see and appreciate a pretty girl. *This boy'll do fine, and he's right. Barbara is a pretty girl, just about ten years too old for him,* and he chuckled, getting wood stacked and a fire lit.

"Day one, nobody hurt or killed, some hard lessons learned, and we'll start making good time, now," Travis said, pouring some coffee. "Elaine had some words for me, and you were right, Zeke. I should have done what you and Hiram did, and worked the team some. Guess Sandy learned a thing or two, also."

Travis smiled one of those damn me smiles men get when they know they could do better. "Old Whitewater Bill had no problem with my second wagon, because, guess what, he knows what the hell he's a'doin'. We got all the bumps and jogs out of the system, and it's off to Oregon with us." Elaine sat quiet, next to the fire, a broad smile on her pretty Shoshone face.

Barbara, on the other hand, didn't let Travis or Sandy Trehane off the hook. "Old Foghorn Hiram showed you boys how to do it right. I was watchin' him all day and he got those mules put where he wanted them, got across the river without getting his boots wet. You men could learn from that fine boy," she jibed and snickered. Moose brought the council to order.

Moose settled down close to the fire and grabbed some coffee also. "We're going to be crossing Crow country for the next few days. I think it will be best if we all keep our rifles loaded and at the ready. This part of the trail that Old Gabe laid out is pretty rough, too. It's best that we keep the wagons close to each other, just in case.

"Hiram, you and George Felix be the lead wagons. We'll put Mr. Trehane in the middle, and you bring up the rear, Pa, with your two wagons. Have Whitewater Bill be last in line. If we run into trouble, pull your wagon up hill, Hiram, and Sandy could stop right behind, and Pa, you pull up hill behind Sandy. That would come close to making a stockade.

"I'll never be more than half a mile in front of you,"

Moose finished, pouring another cup of boiling coffee. "How'd that fancy chair work out for you, Sarah? You sure looked nice sitting up there behind Hiram."

"I was just as comfortable as I would have been in the cabin, Moose, if the cabin had been thrown about in an earthquake, that is."

The group was still chuckling as they made themselves ready for the night. "I'll take first watch," Zeke said, and give you a gentle shove in a couple of hours, Sandy."

THE STORM GAVE out during the night and sunrise in the Rocky Mountains was breathtaking. The high peaks glistened with fresh snow, and all the trees and brush at the lower elevation were brilliant green, sparkling in the sunlight. "Fire feels good this morning," Zeke said, putting the coffee on. "George, you and Hiram better bring the animals in while I fix Mama some breakfast."

He poured a cup of coffee for Sarah and took it to the back of the wagon. "Just look at you, all snuggled in that nice bed. Sleep good, did you?" He handed her the cup, and snuck a quick kiss.

"Like a baby, but I can't say the same for the babies. They kicked and squirmed all night. We'll be okay, won't we? Moose kind of scared me with that talk of the Crows, last night."

"It was good for him to make us all aware of what could happen, and good the way he will have the wagons spaced, with Sandy in the middle like that. We'll have to keep our eyes open and be ready, just in case. Want some fried sidemeat?"

"Just a little bit, with a biscuit. Pull that tarp down and I'll get dressed and join you."

The wagons were underway within the hour, and without wind lashing buckets of rain and trees whipping their branches to terrorize the animals and drivers, the morning went well.

"I've seen what I thought were Indians lurking in the trees, Moose. Are we being watched by the Crow?"

"You have good eyes, Zeke. No, it is Slow To Fight and some warriors, giving us a safe escort out of the mountains. I'll have to tell Slow To Fight that he's lost his touch, that a white man could see him in the forest." They chuckled over the comment.

"The Shoshone scouts will have to turn back, maybe later today, maybe tomorrow. I don't think even Ma and Pa have seen them."

"Always appreciated insurance," Zeke grinned. "This is beautiful country we're riding through. Will there be good grass and water like this all the way?"

"We'll pick up the Snake River and follow it west to Fort Ross, and then continue along the Snake to Fort Boise, then northwest and into Oregon. Then west again to the Willamette Valley. To answer your question, yes, we'll have mostly good water and forage for the entire trip.

"Those that follow us later in the season might not be so lucky. The Snake River has carved itself a deep gash in the countryside, and there are places we won't be able to get anywhere near the river but it will be completely visible, way down in the gorge. It's frustrating, knowing fresh water is right there and you can't get to it.

"Because it's early spring, we'll have grass, though. It

dries up fast on the flats above that river gorge. There isn't any summer grass, just dried stalks and brush for those that will come later."

"The Columbia River," Zeke mused, a smile working its way across his face. "Lewis and Clark followed that large river all the way to the Pacific Ocean. Have you seen the ocean?"

"I rode all the way to the ocean with Bridger once," Moose said. "We rode canoes down the river. I was scared to death," he laughed, turning his face away from Zeke. "Old Gabe made me taste the water when we reached the ocean. Salty and cold is what I remember.

"Bridger said because of the gold in California and good farming in Oregon, that there would be thousands, maybe hundreds of thousands of people coming through our country. I'm not going to like that, I'm afraid."

"There will be some massive changes to this country, Moose. I think you're right to be afraid. Your people's lives are going to be changed, and I doubt that change will be for the better."

They rode in silence for the next several hours, enjoying the beauty of the western slope of the Rockies. The trail was incredibly wet, with mud sometimes as much as two feet deep. Zeke's mules were pulling good but Trehane's horses were not in good shape and he needed to stop and rest them often, slowing the movement west. Along with being out of shape they were more than green in harness, which added to their anxiety.

"Good grass, plenty of exercise, and those boys will be fine. My horses aren't exactly up to Zeke Hawthorne's standards either," Travis laughed that night over supper.

"We'll just go a little slower until all the animals are muscled up."

"I'm going to let Zeke lead for a few hours tomorrow morning," Moose said. "We need camp meat and I don't think we want to use the rifles yet. We'll be in Crow country for anther day or two, so I'll use my bow. We're low enough that the animals have been in fresh grass all winter, so should be good meat."

"Wish I could go with you, Moose," Hi said.

"I'll tell you what, Hi," Travis said. "I'll lead for a few hours in the morning and you and Moose go hunting. Elaine and Barbara can guide our wagon and Zeke can run his mules. Any problems with that?"

"I've watched Moose and Hi shoot their bows and there won't be a deer feeling safe tomorrow," Zeke chuckled. "I think it's a good idea. Just remember, boy, to do exactly what your uncle Moose tells you to do. We're still in dangerous country."

"I will Papa," he said, still smiling. "Like Moose, I'm half Shoshone, and many of the men in the village have taught me hunting and being in the forest. I'll bring us a good deer for camp meat."

NIGHT CAME EARLY and fast on the trail. "Seems like the sun's up when we stop but by the time we get the animals taken care of, get cooking fires going, and supper taken care of, it's late at night," Zeke said. "I guess we better get used to it, though. Which is it, I wonder, night coming fast or morning coming early?"

He was snuggled under a heavy buffalo robe, his hands rubbing Sarah's tummy, feeling the babies squirming around. "I can sure tell there are two babies," he whispered, giving her a kiss on the ear.

"We will need to find a good camp sometime next week, Zeke. We'll need to stay a day or two, I think, but those little kits are moving into position. They want out," she snickered, trying to get comfortable. "I want them out, too," and she snuggled deeper into the blanket.

Hiram had his bedroll and buffalo robe under the wagon, in some soft new grass, set so his head was far enough to the side he could watch the stars move through the open sky. The fires were down to embers when Hi thought he heard something or someone moving cautiously through the camp. Sandy Trehane was night guard, but he was sitting next to fire and apparently didn't hear anything.

"Who's there?" Hi said in his new big voice, but there was no answer. He lay very still, listening. There, again, a rustling, so quiet, so soft, and he was about to get out from his bedroll when hands grabbed him.

"Let Go!" he howled, fighting whoever had hold of him. He was hit on the head, hard, and knocked unconscious. Zeke came out from the wagon, knife in hand, and saw Hi being dragged off by an Indian warrior. Trehane stood up at the fire but didn't seem to respond to what was happening.

Zeke dashed through the brush, howling at the Indian to stop, and waking the camp too. He tripped and almost fell once, then in a sprint, caught up and tackled the warrior. The painted Crow warrior, holding Hi's limp body, jumped to his feet, flailing his steel ax to face Zeke.

"Let him go," Zeke said, thrusting the knife so it would be seen. Moose came up fast behind the man holding

Hiram and smashed his steel ax into the man's skull. Zeke, turning, saw a second Crow warrior who was about to attack when two arrows split the warrior's chest and he fell to the ground, dead.

Slow To Fight and another Shoshone warrior emerged from the darkness to make sure the two were dead, and take scalps. "We followed these two, Moose, just not quickly enough. There are more skulking about, but not enough to attack, now that they know we are here.

"How is Little Eagle?"

"He'll have a roaring headache, I'm afraid, but he's okay." Zeke laid the boy back into his bedroll and wiped away the blood from the bash on the head. Travis and Elaine, and Sandy and Mavis Trehane were milling about, Travis working to get one of the fires burning again.

"Sure glad you were with us, Slow To Fight," Zeke said, shaking the man's hand. "We could have lost Hiram that fast if he hadn't given the alarm."

Sarah was out of the wagon and on the ground next to Hiram, with water and a cloth to clean his wound. "He's got a good lump, but I don't think there's a fracture. He's coming to…" she said, cradling her new son. "Thank you, Moose, and thank you Slow To Fight. Thank you," and the tears ran down her cheeks.

Barbara was right there with warm water and more clean cloth. "Here, Sarah, you get back to bed, I'll take care of Foghorn." She lifted Hiram's head and put it gently in her lap, using the warm cloth to wipe more blood away and clean the wound. "Come on, you with the big voice, wake up and be well," she whispered.

Hiram moaned a time or two, but clung as tight as possible to Barbara, and she rocked back and forth, singing an old Shoshone song, wiping his wound, carefully. She felt him stir and watched as he slowly opened his eyes. "Hello, my brave little man," she said, giving him the smile of his young life. "You're going to have one huge headache come morning." He simply left his head in her lap and gave her the best smile he could manage.

An angel is holding my head. I'm dreaming. He was only about half conscious.

"I'll keep the fire going and stand guard the rest of the night," Zeke said, putting more wood on the blaze. "The rest of you, get some sleep if you can."

15

JUST AS SARAH PREDICTED, TWO DAYS LATER SHE TOLD ZEKE they would need to find a place to stop, the babies wanted to join the world. Moose and Zeke had discussed that at breakfast and Moose had a place already in mind, along the banks of a stream running high and fast with spring melt.

"We'll be there within the hour, Sarah. What can I do?"

"Ask Mama to ride with me, just in case," she said, grimacing as she felt a spasm sweep through her. "You might want to hurry," she smiled.

Zeke had Travis into the driver's seat of his wagon and Elaine in the back of their wagon with Sarah in quick time. He rode up alongside Hi, smiling, but serious too. "Your mama is about to give birth, Hi, so pick the easiest way and follow Moose into a camp area he has picked out. Nice and slow and gentle," he said.

"Oh, Papa, this is wonderful. Is Mama okay?"

"She'll be fine, Son. Just fine." Zeke rode ahead at a solid trot to catch up with Moose and let him know what was going on. *Slow To Fight and the Shoshone braves left for home this morning, and now, it's just us. I'm scared, happy, fearful, and proud all at the same time. I have my family, and now I must get us safely to Oregon and build our farm. I left Missouri with nothing, and just think, I have a beautiful half-Indian wife who is about to bring us two children, and we have adopted one as well. I'm blessed.*

He and Moose were at the side of the trail waiting for Hi and the wagons, after tying off their horses and gathering wood for fires. "I think we'll have fresh trout for supper, Zeke," Moose said, watching the stream cascade through the rocks and jumble of deadwood. "That is, if you still know how to catch them."

"I think I might be a little busy with Sarah and the babies, Moose," Zeke said.

"Those women won't let you anywhere near them, Zeke. We'll get the wagons parked, the teams taken care of, and they'll chase us off like we were skunks on the trail. You just watch."

Hi led the wagons into the clearing and the others followed to form a stockade of sorts. Zeke, Moose, Hi, Travis, Sandy, and the two teamsters got the animals out of their harness and hobbled in lush grass. As they walked back toward the wagons, Mavis Trehane stepped out of Zeke's wagon and told them to stay away.

"Go do something that men do. This is woman's work, now," she said, and there wasn't the normal Mavis Trehane smile to go along with the words. She tucked her head back inside the wagon, with a big smile on her face. "Got rid of them, easy enough, now let's get you taken care of, sweetie."

Sarah had her sister, Barbara sitting at her head and

her mother, Elaine to help bring the babies into the world, with Mavis being ready to help with whatever needed to be done. The first baby had crowned before Hiram had the mules unharnessed and was being cleaned up and dried off before the men had been dispersed.

"You're doing just fine, Sarah," her mother said, watching as Barbara wiped the new mama's face wit a damp cloth. "That went very well and very fast," and she started singing the Shoshone birth song, softly, and Barbara joined in. In between spasms, Sarah was trying to sing along.

Mavis Trehane had the first baby all cleaned and wrapped in soft doe-skin covered with a blanket. "Here, Mama," she said, handing the little one to Sarah. "Your first born, warm and well." Sarah held her, looking deep into her face and in particular, her eyes.

"You look just like your father," she cooed, letting the baby suckle for the first time. The second was a little slower coming along, but with Elaine and Barbara singing the slow Shoshone birth chant and song, Sarah found herself softly singing along, and that second little Hawthorne child joined the world. The women oohed and awed, held, cuddled, and sang the praises women do, before finally wrapping the babies and letting new mother Sarah have them.

"I TOLD YOU SO," is all Moose said, walking toward the creek. "Better catch some fish, Zeke. That's what men do," and they all laughed, looking first at the creek, then back toward the wagons.

"Hi, let's me and you take a little walk up the creek.

Bring that new rifle of yours and we'll see what's around these parts. May even catch a fish or two," he chuckled.

"Shouldn't we stay and help, Papa?"

"What is it you think we could help with? I think they're right, shooing us away," he laughed, tousling Hi's hair.

"I guess you're right. I sure wouldn't know what to do. I'll bring my bow, Pa. I want to get a fish with my bow."

Moose, Travis, and Sandy were left behind as the two wandered up the stream, doing its best to go over the banks because of spring thaw. "I think this is a good time for us to get to know each other a little bit better," Zeke said. "We've had some good talks since you have come to live with us, but you need to know more about my family and how I was raised.

"You're a very lucky boy, being raised in two considerably different cultures, but I'm afraid that the white culture won't always look at it this way. As you grow into maturity, I'm afraid you'll find people who will resent your Shoshone blood, and there may be other Indians who will resent your white blood. It's because of this that you need to know as much as possible about your own background and what it will mean to you through life.

"With your new Grandma, Elaine to help, you need to know everything there is to know about being Shoshone. Barbara and Moose, and of course, Sarah will be a big help. Never ever forget your heritage, it's something to be proud of, something to stand up to, and that's on both sides."

"Is Mama gonna be okay?" he asked, looking back over his shoulder as they walked near the stream. "Is she really going to have twins?" He had been listening to what Zeke was saying, trying his best to understand, but was worried about his new Mama. He knew he didn't have sisters and brothers because of problems during birth, and what was happening was more than just a worry, it was serious.

"She'll be fine, Son. It sure looks like we'll have two new members of the family soon. With all those women around her, she'll be just fine, and soon you'll have brothers or sisters, or one of each," he chuckled. "This is a trip we'll never forget, Hi. Never." It was Zeke's calm that helped Hiram, and soon, with more talk and good fishing, Hi was feeling good about what was happening back in camp.

They returned from their jaunt up stream about two hours later, each with a nice string of four or five large trout slung over their shoulders. Hiram surprised Zeke with the amount of knowledge he had about the white culture and told him that Sarah taught the older children history along with their language and arithmetic lessons. "My real Pa has been to some of the places we'll be going through, and I've read about some of them in the books Mama has."

Zeke was more than pleased that Hi was interested in the Lewis and Clark expeditions, and the two planned on keeping a journal detailing everything they encountered, once they started through that country.

Zeke put his fish down in the fresh grass and walked over toward his wagon, not hearing any noises coming from that direction. Moose motioned Hi to come with him, and they headed off to gather some green wood to smoke the trout.

"Everything okay in there?" Zeke asked, quietly.

"Come in, Zeke," Sarah called. "Everything is just fine."

Zeke stepped into the back of the wagon from the ladder he built, to find Sarah tucked into the bed with a baby, wrapped in warm blankets on each side of her. Elaine, Barbara, and Mavis were crowded around, everyone with wide smiles. "You are the papa of two daughters, Sharp Knife," Sarah said. *This is the most beautiful sight I've ever had,* the big man mused. *She looks very tired, but radiant, gorgeous.*

Zeke just stood still, not saying a word, and stared back and forth, smiling at the girl on the left, then the girl in the middle, and finally the girl on the right, before beginning the process over again. "So beautiful," he murmured, even more softly.

Elaine got the other women out of the wagon, kissed Zeke on the cheek and left as well. "You did good, Zeke," she smiled.

Tears rolled down his cheeks as he slowly sat down on the edge of the bed, a smile bright enough to flood the wagon spread the full breadth of his face, and he bent to kiss Sarah. She thought he was trying to say something, but the words weren't there, just that wonderful smile, and kiss after kiss. His big, gnarly hands slowly caressed each baby's face, Sarah's face, and still, he didn't speak.

Sarah picked up the baby wrapped in a yellow blanket and cradled her close. "This is Susanne," she said, offering the child to Zeke. He carefully took the less than an hour old daughter in his arms, kissed her gently on the forehead. "She's your eldest daughter."

"Hello, Susanne Hawthorne. You're beautiful, little girl." He couldn't stop the tears, rocking back and forth with Susanne, and handed her back to Sarah. Sarah, after getting little Susanne tucked back under the buffalo robe, picked up her other daughter and offered her to Zeke.

"Say hello to your baby daughter, Joanne," she said, softly.

"Hello, Joanne Hawthorne. Welcome," he said, again rocking back and forth, kissing the little girl on the forehead. "You're so beautiful." He handed her back to Sarah and watched as she tucked little Joanne back under the covers.

"How are you?" he asked, taking Sarah's hand and kissing it lightly. "I was so worried, so anxious. What do I need to do? Are the girls, is there anything, oh, Sarah, I'm just so happy I can't even talk right."

"I'm just fine, Zeke. I've very tired, I've never been happier in my life, and if you really want to know, I'm starving. I want a big piece of meat roasted the way you do it. A really big piece," she laughed, giving the big man a hug and a kiss. "We make nice babies, Papa Zeke."

She got contemplative for a couple of minutes, looking at each of the girls, looking at Zeke, trying to hold back tears. "Just a few months ago, Sharp Knife, you built us a cabin and filled it with beautiful furniture, and look, now we are a family of five, on our way to a whole new life in Oregon. I love you so much, and I'm so happy," and she bawled, letting the tears flow, hugging and kissing Zeke over and over.

After a few minutes, she pulled back, settled under the heavy and very warm robe, and said, "Bring me meat, Mr. Hawthorne, before I starve."

"WHAT IS THAT?" Zeke asked, as he and Moose topped a

small rise in the trail. He was pointing at smoke off in the distance. "Hope we're not riding into a forest fire or some other kind of trouble."

"When was the last time you had a hot bath, Zeke?" Moose laughed. "That's what the white man is calling Soda Springs, known as a gathering place for Snake, Bannock, and Ute tribes for hundreds of years.

"We'll be there in time to set up camp tonight, and we'll all get a nice hot bath." He was still laughing as Zeke just sat on his mule, watching the hot steam rise into a cold atmosphere, still many miles distant. "Almost every wagon train that comes along the trail stops for at least one day, everyone takes a bath, and just about everyone washes their clothes."

Zeke let Moose ride on ahead and he rode back to the wagons to tell what he saw. *That must be a large hot spring to put that much steam in the air. A hot bath and clean clothes will be mighty nice.*

Moose got the wagons spread into a wide circle, and everyone spent the next several hours getting animals taken care of, wood gathered for fires, and camps made comfortable, thinking mostly about a hot bath.

The area was covered in salt grass around springs and they had to set up their camps away from the hot springs. "It's best to camp with the animals," Moose said. "There are many Bannocks that come to these springs, and they love to steal horses and mules. We'll need to have night guards again."

"You men just do what you have to do," Barbara said as soon as the horses and mules were unhitched. "I'm going to spend an hour in hot water." She danced up the trail toward the hot springs, Elaine and Mavis right alongside. "Are you coming, Sarah?" she called back.

"Not right now," she said, busying herself in the back of the wagon. Zeke walked over after posting the mules and horses.

"Is everything okay?" he asked.

"Just fine, Zeke. I want you and me and the babies to go to the hot springs together, if that's all right. It seems like we never get any alone time and I want to be alone with you and the babies."

He climbed into the wagon and held her tight. "We can take a lantern and go to the springs after supper. I think that would be the perfect ending for a wonderful week. Moose said we're just a few days from Fort Hall and the Snake River. This is beautiful country we're riding through and Moose and Travis both say it gets even better the further along we get."

When Barbara and the ladies returned to camp, the men, with the exception of Zeke, took their turn in the baths, and then fires were lit and supper was cooked.

"IS IT SAFE?" Sarah asked, holding a baby in one arm and a lantern in her other hand.

"Moose rode all the way around the area and said there is no sign of other people in the area. We'll be very safe." Zeke was carrying Susanne and a lantern in one arm, and cradled that big rifle in the other, as they made their way through the salt brush and sage toward a large pool of steaming water.

"Elaine said it's very hot but it soothes," Sarah laughed. "We don't want to put the girls in the water, Zeke. It's too hot, so we'll wash them off and bundle them back up, then take our bath."

Since leaving Fort Bridger, they had moved rapidly into lower elevations of the western slope of the Rocky Mountains, and were enjoying a real springtime. "Just a few weeks ago and we would not have thought about taking our clothes off outside," Zeke laughed, wading slowly into one of the steaming ponds.

"Just look at those stars, Sarah. So bright. I wonder how far away they are? I wonder what they are? Do you ever wish on a star? I did, once, and do you know what, I got my wish. Yes sir, and I'm talking to her right now."

He lowered himself into the water, feeling the affects of hot mineral water immediately. "Maybe we'll just build our farm right here," he chuckled, watching his wife slowly enter the pool.

She splashed him gently, then moved into his arms, letting his hands roam all over, feeling the warmth of the mineral water ease her tired and sore muscles. "It didn't come from a wish on a star, but I'm holding my wish, too," she murmured.

"Mavis Trehane is not enjoying our trip at all," she continued. "I don't think she has ever been anywhere before in her life. Never been hunting with the men, never been moving a village from winter to summer country. As long as I can be with you, I'll never complain.

"It's wonderful, sitting in my beautiful chair, watching Hiram drive the team, seeing you ride out with Moose or Travis, having you come alongside the wagon, just to say hello. And, what makes it all worthwhile, Zeke," she said, "is knowing you will build us a new home." She was snuggled deep into his arms, letting the hot water soak all the way through her tired bones.

It was an hour or more before they got back to camp, with two young ladies demanding a late-night supper from mama, and Zeke putting more wood on the fire. He settled down near the fire, taking an offered cup of coffee from Travis. Moose, Sandy, and Hiram were also gathered around the blaze. "Looks like the ladies are all getting their beauty sleep," Travis noted, handing around the rum jug.

"THINK we can make Fort Hall in two days, Moose?" Travis asked. A couple of days at the hot springs and they were back on the trail, fresh clothing and all.

"Three for sure, then another week or more on to Fort Boise. Hall is still run by the Hudson Bay Company, Papa. Even though this country, even Oregon, is now U.S. Territory, Hudson Bay stays around. Will you be okay meeting those Hudson's Bay men?"

"I'll be fine, Moose. All the animosity from the time of the American Fur Company and them is water over the falls. Trapping is over with, I'm afraid, and these old forts will become stops for all the people emigrating into these western areas. Hudson's Bay was a good company," he said.

"Well, Son, we have to remember that they got here first. The U.S. got Oregon from the British, you know, and the Russians have been around, as well. Hell, the Spanish knew about this country before Lewis and Clark, but didn't actually come into it. Bridger says the Spanish got whole big cities in California and New Mexico.

"Won't be long, I'm afraid, there'll be big cities in this country too. Getting an early start out of Fort Bridger is good for us, but this trail will be busy later this year. We'll get the good grass all the way to the Willamette Valley."

They met the Snake River and Zeke saw for the first time the deep gorges that Moose had talked about. The wagon train was on a plateau, hundreds of feet above the raging river, and the sides of the gorge were almost vertical.

"Ain't no way we could get down there to get water for the animals," he said. "Even if we did, we'd have to come back up to move along the trail. Is it like this all the way to Fort Hall?"

"Pretty much, Zeke," Moose said. "We'll have water and fresh grass because we're so early. "That's a lot of water moving along mighty fast. We'll have one big ford up ahead, and it is usually dangerous. We'll have to cross the Snake where it broadens out, and there are three islands that we will use to get all the way across.

"I know Hi will be okay, and the Frenchmen, but I'm worried about Trehane. He's still rough on his animals, and Mavis just spends most of the day complaining. She has him convinced that they should stop at Fort Hall. I know I wouldn't, but Trehane, he does pretty much what she tells him to do."

Zeke and Moose chuckled over that for a minute, before riding back onto the trail, watching the wagons slowly catch up to them.

16

"Fort Hall," Moose said, pointing at rising smoke way in the distance. "We've made good time despite the spring thaw and raging damn rivers. We'll be fording creeks and streams now for the rest of the journey, so I guess complaining isn't going to do much good."

Zeke had to laugh, and said, "We've spent more time in the water since leaving Soda Springs than we have the whole rest of the trip, so far. That's what makes the grass grow, Moose, so we shouldn't complain too much. I asked Sarah to make up a list of what we should stock up on when we hit Fort Hall. Give her your list, too."

"She already mentioned that. Seems we might be losing Sandy and Mavis Trehane. She really hates this trip and is demanding that they stay at Fort Hall. I guess we'll just have to let that play out. Sarah and Mama were born to this. Mama has said a couple of times that she wished she had made a travois and could walk along with a pony."

"So that's what Sarah was talking about the other evening. Interesting." They rode along, about a mile in front of the wagons, trying to keep as much out of the mud as possible. "That Trehane wagon is going to have a hard time when they reach this boggy country, Moose. I think I'll drop back to give old Sandy a hand with his team."

They had been following the Snake River since leaving Soda Springs. The river was fed by hundreds of streams and rivers boiling their way out of the mountainous country of the eastern Great Basin. Fort Hall was located near where the Snake and Portreuf Rivers join.

Every stream and creek that fed the Snake was running full or over the banks with the spring thaw, and every one of them had to be forded. In some places, the ford was relatively easy, in others, either Moose or Zeke had to ride up and down the creek to find a ford. All around the streams the ground was boggy and muddy, making the mules and horses work hard, wheels digging deep into the mud.

"Muddy enough for you, Sandy?" Zeke called as he rode alongside the Trehane wagon. "Besides the heavy snow we had this winter, it appears this country has also had a pretty wet spring. Looks like we'll have good grass the rest of the way, for sure."

"Don't rightly care if I ever see mud again," Trehane snarled. "Horses hate it as much as I do," and he had to snicker just a bit. "How much longer before Fort Hall?"

"Just a few more hours. I could see smoke from their fires when I turned back to the wagons. We'll be camped at the fort tonight. Need any help with the team?"

"No, thank you, Zeke. We're gettin' along just fine. That last ford back there was a tough one. Fast water and deep too. Your mules and wagon just ploughed right on through, and my horses balked and the wagon got twisted some in the current. Don't much care for makin' this trip. If I ever go on a trip again, it'll be saddle back with pack animals, no damned wagon."

He pulled a plug of tobacco and bit off a chunk, yelled at the team and Zeke took that opportunity to wave and turn toward his wagon. "Hello, little mama," he called, riding up to the back of the wagon. "How are all my ladies?"

"All of us are just fine, Zeke. How much longer before we reach Fort Hall?"

"We'll be camped there tonight, Sarah." He rode up to the front of the wagon, and called to Hiram. "How's things going, Son?"

"We're not having any trouble, Papa. That last ford was fast and deep, but Ruth and Tobias pulled us through without a hitch. Heard you tell Ma we'd be at Fort Hall tonight."

"You'll see smoke from the fort when you top that little rise up there. Want me to spell you for a time?"

"No, I'm doin' fine. Ma's telling me Shoshone stories and I can hear the girls making noises too. I like this, Pa. We're a real family, and I like that."

Zeke sat tall in the saddle as he rode back toward the Travis wagon, his heart swelled to bursting at what Hiram had said. *This is why I left Missouri. Yes, I have a real family. A half-grown son, two beautiful daughters and a fine and beautiful wife. A real family.*

"Hey, Travis, you gonna tell me how deep and fast the water was at that last ford, back there?"

"Damn right, I am," Travis said. "You pick that ford or Moose? Old Sandy damn near lost his wagon on that one.

Twisted around and floatin' some. His horses just ain't up to snuff yet."

"Want to let Barbara or Elaine drive for awhile and ride up with me and Moose?"

"Yeah, I do. And I'll pick the next ford," he laughed, and motioned for Barbara to come up and take the reins. "Barbara's a good teamster, Zeke. I'll jump off and grab my saddle horse."

They rode at a fast trot, passed the wagons, and caught up with Moose in short order. "Old Fort Hall. What a wreck of a place that was when I came west," Travis said, seeing the smoke as soon as they topped the rise. "Nate Wyeth built the place and then the Hudson's Bay Company came along and built Fort Boise, down river from here, and drove him right out of business.

"Hudson's Bay took over Fort Hall and still run it today. Britishers and Frenchmen, Zeke, that's who we'll be dealing with. We'll move down river to Fort Boise and then that long trek north, out of the Snake River Valley and into Oregon. Some of the most beautiful country I've ever seen."

"I don't think you've talked this much since I met you," Zeke laughed. "You really do like this country, I'm thinking."

"Man wouldn't go wrong building a ranch in that valley, Zeke. Wouldn't go wrong for a minute. Good grass, good water, and good climate. Hell, man, if I didn't know just how good the Willamette Valley was, I might be tempted to put down my stakes right here. You'll see, the Snake River Valley is beautiful."

The two men rode up on Moose and Travis gave his son hell over that last ford, but kept a sense of humor as well. Moose gave it right back to his father when he said, "I didn't have any trouble."

"We'll have one more ford up ahead and then into Fort Hall, unless, of course, the Hudson's Bay Company put up a bridge. There'll be a lot of traffic on this trail as spring and summer wear on." Moose pointed out some antelope racing across the sage plain, and the men halted their horses to watch the show. "Wolves can't catch 'em when they're runnin' like that. Seems even the babies can run faster than the wind."

There was a toll barge across the river, which everyone happily paid, and the small wagon train arrived at Fort Hall. "We had that well-deserved lay-over at Soda Springs," Travis said, "and I don't think we need but a day or two to restock and move on toward Oregon. Fort Boise is up the road a piece, then the long haul to the Columbia."

RESTOCKING WAS QUICK, and Sandy and Mavis Trehane decided they would rather not continue the journey to Oregon. Within two days, the rest were back on the trail. Travis ran into several old trapper friends, and there were a few local Shoshone Indians in the compound, but they weren't friendly to Moose, or anyone else.

"Many of the Shoshone in this country run with the Bannocks and they have a great dislike for white men and their wagons. They do have a great like for horses and mules, however," Moose said as he, Travis, and Zeke enjoyed a tin cup full of rum.

"This is not the dangerous country that the Plains and the Rocky Mountains are, but we should continue to maintain night guards and ride with our eyes open," Moose said as they got underway.

"We're riding through Bannock, Ute, and Snake country, and while they won't be looking to take our scalps, they will be looking for an opportunity to take our stock. We shouldn't have much problem keeping camp meat in the barrels, though."

Barbara had bought a saddle horse at Fort Hall and rode point with Moose. "It's been a long time, brother," she said as they moved alongside the Snake River. "We used to ride in the open country a lot when we were growing up."

"You surprised the whole family with your sewing machine and your knowledge of engineering. You've changed, but I think I like you this way. I have many friends in the village, but when I get back, I won't have any family. That bothers me."

"I have just spent two years back east, living and working with strangers, and I don't want to go back," Barbara said. "At least, Moose, you'll have friends. Sarah found what she has always wanted, a loving husband, and now, my goodness, a full-fledged family.

"I'm not ready for that, and don't know if I ever will be. I guess I'm pretty independent, at least that's what Mama says. Will you be happy going back to the old ways, not living in a building with a big fireplace and warm bed?"

Moose wasn't sure if Barbara was teasing him or if that was a sincere question, but it did make him think for several minutes. He gave her a long look before he started talking. "I'm half-Indian, half-mountain man, and half-educated," he chuckled, enjoying the giggles from his sister as well. "And I see horrible changes coming to my Indian people, changes that will alter their way of life forever. I want to be there to help them through the transition.

I have to stay with the people, Barbara. What we've seen just these last few years, with thousands of white people from the east coming through this country, not even caring that someone else lives and depends on the country, is just the beginning. There will be millions, and my people will suffer. I have to stay."

"You've always been so close to the other half of our family, Moose. I never have felt that way, but I will support your decision completely. Slow To Fight has been a wonderful leader and he depends on you, needs your knowledge. You'll follow as the next leader of the people. I'm very proud of you, brother," she said. "Very proud."

THE GROUP HAD GOTTEN into the habit of not stopping for mid-day meal and rest, and now, following along the river, they found they were making excellent mileage each day, reaching Fort Boise in just about four days, spending only one day there, re-stocking on a few items, and moving north along the Snake River.

"I kept hearing talk about the Bannock and Shoshone getting ready to raise hell when the wagons start coming through," Travis said as they sat at evening fire. "I thought you said the Bannock were more interested in stealing our stock, Moose."

"All I know is what Slow To Fight said," Moose replied.

"I CAN'T BELIEVE how those girls have grown in just a few weeks," Zeke said one evening as they sat around a large fire after supper. "They'll be walking and talking by the time we reach the Willamette," he joshed, tickling Susanne. She was wrapped in a deerskin, nestled in his arms, and he was rocking her gently, watching her slowly close her eyes and go to sleep. Sarah held Joanne, and that little girl had decided she was not going to go to sleep.

"They are so alike and so different all at the same time," Sarah said, rocking back and forth as well. "They are both hungry all the time," she laughed, letting Joanne nurse, and maybe get sleepy.

"They're big, like you and Grandpa," Hi said to Zeke, as he settled in next to Sarah. "I'm glad we picked up that extra pot of grease, Pa. I think the right front wheel of the wagon is wearing fast. Can you take a look at it in the morning? It's making some funny noises."

"I sure will. When did that start?"

"Second day out from Boise, when we had to drive through all those rocks. I greased heavy this morning, but it made noise all day."

"That's not good, Son. We'll take a good look at it in the morning. Might just be a nick on the axel. Maybe I'll drive after, to give it a good listen. You can ride with Moose for the day. I know you'd like that."

"Oh, yes, Pa. Barbara's been riding too, maybe I can ride with her for a while," and he blushed as bright as Zeke and Sarah had ever seen. They tried not to chuckle, but Zeke couldn't hold it back, and finally had to get up and throw some wood on the fire.

"That would be fine, riding with your aunt Barbara and uncle Moose," Zeke smiled, poured some coffee, laced generously with rum. "Let's plan on fixing that wheel first thing, and then maybe we can stop early tomorrow evening and see if there are any fish in the Snake River."

"We need to do that more often," Sarah said. "Fresh trout the day you catch them and then several days of smoked trout sure is good. I've never had what Moose has been calling salmon, have you?"

"Never had any salmon in the Ohio Valley or in Missouri. Moose said it's a little bit like trout, but red, bright red, and very rich tasting. I'm looking forward to seeing and eating some. This is a pretty big river so the trout could be good-sized also. That would be nice for smoking. Moose said he saw some antelope late today, so we might get some fresh camp meat as well. This is sure a better way to travel than when I came west," he snickered. "I trapped little rabbits and those big prairie chickens, but I like red meat."

"You know how I feel about that," Sarah joked. "Bring me fresh meat, oh mighty hunter of mine," and they laughed loud enough to waken little Susanne. "Oh, now we've done it," Sarah joked. "I better get these girls in bed and get under a warm blanket myself."

Zeke carried Susanne and Sarah had Joanne, and he helped her into the wagon and got the three settled in before returning to the fire. Travis came over from his fire to join him in coffee and rum. "How you holding out, Travis? Everything okay?"

"We're doing fine, Zeke, just fine. You're more than a son-in-law, Zeke, you're probably the best friend I have, next to Jim Bridger. I just wanted you to know that, besides the fact you saved my life. Probably saving it again, right now, with this move to Oregon."

"You've proved yourself to be my best friend, Travis, over and over. We'll do fine in Oregon, I know it. Got a little problem with the front right axel on the wagon, so let's not plan on pulling out in the morning before I have a chance to check it out. Hi says it's making a hell of a racket."

"Probably busted it going through those rocks, Zeke. I'll give you a hand soon's it's light enough to work. Everything else okay with your family?"

"This has been a lot easier journey than I thought it would be. Sarah and the babies are doing fine, Hiram is a fine son and does more than his share around camp and with the wagon and team. I don't think he got along too well with Ben Pierson but I know he misses White Flower."

"Old Ben can be hard to get along with even for me," Travis chuckled. "I know Hi is calling you and Sarah Ma and Pa, and he calls us Grandpa and Grandma. But I don't think he'll ever call Barbara Auntie," and both men broke out laughing.

"That boy is in love, Travis. That is a great truth, right there. That boy is in love."

"THAT'S A REAL MESS THERE, ZEKE." Travis muttered the next morning. "Lucky Hi said something last night or we'd be facing a wheel falling right off that wagon. She's busted almost clear through." Travis was holding the axel that had bent at a bad angle with steel edges as jagged as broken glass. "Can you fix it?" he asked.

"Could if I had a forge all fired up, sure enough," Zeke replied. "Damn," he said, walking back and forth in front of the wagon, jacked up with logs and rocks. "It would take me two hours and I'd have that ready to remount. Damn," he said again, then stopped his pacing.

"Only thing to do is for me to ride back to Fort Boise and either have it fixed or try to find one ready to mount."

"Can't go by yourself, Zeke. Too dangerous. Neither Moose nor Hiram can go with you because Moose needs to stay for protection and Hi needs to stay and act as camp boy for wood, water, and fires. George and White-water need to stay for protection, and, old friend, that only leaves one person..." he said, smiling ear-to-ear.

Zeke chuckled, taking the broken axel from Travis and walking over to the morning fire. "We better get packed and on the trail, then, Mr. Travis, Sir." He poured each of them a cup of coffee. "Let's ride as light and fast as possible. I'll ride Ruth, she's really a fine trail animal, and your horse will not have a problem with a fast ride. We should be back at Boise in three days, doncha think?"

"We'll take coffee, beans, and smoked meat, some hard biscuits, and we'll be there in three days for sure," Travis said.

The two were packed, the broken piece of axel riding in Zeke's saddlebag, counter balanced with coffee and beans, and on the trail in less than an hour. "Don't you be getting' in trouble, Mr. Travis," Elaine said, half smiling, and Barbara laughed at her mama.

"That goes for you, too, Zeke," Sarah yelled as the two rode out of camp at a fast trot. She turned to Hi after losing sight of the men. "Better get that fishin' pole of yours working, Son. Trout for supper, okay?"

"Yes, ma'am," he said, rummaging around in the back of the wagon. Right away, Mama, right away," he yelled back, grinning. The women, along with Hi, were looking at the delay as a respite from the long trail. Only Moose was looking at it as dangerous.

He called to Hi to join him at the fire before heading out to fish. "This is not a picnic, Hiram," he said, "despite the fact the women want it to be. Go fetch George Felix and Whitewater. We will have to be prepared to defend this little camp. It won't be but a short time before the Bannock or Shoshone in this area discover us, and that means danger."

17

"YOU'VE BEEN PRETTY QUIET SINCE WE LEFT FORT HALL, Travis. Something bothering you?"

"Yeah, I suppose so. I never did like Fort Hall, when the American Fur Company had it and after, when Hudson's Bay took over. When we were at Fort Boise I kept hearing rumors of trouble with the Shoshone in this area. Seems as though many of the emigrants that have been coming through have been worse than rude, shooting and killing indiscriminately.

"Some of the old trappers living around Boise, men I've known for twenty or thirty years are saying that there might be a war in the near future. We need to get that axel fixed and get back on the road as soon as possible."

"I thought Moose said the Indians in this country were peaceful."

Travis harrumphed a couple of times. "He's relating what he knows from Slow To Fight and I'm telling you what I know from talking to the trappers right there at Fort Boise. The Shoshone in the western hills of the

Rocky Mountains are a different tribe from the Shoshone here in the Great Basin. These people are influenced by the Bannock and the Ute or Paiute tribes, both of which hate the emigrants."

With their animals in a long trot, the men made Fort Boise on their third day and Travis went to the Suttler's Store while Zeke found the blacksmith shop, run by a French-Canadian gentleman named Fournache. "Didn't expect to see you back, Mr. Hawthorne. Problems?"

Zeke pulled the axel out of the saddlebag and showed it to the man. "Got into some rocky country and she split on us. Got another or can you fix this one?"

"Got this wheel to mend and then I can fix that for you. I can't remember what you said, you're heading for California or Oregon. If it's California, I want to warn you that there's Indian trouble on that trail. Shoshone and Bannock unhappy as hell with all the wagons passing through their country.

"Too many people coming out this way, Mr. Hawthorne, too many. They shoot the deer and antelope and don't eat all the meat, they shoot an Indian just because he's an Indian. I tell you, sir, things are gonna get damn hot around here in the next few years."

"We've been feeling the changes at Fort Bridger as well, Mr. Fournache," Zeke replied. "The emigrants making problems, in particular the Mormons in the Salt Lake country. They even threatened to burn out Jim Bridger's place."

"Old Gabe was through here some time ago. Said he was givin' it up. Mormons want it? Let 'em have it, he said. You bein' with Travis kinda proves that Bridger is really serious."

Zeke left the Frenchman to do his work and made his way to the suttler's. That little store was packed to the rafters with merchandise, everything from hundreds of traps to bolts of silk and cotton, wools and canvas. He found Travis at a makeshift bar, just a couple of planks laid across some barrels, in conversation with an old trapper.

"This is who I was tellin' you about, Tom," Travis said as Zeke joined them and motioned for some rum. "This here is Ezekiel Hawthorne and he trekked all the way from Missouri to Fort Bridger by himself. That's the way so many of us did years ago, but not today, no sir. But old Zeke did.

"Zeke, this here be Tom Thomas; lived with the Crow for many years, worked with Old Gabe for a dozen seasons at least, and just hangs out near the rum jug these days."

Tom Thomas whacked Travis with one big hand and stuck the other out to shake with Zeke. "Any friend of Travis here, is someone I gotta watch out for," he said, with a twinkle in his eye. "So you be heading for the Willamette Valley, eh? Ain't much for farmin' myself, but I do like to eat what them farmers grow, long as they be some venison or buffalo near-by."

"What's the word on Indian trouble, Tom?" Travis asked.

"Been lots of talk, but that's all. Some say the Bannocks are behind the problem. They've lost people, angry as hell about all the game being shot up, but the Shoshone will probably get something started, either this year or in '53. Lots of bad talk, Travis, lots."

"Sooner we get that axel fixed and get back on the trail

to Oregon the better," Travis said. "What did the black-smith say?"

"We'll have it this afternoon and we can head out then or first thing in the morning."

"Let's get on the trail as soon as we have it," Travis said. "We get up on that plain above the high-water mark and ride like hell, we can be back with the wagons in two days, not three."

Before picking up the axel, they filled two sacks with smoked meat and hard biscuits, not planning on making regular camps, just throwing bedrolls out for a few quick hours of sleep. "We can eat in the saddle, I think," Travis said, "and only worry about water for us and animals."

It was a long two days back to the wagons, in the saddle from sunup past sundown, and the two rode in in time for a fried trout supper.

"Glad you two are back," Moose said, taking the lead ropes from the animals. "Women are driving me and Hi crazy. Didn't know three women could talk that much."

Travis and Zeke chuckled as they stepped out of the saddles. "Glad everybody's safe," Travis said, giving Elaine and Barbara hugs. "Soon's we get that axel fixed, we'll load up and get back on the road. Lost a week with this problem and don't want to get caught up by those might be behind us."

"What's the big hurry, Papa?" Barbara asked.

"They're talking Indian trouble at Fort Boise, and they mean it. It's serious. Since we're heading north, we'll get the hell away from the problem. Even Tom Tom is worried. Seems the Bannocks are raising hell on the California trail."

"Slow To Fight never said anything about trouble."

"These are Western Shoshone, Moose. Different people, and closer to Bannock and Paiute. Them folk heading for the gold in California shoot all the game, shoot Indians just because, and they say there's gonna be hell around here."

Travis, Moose, and Hiram joined Zeke at the wagon, got the new axel mounted and the big wheel greased and in place well before dark. "Let's get the wagons repacked now and we can hitch up and be on the trail at sunrise," Travis said.

Sarah and the babies were wrapped in buffalo robes, sitting close to the fire when Zeke and Hi got back from the wagon. "I was worried about you, Zeke. This has been the first time that we've been apart since we got married. I'm glad you're back."

Zeke picked up one of the girls and hugged and kissed her, then did the same with the second. "Ain't the same, out on the trail, I mean, without you, Sarah. We'll probably move fast for the next day or two, get out of Bannock territory, then back into that rhythm we had. Hi, I want you to drive and lead, with Travis's two wagons following. It was a mistake for him not to buy Sandy Trehane's rig, but that was his decision. His men are doing well with the wagons, but he could have made the load in those wagons lighter with Trehane's in the mix."

Elaine and Barbara cooked up pans full of fresh trout and had potatoes roasting in the coals. "I have a little surprise," Barbara said, bringing out one more large cast iron kettle. "While you boys were off playing at Fort

Boise, I made up a new starter-dough mix and we'll have fresh bread with our suppers from now on. Don't know why I didn't keep the other starter going."

She pulled a large loaf from the Dutch oven and it all but disappeared within minutes. "When we first got started, I made a loaf or two every night before we turned in. Well, from now on we'll have fresh bread in the morning. No more of those hard, old biscuits."

AFTER LEAVING FORT BOISE, the group headed northwest, across the Snake River, toward Columbia country. "That country behind us," Travis said, "they can have it. From when we reached the Snake River, all the way to Fort Boise, they can have it." He stormed about the camp, getting his teams ready, chasing Elaine and Barbara about to make sure everything was packed.

"Who are these people you're calling 'they'?" Zeke finally asked after hearing the comment for the tenth time.

"Anybody that wants it," Travis said. "A river filled with spring run-off that you can't get near because of shear drop-offs, and streams that simply disappear, and angry Indians. We're going to be in Oregon country and away from this horrible country."

"Okay, Papa, you need to get away from driving the wagon," Barbara said with a warm smile and hug for her father. "You have too much time on your hands driving this team. You ride up front with Moose and I'll drive for a day or two.

"Papa used to be the same way in the trader's store at the fort," she said. "Mama and I had to chase him off sometimes so he didn't chase off whatever customers we might have."

There was general laughter around the camp as things were put in place, teams were hitched, and Moose finally called out, "Let's move 'em out!" Harnesses tightened, wheels broke free of mud and turned, and whoops and hollers filled the air. All thoughts were probably the same, "Oregon, here we come!"

Zeke was riding alongside the Hawthorne wagon so he could talk to Hi and Sarah. "Moose says the country won't be that much different than what we've been in, despite all the howling by Travis. Lots of sagebrush, but since we're so early in the wagon train season, we will have good grass. And," he said, "the rivers will be accessible. Some of those bluffs on the Snake were fifty feet deep. We won't find that."

"Moose said that the more north we get, the better the grass and there will be more water from streams and rivers," Hi said. "Mr. Travis is really worried about the Bannocks and how they have stirred up the Snake tribes."

"We got some good information about that when we were back to Fort Boise for the axel, Hi. But we're moving out of their territory right now. We'll need for you and Moose to keep us in camp meat with your bows. A gunshot can be heard for a long distance, and there's no sense in creating a problem."

ON THE FIFTH day after crossing the Snake, the wagons were stopped in a clearing for the night. Hi and Zeke were about to take their animals into the grass to be hobbled when three Indians appeared on the trail in front of them. "Look!" Hi said, pointing.

"I see 'em. Take the lead ropes and slowly walk back to the wagon, I'll stay back and guard. Spread the word. Don't panic, just go straight back to camp." Zeke waited until Hi had turned the animals and fell in behind, keeping a close eye on the three Indians.

Looks like a family, not warriors. That's a woman for sure, and a man, and that third one must be a child. Hi walked the animals into camp and called Travis and Moose to tell them about the Indians. Zeke came slowly into camp, and chased all the women back into the wagons.

"They're Bannock," Moose said, "not Shoshone."

"Go talk to them, Moose. You might have to sign if they don't speak like the people." Travis had his rifle in hand and Zeke pulled his from the wagon. Hi got his shotgun out of the wagon, and they all watched as Moose walked up to the three, his hands at his side, palms open and facing forward to show that he was unarmed.

Using the sign language of the native people Moose said hello and asked what they wanted.

"We are hungry," the man signed, "and cold. We have lost our people and we can't hunt."

Moose told them to stay where they were and came back to where Zeke and Travis were standing. "Something wrong with this," he said. "They say they left their people, can't hunt, and are cold and hungry. This is a trap," he continued. "They are well fed, and the man has a bow and a quiver full of arrows. They are supposed to let us get them into camp and all of us be around the fire, then the warriors will arrive, and we will die."

Travis motioned Hi to get under the Hawthorne

wagon, motioned his drivers to get under the second wagon with their rifles, and had Barbara join him under their wagon. "I'm going to move under our wagon with Hi, Moose. Then what?"

"I'm going to force these three to leave, and then we watch. The attack will come sudden, fast, and deadly. Make sure your weapons are ready, Zeke." Moose turned and started back toward the three, noticing that they had separated some, no longer standing in a tight group.

With his rifle cradled in the crook of an elbow, Moose signed that the three must leave immediately. After signing, he took the rifle in both hands, and made sure they understood that it was cocked and ready. He waved the rifle once, as a gesture for them to leave, when the man pulled an arrow and tried to get it notched. Moose turned the rifle, not bothering to bring it to his shoulder and fired, dropping the Indian with a shot to the chest.

The other two turned and started running toward a stand of trees just off the trail and Moose bounded back to get behind some rocks near the fire ring. Half a dozen arrows flew through the air as he dove behind the rocks and worked to get his rifle reloaded.

"Catch," yelled Hi, and he threw a bow and full quiver of arrows toward where Moose was hidden. Hi had his own bow and quiver at the ready. He notched an arrow and had three others in his bow hand at the ready, when four warriors tried to rush Moose. He loosed his first shot, directly into the middle of the lead warrior, and Travis fired and brought the same man down. Zeke fired his rifle and hit a second attacker, and Moose took a third on, hand-to-hand, using his big knife to end the fight. The fourth man turned and raced back into the trees.

"It's not over," Zeke said. "There's more of 'em up there. Anybody hurt?" he yelled out and Moose and Travis answered back that they were okay. Travis's driver was ever quiet, as usual. "Let's get moved so we can fight from any direction. They'll probably circle around us.

"It'll be dark soon, and we'll need to get that fire blazing good. You ladies stay in the wagons."

"I see three, no, four men moving through the trees, moving away from us," Hiram said. "One of them is limping, and one might be that young boy that was with the first three that came into camp."

"You've got one hell of a set of eyes, Son," Zeke chuckled. "Are they on horseback?"

"Two are on horses, and one is helping the one that is limping."

"We're missing at least one person and one horse, then," Zeke whispered almost to himself. "They probably want us to think they're leaving, but will circle back on us."

He hadn't quite finished saying that when two Indian warriors charged out of the trees, not twenty feet from Moose, and to his left. Moose turned fast and shot one, but the second one pounced on the big man, his knife flashing in the air. Zeke was out from under the wagon and on top of the two in three fast strides.

Zeke's knife found soft flesh and he drove the blade deep twice before feeling the brave go limp. "Moose," he cried, "Moose, are you hurt?"

"Yeah," Moose gasped. "My side, Zeke. He stabbed me deep." Travis and Hi were there within seconds, moved the dead bodies aside and got Moose laid down and as comfortable as possible. Elaine and Barbara were there right away as well, and began working on the hurt man.

Zeke motioned for Travis, Felix, and Whitewater to keep a close watch. "I don't think this is over, so let's keep our guard up tight. This was a pretty small hunting party, but I bet they have friends somewhere close."

Moose was wearing a regular shirt, not his buckskins, and Barbara opened it up and found a knife wound at the bottom of the ribcage, bleeding heavily. She used part of the shirt to cover the wound to stop the bleeding. "The wound is under the skin along one of his ribs. It did not go into his lungs or anywhere near his heart." She motioned for a bowl of warm water and more cloth.

"That's gonna be sore, sure as hell, little brother," she said, "but you're gonna live. The rib bone deflected the knife, but it did a lot of muscle damage." She washed the wound down good, poured some of Travis's rum over the wound, bringing a muted howl from the big man, then sprinkled some powders that Elaine brought over the wound and bandaged it up.

"Get wood for the fire, Hi, and get plenty of water for the women." Zeke was putting wood on the fire, getting it burning high and hot. He motioned for Whitewater to take up a defensive position and he did the same, just in case there was another attack. "I don't think there's anymore of them," he said. "They would have hit by now, but let's be damn careful."

"It's almost dark," Travis said again. "They'll try to steal the animals tonight and then hit us in the morning. Get those horses and mules tied to wagon wheels inside the half circle, and us men will sleep under the wagons with our rifles ready.

"Me and Felix will take second shift, you, Whitewater, and Hi take the first, Zeke. Don't ask any questions. If you hear a noise, shoot it. The Bannocks are known all over this country as being able to steal a horse while a man's still in the saddle."

"Let's get Moose settled in your wagon, Travis, then we better get us fed. It's gonna be a long night. How you holding up, Hi?"

Hiram was sitting next to the fire, being very quiet. Zeke sat down next to him and put his arm around the boy. "You were very brave, Hi. You acted and did what would be expected of a full-grown man. I'm very proud of you, Son. Very proud."

"Thank you, Papa." He sat still, gazing into the fire, tears slowly trickling down his cheeks. "I killed that man, Papa," he said, so soft Zeke had to strain to hear him. "Was I wrong? But what else could I do? He was going to kill Moose."

"You did what a man has to do, Son. You protected your family. You saved your Uncle Moose's life. That's a very brave thing for a man to do."

Father and son sat together, ate some venison and fresh bread, drank many cups of coffee and kept the fire going for several hours. Every half hour or so, one of them would get up and walk around the inside of the wagon circle and then settle back at the fire. It was either late at night or early in the morning that Travis and his driver relieved them and they slipped into their bedrolls.

18

THE CAMP WAS ALIVE WELL BEFORE SUNRISE, THE ANIMALS were harnessed, a quick and mostly cold breakfast was eaten, washed down with cups full of boiling coffee, and the group was ready to move out. "I'll lead, but not way out in front," Travis said. "Probably just twenty or so yards in front. Zeke, you ride about twenty yards behind my second wagon."

"Keep us on this main trail, almost due north, now," Moose groaned, letting Barbara clean the wound and redress it. "Should be good grass and water for the next week or more." Barbara shushed him and motioned Travis and Zeke to get out of the wagon and let her do her work. They smiled, patted Moose on the shoulder, and left.

"We will not meet any friendly people on the trail today. If somebody shows up, shoot 'em dead. Hi, you have your shotgun and bow, Barbara, you have your shotgun, and Felix, you and Whitewater have your rifles? Good. Let's move 'em out," he yelled, and the wagons began another long day on the Oregon Trail; this time short-handed with a wounded man in great pain.

After several hours without a sign of trouble, Travis and Zeke ended up riding together about a hundred yards in front of the wagons. "This is nice country," Zeke said. "Good grass and water."

"This is eastern Oregon Territory, and the area became a territory just three or four years ago. Probably the driest part of Oregon," Travis said. "To the west are the Cascade Mountains, with active volcanoes that you can see when we get over into the Willamette Valley. And to the east are the Rocky Mountains. This in-between section doesn't get a lot or rain or snow. We're seeing good grass right now because it's still spring. Those following along behind us won't get this good grass.

"We're leaving an area where several tribes are most unhappy and moving into an area where the tribes are even more unhappy. This trail takes us to Whitman's Mission, of which, nothing stands today." He was grim-faced saying that. "For the next few days, we should watch for the possibility of some roving bands of Bannock or Shoshone, and then we'll move into Cayuse country."

"Have the Cayuse been bothered by all the immigration?"

"More than bothered, I'm afraid," Travis said. "Damn near wiped out. It's the same story the Crow tell, and many of the tribes throughout the plains." Travis spent the next hour telling Zeke the story of how Whitman and his wife had set up a mission, and how they had accidentally introduced measles. Fully protected themselves, the measles spread through the tribe, killing most of the Cayuse.

"The tribe was more than angry, Zeke. To this day, they believe the introduction of the dreaded disease was done on purpose. There is hatred in that tribe. They burned that mission to the ground and killed every white person around it, including Whitman and his wife. Some called it a massacre, others called it retribution. Whatever name you might put to it, the Cayuse today aren't particularly welcoming."

"It's a dilemma, Travis, that all of us moving into Indian country will have to live with. I support the Indians in their fight to protect their homes and their food supply, but at the same time I feel a huge obligation to protect my family from attack by those same Indians.

"We just came out of a fight with Bannocks that feel they are protecting their homes and families, and we killed them protecting our families. Your wife is a Shoshone, an ally of the Bannock. Yet, there is no way we could have avoided that fight, no way we could have established a dialog and come to an agreement of some kind that did not involve death.

"There is no real answer, Travis. They believe they are right, and we believe we are right. They are right, and we are right." He just sat deep in the saddle and rocked his head back and forth, sadness spread across his face.

They rode in silence for the next several hours, Zeke in deep contemplation, until finally Travis broke into his reverie. "We'll follow the Columbia River from Whitman's Mission down to The Dalles, and then we'll have to make a huge decision. I doubt that Moose has been much past Whitman's or he would have said something before this. I remember, he said that he and Old Gabe went down river in canoes. He knows about the problem, just doesn't talk about it."

"You can't just say something like that and then just quit talking, Travis. You make it sound mighty serious, whatever it is you're trying not to talk about."

Travis gave a soft chuckle before he continued. "The Columbia River is a big river, Zeke. Really big, and from The Dalles, which is where there is a great falls, down river for many miles is the Columbia Gorge, with incredible rapids and whirlpools, and just roiled up water. Killed a lot of people over the years. Old Gabe said he rode a raft down through the rapids one time and won't do it again."

He was interrupted by a long, loud whistle coming from the wagons. "That's Barbara," Travis said, turning his horse back and spurring it into a hard gallop, Zeke following right behind.

"Indians," she shouted, pointing to the east. Hiram had spotted them as soon as Barbara whistled and began moving the Hawthorne wagon into a circle, Felix following, then Barbara, with Whitewater Bill closing the gap. The entire procedure took less than five minutes.

In the meantime, Zeke and Travis were off their mounts and had rifles at the ready. They were soon joined by Hiram, Felix, Whitewater, Barbara, and Elaine, all armed. Barbara pointed to a stand of juniper bushes about two hundred yards off. "See the piñon pines way off behind the juniper? Watch close and you'll see movement from what looks like several men."

Zeke picked up the movement first and estimated the distance at about half a mile. "It looks like five, maybe more. Let's spread out, Travis, not have everyone inside the wagon circle. Hi, you stay inside the circle, and Whitewater, you go outside the circle to the left. I'll go outside to the right. If they are hostile, they won't expect anyone to be outside the protection of the wagons."

"Somebody get my rifle," Moose yelled from the back of Travis's wagon. "I might be hurt but I can still shoot." Barbara jumped up and got it and a powder horn, patch and ball pouch for him, then got back under the wagon with her shotgun.

"Looks like they've hunkered down after seeing us circle-up," Hiram said. "I think there might be seven or eight of them, and they're spreading out now."

"Those young eyes of yours are good," Travis muttered, "I have yet to spot a single, one." He was laid out in the dirt using a wheel for protection and didn't want to raise up to look. "You just keep us posted," he said, trying not to sound upset.

"They're spread way out and coming up fast. They're keeping really low. They're just behind the juniper bushes, trying to get closer. They'll have to crawl through the sage to do that." He had been holding his shotgun but put it down and picked up a Hawkins that Zeke had brought along for him. He stopped talking and raised the rifle closer to his shoulder. *I've got one rifle shot then I'll grab my bow and quiver,* he thought, watching one big Indian scuttle up to a sage not a hundred yards from the wagons.

"If they were friendly, they'd have come up waving and smiling," Moose hollered. "Don't anyone hesitate and wait for a smile." Then his Hawkins went off with a loud blast, followed by a scream that ended fast. Hiram fired next, then a volley of shots from everyone else.

This is when the Indians counter-attack, Zeke remembered. *While we reload, they have their bows and fire one shot right after another.* He heard a scream without hearing a shot and smiled as he drove a ball into the muzzle of his rifle. *Hi has his bow working. That boy is something.*

One more volley from the wagons, a few more arrows from Hi, and the fight was over. They watched two Indians crawl back through the sage toward the juniper bushes. "Let's get these wagons moving, folks," Travis hollered. "The Indians will want to gather their dead and wounded and that'll give us time to make some miles. Move 'em, folks!" he said several times.

"They broke off fast," Moose said as Travis rode up alongside the wagon. "This was probably a hunting party, and now the survivors will spread the word. This isn't over, Papa."

"I'm think you're right. Did you get a good look? Were they Bannock?"

"I think so. We need distance, Papa. You'd better get back out there and keep these wagons moving. Usually when they break off fast like that, it's because there was great loss. That is to our benefit," he snickered, giving his rifle a little pat.

TRAVIS AND ZEKE kept on the trail until almost sunset before finding a place where the wagons could be turned into a stockade of sorts and be defended. "No fires tonight, folks," he said to many groans. "If you're of a mind to smoke a cigar or pipe do it now before the sun goes down, otherwise, no smoking either."

Supper consisted of whatever meat had already been cooked, bread, and corncakes. Cold water with a splash of rum washed everything down. Sarah and Zeke sat on a blanket, their backs against a wagon wheel. Hiram sat across from them holding Joanne. Zeke held Susanne who had developed a cough during the day.

"She has a fever, Sarah. We have to keep her warm, even though we won't have a fire." Sarah had wrapped her in warm blankets and Zeke held her tight. *I will not lose another child. I won't.* Zeke's thoughts were back in Missouri when he held a small little child as it breathed its last. *I'm not a religious man. I don't get on my knees and beg things from gods, but I simply can't stand the thought of losing another child.* He closed his eyes and rocked back and forth for an hour before Sarah said it was time for bed.

She and Zeke got the girls under the buffalo robe, Sarah with them, one cradled on each side of her. "They can sleep with their mama tonight, even though that beautiful cradle you built for them would be fine."

"They need your warmth, Sarah," he said, so softly she almost couldn't hear him. "Hiram and I will be right outside if you need anything. Stay warm," he said, kissed each in turn, and climbed out of the wagon.

"Will Susanne be okay, Papa?" Hiram asked.

"We'll do anything we have to do to make sure of that, Son." They wrapped up in blankets and crawled under the wagon. "We'll take second watch tonight, so let's get some sleep while we can."

TRAVIS AND WHITEWATER BILL took the first watch and without a fire to shed light and heat, found it difficult. "I've tripped over everything there is to trip over, so far," Travis grumbled, catching himself after kicking a harness. Whitewater sat outside the circled wagons on the west side, only getting up occasionally to walk about.

"Why don't you just sit and watch?"

"I'd go to sleep, that's why," Travis snarled back.

"If there are Injuns out there, they know where we are. Just follow the sound of an old angry trapper. Hush, now." Whitewater Bill had been in hundreds of Indian fights over the years and had to get Travis to quit talking and making other noises.

Later, it was Moose and Felix who relieved them. "Decided to give Zeke and Hiram a full night's sleep," Moose said, joining Travis. "Go get some sleep yourself, Papa, and be quiet about it," he chuckled. Moose settled in, leaning against a rock, taking pressure off his wound. Barbara had changed the dressing a couple of times and sprinkled herbs and other medicines that Elaine had brought, but there was considerable pain, and he winced some as he sat down.

Travis grumbled all the way back to his bedroll under his wagon and was fast asleep within minutes. Whitewater made one last turn around the wagons and found his bedroll too. "It's mighty dark tonight," Moose said, leaning against the rock, watching off to the west. "If they come, we won't see 'em, Felix. We can only hope we hear them in time."

The hours seemed to creep by, one hour more like two, and finally the first hint of light eased its way across the eastern sky. "Let's get everyone up and get moving," Moose said, "before anything can get started. If they didn't hit us last night, it's either because they wanted to wait for daylight, or they aren't actually here."

"Moose, can you come here, please?" Sarah called from the back of the wagon.

"Good morning, pretty sister. Watcha need?"

"Susanne has a bad fever, Moose, and I need a good strong tea. Can you find some herbs for it? You know which ones I need. Sumac makes the best for a fever, and I'm sure there's sumac around here."

"Right away," Moose said and went out from the wagons, his rifle at the ready. Elaine and many of the women in the tribe taught Moose and all the children the healing herbs and medicines that are found in the wild, including the ubiquitous sage and juniper. Moose gathered sumac leaves, some roots, some twigs, and found some wild roses, gathering the rose hips. He came back to camp quickly.

A small fire, some ground herbs, a bit of water, and a delightful aroma spread through the camp. He filled a canteen with the tea and brought a tin cup full to Sarah. "She won't like this at first, Sarah," he snickered, handing her the cup. "It's hot, so let it cool some before you try to giver her any."

"Thank you, Moose. How's your wound? Are you going to be okay?"

"I'm fine," he said. "We're going to start moving right away, so don't let that spill." He gave his sister a kiss on the top of her head and jumped down out of the wagon, gave a hearty groan, and hurried to help get all the animals harnessed up for another long day.

He found Zeke and Hiram putting the mules in harness. "I just made a good medicine tea for Susanne, Zeke. Sumac will bring that fever down and rose hips will give her plenty of energy. I'm sure she's just catching a slight cold. Did your mother teach you about the herbs and roots, Hiram?"

"I was telling Papa about making a tea when you walked up," Hi answered.

Zeke was looking like he wasn't that sure of the benefits of brewing tea from plants growing in the wild. "The people have been making medicine for thousands of years, Zeke. You'll see, Susanne will not have a fever soon."

"I need to redress that wound, Moose," Barbara said, holding some clean cloth. "Look what you've done," she said. "Almost healed and you did something to make it bleed some more. Just like a little boy," she continued, watching Moose cringe from the slight pain of removing the old dressing.

She smeared a blend of herbs and grease on and attached the new bandage. "Now quit trying to do everything. Let some of these other boys do some of the work."

She was smiling, most of the others were chuckling, and all Moose could say was something about thank you, and it's fine, and I love you little sister, and walked off to get some peace and quiet.

19

Moose and Zeke rode lead all day, sometimes hundreds of yards in front of the wagons, sometimes, when the trail led through deep forest, very close in. "I think that was a small hunting party that attacked us," Moose said late in the day. "They won't be missed for some time, maybe days. By then, we'll be in different country."

"Let's not forget that at least one, maybe more, are still alive. When they get back to their village, they will want revenge. We need to make as much distance as we can," Zeke said.

"Travis was telling me about the terrible situation at Whitman's Mission. An entire tribe almost wiped out by measles? That must have been horrible." Zeke had had that on his mind ever since Sarah told him about Susanne's fever. First, Travis talked about a devastating disease and fever that all but wiped out an Indian tribe and, then his daughter comes down with a serious fever.

I've lost one entire family to disease and lack of medicine. I can't think about losing even the tiniest part of my new family.

"The Cayuse tribe believes the illness was purposefully introduced," Moose said. "The white man's illnesses have killed many Indians, Zeke. Smallpox is just an example, but measles have been devastating as well.

"The Crow have suffered more than most, I think, but the Cayuse situation was very bad."

"We'll be reaching the Columbia River soon, I think, Moose. Will we run into even more trouble?"

"We'll skirt around where Whitman's Mission was and ride straight to The Dalles. The Cayuse are not belligerent; they are very angry, but should not give us any problem. We are leaving Bannock country now, so the next few days should be peaceful," he said, his smile more wry than genuine.

They pushed the wagons hard until late in the day, trying to get as much distance as possible from the morning's problem, and found a small meadow near a creek where they could form the wagons into a small stockade. "Let's keep the animals inside the circle. There's plenty of grass for them, after we take them to water. We should be safe enough to have fires tonight," Moose said, after the wagons were stopped.

Zeke hurried to the back of his wagon while Hiram took care of the mules. "How's Susanne doing?" he said, climbing in. Sarah was sitting in her rocker and the two babies were tucked into the double cradle Zeke had made for them. "I've been so worried all day. Is it a cold or is she coming down with something more serious?"

"The fever is way down and she's got her appetite back. Moose made a fine pot of tea. I gave some to Joanne also, just in case. We'll just have to keep nursing our little ones, Zeke. I think it's just a cold, but we'll keep the tea going."

"I'm so glad," he said, bending over to give her a kiss. "I'm glad Moose knew what he was doing, but I was worried."

"For nothing," she smiled back. "When I was back east at school I learned how the white man's medicines are made. Guess what, husband of mine? They're made from herbs and spices, but with technical names, just like ours," and she chuckled, watching Zeke get a small frown. "It's all the same stuff, Zeke."

She laughed at his little frown, and then he did too. "I'll have Moose make a nice pot of rose hip tea and we can all have some before bed tonight. My grandmother, Mourning Dove said rose hip tea will stop a cold dead in its tracks, and there are plenty of wild roses in this country."

"Wild roses for my little hummingbird," he chuckled, giving her a kiss, before climbing out of the wagon. "You stay in here with the girls, nice and warm, and I'll bring you your supper."

With a big fire, the group enjoyed a hot meal, had a good supply of wood for the night, set the guards, and called it a day. Moose had made a large pot of rose hip tea and everybody had a tin cup full before bedtime, even the Frenchman. Travis and Zeke laced theirs with a touch of rum.

Zeke helped Sarah get comfortable in the big bed, surrounded by the twins, and crawled under the wagon to join Hiram. "We'll take the late watch again, Hi. Let's get some sleep."

"Moose said he can feel a difference in the air. I'm not sure I can. Can you?"

Zeke was looking almost straight up at billions of stars splashed across a moonless night sky. "This part of Oregon is between two large mountain ranges, Hi, and is dry because of that. We're moving north and getting lower in elevation too, and because of that the air is denser.

"I think he feels more humidity as we get lower and closer to the Columbia River. He says it's a very large river. I grew up near the Ohio River and I've crossed the Mississippi River, and they are very large too. I've read what Lewis and Clark wrote about the Columbia and I think we'll get to see some big scenery."

It only took another couple of minutes and the two were fast asleep, Zeke thinking about the Columbia and Susanne, and Hiram trying to understand a river even bigger than the Snake, the biggest he had ever seen or imagined.

IT WAS a solid week on the trail without any trouble from Indians, mechanical problems, or sickness, and the wagon train moved onto a plain fronting the Columbia River. They stopped for a mid-day break for the animals and to have something to eat.

"We'll have to give Moose a new name," Barbara teased as he made one more large pot of tea for the group. "El Doctoro, the mighty Moose of rose hip tea," she laughed, dancing around the fire.

He took a playful swat at her but she danced away, still laughing. "You laugh, dear sister, but no one in this little wagon train has a cold or a fever." Sarah sat by the fire with the two babies in her lap, smiling as they giggled and made happy baby noises.

"When can we see this big river?" she asked. "All I've heard this week, from Zeke, from Hiram, even from you, Moose, is how big this river is. I want to see it."

"I think we'll get our feet wet in the Columbia River before the sun sets," Moose said, "and you'll hear it before you see it."

"Why would we hear it?" Sarah asked.

"Wind," Moose said. "The Columbia Gorge is just downriver from The Dalles and the wind howls through that gorge. It turns rafts over, blows structures down. It's fierce, and the wind brings other miseries with it, like rain and ice. I've never been down the river past The Dalles and never want to.

"Bridger and I came to The Dalles on canoes and then went overland to the Pacific, which is probably what we'll have to do as well. There's a huge waterfall that you'll enjoy."

Sarah didn't understand, Barbara looked just as confused, and Travis and Zeke sat listening, not saying anything. "If you haven't been down river, and don't want to go down river, how are we supposed to go down river?" Barbara said, not angry, but with a stern look on her face. "You were supposed to take us to the Willamette Valley, Moose. What do you mean, 'you won't go'?"

"The best answer to that, Barbara, Sarah, everyone," Travis said, "is to wait two more days, and everything will be clear. When you see the gorge and what the river looks like, you won't want to be on it either.

"The trail from The Dalles is overland, again, and this

time, long, steep, and hard. It's called Barlow's Pass or Barlow's trail, and we'll move along the flanks of Mt. Hood, which if you really want something to worry about, Barbara, is an active volcano." He gave her a fun little smile before continuing. "Then, we'll drop into the very north end of the Willamette Valley and the end of the trail, Oregon City." He took a deep breath, looking around the camp fire.

"So," Travis continued, "that being said, let's get these wagons moving. We're deep into Oregon Territory, and almost home."

IV

BOOK FOUR: OREGON
AT LAST

I<small>T WAS A CHILLY, BLUSTERY, EARLY SUMMER DAY WHEN THE</small> four wagons made the final run along the Columbia River to The Dalles, Moose and Zeke leading the way. "Quite a little community," Zeke commented seeing the many buildings and activity spread out on the river's banks. Many of the business signs were in French while others were decidedly British.

The falls captivated the women, all commenting on just exactly how much water was flowing. Moose spoke about watching salmon jumping, some "as long as your leg," with hooked jaws. "The bears come right down to the water's edge and are willing to fight you for their share."

Indians had weirs and traps set up all along the big river, ready for the two runs each year. "Salmon is a staple of their diet," Travis said. "I remember at one rendezvous, a tribe brought great baskets full of smoked salmon and it was gone just that fast.

"This was a big Hudson's Bay Company town," Travis

said, "so there are French and British influences, several Indian groups, and it's all changing now that Oregon Territory is part of the United States."

Travis pointed out some large slabs of salmon on drying and smoking racks along the river. "Salmon continues to be a major part of the Indian diet along the river, and for the trappers and traders as well." Travis and Zeke each bought large smoked filets.

"We'll need to bring fifty pounds or so when we make the push over the mountain," Zeke said, slicing a mouthful off a slab and munching on it.

Most amazing was the size of the river, and the narrowness of the channel as it sped it way westward. "So that's the Columbia Gorge," Hiram said. "I've never seen anything like that. How fierce is that current?"

"That's just the bare beginning," Moose said. "It gets narrower, and fiercer down river. Feel that wind whistling up the gorge? It gets worse, too."

They drove the wagons through the community and out to the southwest a bit to find a place to encamp. They were among the very first of the new season, so grass for the animals was available. "Let's get the wagons in a semi-circle," Zeke said. "We'll be here for about a week, I think, getting resupplied and finding a guide to take us over the mountains."

"You found that guide," a man said, riding up to the group. "Been sitting here waiting for you, Mr. Hawthorne."

"Well, hello, Mr. Rutherford Johnson. What a wonderful surprise to see you!" Zeke exclaimed. "There was still snow on the ground when we left Fort Bridger, and it was a late start. Just couldn't wait for you, I'm afraid."

"There was heavy snow in the Sierra Nevada too, so I couldn't get out early, like I wanted. Came north and across Barlow's Pass to meet up with you. I've had time to make that crossing twice, so I know I can get you through without much trouble, but it is one difficult journey you be looking at.

"Late spring storms will be the biggest potential problem, but I'll tell you right up front, this is gonna be a mean trip. This Cascade Range is nothing but rocks and it seems to go straight up, all the time." He was chuckling all the time he was talking, his eyes dancing and twinkling, like he was telling a secret.

Johnson hadn't changed much, Zeke noted, still all positive and full of good humor. "When we get across on the other side of the Cascades, we'll come down into the Willamette Valley along the flanks of Mount Hood, a volcano. It's a rocky, steep trail we'll be navigatin' Mr. Hawthorne, but I know I can get you there."

Zeke spent every day working on the wagons, fixing things that were broken and making things that might break stronger. He took the time to set up his forge and was doing considerable work with it. "I'm amazed at how many people have stopped by to watch me," he said one evening. "As if they had never seen a blacksmith before. I did shoe one man's horse for him. He paid me in salmon," he joked.

Johnson and Moose spent hours working on mapping out the trail they should follow. "I'm glad you know that country, Johnson," Moose said. "When I came through here, we simply rode our horses and trailed our pack animals and didn't worry about things like whether a wagon could pass through."

"I think you should come on across with us, Moose," Barbara said one evening when everyone was sitting around a big fire. "We might need your strength getting these wagons through all the rocks Mr. Johnson talks about."

"I think it would be a good idea, too," Travis piped up. "We have George Felix and Whitewater Bill, and now Mr. Johnson, but one more good hand sure would make me feel better. Besides," he laughed, "you just might like it. Give it some thought, Son."

"I have been, Papa. I want to get back to my mountains, to my village, and at the same time I want to help my family get across a dangerous pass and into their new homes. I'm also afraid that when I see the Willamette Valley, I might just want to stay," he snickered just a bit. "I know I want to stay with my family here, and with my family back in the mountains, and I don't want to have to make that decision."

Elaine got up from the fire and walked over to her son, sat down and put her arm around the big man. "These are the kinds of decisions that only men get to make, Moose. Boys don't, women don't. You're a full-grown Shoshone, Moose, and whatever decision you make, your father and I will abide."

He hugged his mama tight, got up from the fire, shook hands with Travis, and took a walk in the moonlight. *It was easier being a boy. Slow To Fight needs me at the village and Mama needs me here, and I want to be in both places. I don't want to make this decision.*

"WE'RE gonna need four animals on each wagon, Travis," Zeke said one morning as the two stood near the river watching it cascade into the gorge. "Look at that water. An old guy at the blacksmith shop said many people are saying the Columbia River is the second largest river in the country.

"I crossed the Ohio, and it's pretty big, not this big, and I crossed the Mississippi, and it is bigger, but not by much, I don't think. Just how much water do you suppose that is, rushing out of the mountains?"

"Plant a lot of wheat and corn with that much water," Travis snuffed. "Let's see if we can find some good wheelers for those wagons. Hope we don't have to pay too much for 'em, but we do want good horses. Big, strong, wheelers."

They visited a couple of the stables, one owned by the Hudson's Bay Company, and found good stock available. "Johnson says there's grass most of the way across those mountains, but a lot of downed trees, all busted up from the winter, and rock slides in many places. Let's get those animals today, Travis, get those wagons stocked, and get moving."

TWO DAYS LATER, the four wagons with four up on each wagon, moved toward the Cascade Range and Barlow's Pass, Moose and Johnson leading the way. Hiram was driving the first Hawthorne wagon with Sarah sitting beside him.

"I'm glad Moose decided to help guide us, Mama," he

said. "He always scared me when I was little, but now that he's my uncle, I'm not scared anymore."

"Moose is awfully big, Hi," she said, "and he scares a lot of full-grown men, just because he's so big. I'm glad he's coming with us, too. I'm sure, once he knows we're all in our new home, safe and warm, that he will go back to the village. He's more Shoshone, I think, than either Barbara or me. The village will need him."

"I'm also glad we won't get up into the mountains before tomorrow. Papa gave me a lot of advice and instruction on driving four animals instead of two, but today and tomorrow will give me time to really drive them." He had Zeke's two mules as leaders and two big farm horses at the wheels. Zeke was riding one saddle horse and trailing another.

Sarah climbed into the back of the wagon and settled into her overstuffed chair right behind Hiram, tucked the twins in her arms, and let them nurse. *He looks so good up there, all those reins in his hands. I bet that boy has grown three inches and gained a bunch of weight since we left. He's gonna be long and lanky, but strong as Moose in a few years. He's in his thirteenth year and Zeke is turning him into a fine young man. I am so lucky.*

Felix had a little trouble learning how to drive four up, but Whitewater Bill picked it up right away. Travis fought the leaders for the first couple of miles, but with a little help from Zeke, had the situation in hand by the time they reached the beginnings of steep mountain country. All four people driving wagons felt comfortable sitting around the campfires that first evening.

"Nothin' but rocks and broken trees the rest of the way," Johnson said. "Moose and I will stay well ahead of you folks now, and we'll probably call for help once in a while. We'll be moving rocks from the trail and downed trees. It'll be slow goin', but it's so pretty on the other side, you'll be glad you made the trip. Shouldn't have any Indian trouble at all," he said.

"You might, though," Moose said, glaring at the man. Everyone just stopped what they were doing, wondering what Moose meant by that. Moose let his comment hang in the air for just a couple more seconds, then broke into a chuckle.

"Whew," Johnson said, along with the rest of the group. "A joke like that could give a man heart failure," he laughed, and Moose whacked him on the back, spilling his coffee, both of them laughing hard. "I think that young man just told me I better quit teasing him so much."

"I'm glad you picked up those two big double-bladed axes and that two-man buck saw, Travis," Zeke said when things calmed down a bit. "From what Johnson has been saying, we're gonna need them to clear the trail. I've got them attached to the side of my first wagon so they will always be close."

"I want to learn how to saw with that long saw," Hiram said.

"That's the bucksaw, Hi," Moose said. "I'll teach you now and then for the next thirty years and you'll be cussing me 'cause you know how to use one."

THE MILES CREPT BY SLOWLY, the teams pulling heavy wagons up a steep and boulder-strewn trail. The train had to stop regularly to wedge boulders out of the way, rip trees out from the trail where they had crashed during the winter, and let the teams blow. It seemed like the crest of the range got farther away each day, instead of closer, and the nights were decidedly colder than back along the river.

"I am so sore," Hi said as they sat around the campfire a couple of days later. "I bet we sawed four huge trees into kindling today. Now is when we should find a hot spring," he joshed, stretching and rubbing his shoulders.

"The thing is, Hi," Johnson said, "it ain't gonna get any better. You'll never know it, either, but all the wagons that come along later this season will be saying 'thankee' for clearing the trail for them."

"I just wish they were here to help," Hi said. "When we get to the valley, Papa, let's sell that saw." Moose and the group laughed over that. In the morning, as Hi brought the teams up to harness them, he found the bucksaw tied to the side of the wagon with a big 'For Sale' sign attached.

An early summer storm moved across the ridge top one night after everyone had gone to bed, with strong wind, flashing lightning and deafening thunder. Zeke and Hiram were up and dressed right away to see to the animals, finding Johnson and Moose with them as well. The cold rain pelted them as they settled the animals, and before they could get a good fire going, the rain turned to icy sleet, and then snow.

They made less than four miles before they were stopped dead on the trail by snow drifting and piling up. "We might be here for more than a day, I'm thinking," Travis said. "These animals cannot pull these wagons uphill, through these drifts, and fight the rocks and downed trees too. Let's make ourselves as comfortable as possible and wait out the storm."

"It's a wet snow," Johnson said, helping with the animals. "A little sunshine and it will melt away quickly."

"Yeah," Zeke piped up, "and give us a good mud trail to wallow through."

Barbara saved the day, grabbing Hi and getting a big fire roaring, with pots of coffee boiling within a few minutes. "Looks like beans and crusty bread for supper tonight," she said, having no trouble getting a large cast iron kettle filled with fresh water for the beans. "I'll put a couple of pounds of smoked venison in those beans and you boys'll have strength enough to cut all the trees in the Cascade Mountains."

The blowing and drifting snow made life miserable whether they were in a wagon, tucked under heavy robes, out gathering wood for the fire, or seeing to it that the animals were taken care of. Sarah stayed in the wagon with the twins for the most part, but found that even the little girls enjoyed getting out now and then to get near the fire that was kept roaring.

Hiram took on the duty of keeping the fire hot, and Zeke helped him with the animals. "Will we have to go back, Papa?" he asked the following morning, fighting his way through heavy drifts to find wood for the fire.

"I don't think so," Zeke answered. "We have plenty of food, there's good water, of course, and the animals aren't having any trouble kicking snow aside to find the grass. God knows there's enough wood for hot fires," he laughed. "Nobody's hurt or sick, so I think we just need to look on this as something to endure."

"What are we going to find when we get down in the valley?" Hi asked.

"Only thing I know is what we've been told, Son. Those men at The Dalles talked about that long, broad valley with a fine river right down the middle, good soil, and available land for claiming. Not sure what the procedure's gonna be, but we'll sure find out when we get to Oregon City."

THE STORM WORE itself out on the second day and the sun came out, bright and warm. "Snow and ice are melting fast, just like Johnson said," Travis muttered, gathering in the stock. "We'll be moving tomorrow, folks. Let's make sure we're ready."

Sunrise found the four wagons loaded and teams in harness ready for another day of climbing into the high Cascade Range. "If we don't top out tomorrow, we will the next day for sure," Johnson said that night as they gathered around the campfire. "Wait until you see that volcano, and on a clear day it is magnificent. Still smoking, you know."

"Will it blow up?" Hi asked, his eyes wide, as much from interest as from fright.

"Well," Johnson said, "it has in the past, it surely has. It's the first one I've ever seen, so I don't really know."

"I've read about them," Sarah said. "Some really powerful explosions. There's a big volcano somewhere in Italy that blew up and buried an entire town."

"According to people in the valley, this whole mountain range is made up of volcanoes," Johnson said, "but nobody seems to be scared of them. I think I'd want to keep an eye out."

Zeke laughed, saying, "Just to watch it blow up in your face? I imagine they simmer a little bit before they actually blow up. Volcanic soil is some of the best soil to grow vegetables, grain, and fruit, though. I've read that, so it might be a good thing for us, not something to worry about."

21

"I THOUGHT COMING UP THIS MOUNTAIN WAS HARD," TRAVIS snarled, working his four-up through a maze of rocks and trees on a steep downhill course. The horses didn't much care for going downhill to start with, and to have a heavy wagon pushing them along didn't help any. Brakes on big wagons didn't always help as much as the driver would like, either, and this combination of problems had Travis in a twit.

"We get to the bottom of this mountain, I ain't ever drivin' any wagon again, ever," he howled, snaking that wagon and team along in the mud. Elaine could be heard in the back of the wagon, laughing along with Barbara.

"You want me to drive awhile, Papa?" Barbara hollered.

"On the next break, you take over," he said. "I'm gonna ride a horse way up front with Moose."

"Mr. Johnson said we should be down into the foothills sometime tomorrow or the next day," Barbara said. "The trail is already starting to get better." She and her mother had been having a long discussion over what would happen to them when they reached the Willamette Valley.

"Oregon City is now the capitol city of Oregon Territory, so I guess that's where we have to start. If we're going to have a business, then we'll have to be in town, won't we?" she said. The conversation has been held many times, the first time while everyone was still at Fort Bridger. "I wish we knew more about Oregon Territory. All we seem to know is there is good soil and good water.

"But to start a business," Elaine continued, "we need people. Oregon City seems to be the only town I've even heard of."

"That would be best for Travis and me, and I suppose for you as well," Elaine said. "As a dressmaker, you'll need to be where people are, and the same for us with a dry-goods and farm implements business. Sarah and Zeke will be looking for land to make their farm."

"It would sure be nice if Moose could stay with us," Barbara said. "He built that lumber mill at Fort Bridger, and Mr. Johnson said we will be in heavy timber country. He could start a new mill and have a good business."

"Moose has some big questions to answer, Barbara." Elaine said. "He's drawn very strongly to the village, to the people. He feels a heavy responsibility and knows that hard times are coming for our people. It will have to be his decision, but I too wish he would stay with us. It would be wonderful to have the whole family together, all the time."

She sat back with a smile on her face. "That is probably every mother's dream and wish. Sarah is married and all at once is the mother of three, all within less than a year. You'll never beat that, Barbara," she laughed. "It would be so nice, though..." and she let her thought trail off.

THE WAGONS WERE LITERALLY beat half to ruin when the group finally worked its way to the valley floor and started the trek north to Oregon City and their new life. "We'll probably be living in these two wagons when we find the land we want to settle on," Zeke told Sarah and Hi that night in camp. "It will take us, Hi, a few weeks, at best, to get a cabin built.

"I think we're probably too late this season for any kind of paying crop, but we will certainly have time to get a good garden in. We'll have to control the time we spend on projects because we'll have so many going on all at the same time."

"I understand building the cabin and getting a kitchen garden going, but what else?" the boy asked.

"Well, Son, just think about this. We will be starting out with very little money, so we won't be buying very much. We won't have a home, so that's got to be built. We will have to cut and mill the wood first, just to build the home. We won't have any furniture, except for what's in the wagon, so that will have to be built. We won't have any farm implements, so they will have to be built, and we won't have any cleared land to farm, either.

"Yep, my boy, we will have our days planned out for more than a year, I'm thinking." He chuckled when he added, "On top of all that, your mama will have you studying every night, too."

Hiram groaned a bit as he got up to throw some wood

on their fire. Zeke was giving him a good look as he did. "You've really grown, Hi. My mama had a stretch board, she called it when we were growing up. We'll put one up at our cabin and every year we'll put you kids up against the wall and mark how tall you are."

"Barbara said her first job was going to make me new shirts and trousers. She said my pants are too short and my shirts are too small. She sure is pretty, isn't she, Papa?"

"She sure is, Son," Zeke chuckled. "She sure is."

"You told me that Elizabeth knew how to make pottery and glazed tableware, Zeke. Could you teach me?" Sarah asked. "With the Willamette River and all the streams that feed it, right there, I would think there would be sand and clay."

"Elizabeth taught me, and I know I could build the ovens we would need," Zeke answered. "That's a good idea. We don't have very much money, so if we don't have to spend much, we'll be in better shape to begin this new life."

During the year that Zeke was at Fort Bridger, he'd made money in the blacksmith shop and doing carpentry work. Five percent of that was supposed to go to Jim Bridger, and Zeke kept close track of how much that was. "My blacksmith money was all paid in gold, even though some of those old trappers wanted to pay me in beaver pelts. Our belts may be tight by the time that first crop comes in."

These conversations went on each night until they finally rolled into Oregon City. Each day they marveled at the Willamette River, how broad and deep it was, and particularly how wide the valley was. The forests in the mountains east and west dipped right down to the valley floor and were deep green.

They passed many farms and as they moved closer to Oregon City it was obvious that the farms were doing well. Grains and produce by the ton and in many areas, great orchards were already mature and bearing fruit.

"I think we made the right decision," Zeke said as they drove the wagons into Oregon City. "This is beautiful and bountiful country."

Moose and Travis led them through the city and found a place on the outskirts where they could locate the wagons and make camp. The rest of that day was spent just getting a semi-permanent camp set up, and seeing to it that all the animals were well taken care of. "With sixteen animals, we could almost open a blacksmith shop and corrals," Zeke joked, leading the animals to an operating stable.

"We'll keep the two mules and a team of farm animals, Hi, and I think we should keep a couple of the saddle horses as well. Let's talk with Travis, Johnson, and Moose tonight about the rest of the animals. We might want to sell some of them. We know they're healthy and strong."

AT THE CAMPFIRE that night plans were made for everyone, it seemed. Zeke and Travis had Johnson in a long discussion about the trail he used coming from California to the Willamette Valley. "Would you be able to transport merchandise from California to my store in Oregon City?" Travis asked, and before he could answer, Zeke asked him about moving his farm products south California.

"I think you boys just created the Johnson Transportation Company. This whole section of Oregon needs a lot of merchandise, and I have the knowledge of how to get it here. Most seems to come in from the sea, with some coming north by land.

"To be as honest as possible with you, I don't have the money it would take to get started. Wagons, animals, licenses if we need them, and of course, we would have to pay the teamsters."

"What would you need?" Zeke asked, thinking that he and Travis had four wagons between them and the teams of animals.

"Well, sturdy wagons, strong teams to pull them, and a couple of good teamsters and, of course, suppliers at one end and buyers at the other." He got very quiet for a few minutes, then laughed out loud. "Hell's bells, boys, I have all that, don't I?"

"I say we draw up a contract between the three of us to create the Oregon-California Transportation Company. It wouldn't surprise me if you got George Felix and White-water Bill to drive for you," Travis said.

"You can't have my wagons until Hi and I get something up for all of us to live in," Zeke said, "once we find some land. And that would also give me time to rebuild the wagons. They're in sad shape right now."

Zeke called Sarah over, told her what they were discussing and asked if she would write up the contract that the three could then use to create financial accounts and begin to do business. "Come on, Hiram," she said, "you haven't had a good lesson in penmanship since we began this journey. We have work to do." She gathered up the twins and ushered Hi into the back of the wagon.

"When we go to the land office tomorrow, let's get all the information we can about opening businesses in the territory and in Oregon City," Zeke said. "I think we're off to a good start, Travis. I hope we can keep you very busy, Mr. Johnson, I sure do."

MORNING CAME WITH BRIGHT SUNSHINE, little wind, and a few billowing clouds announcing an early summer day. "We're going to be missing days like these," Zeke said as he, Travis and Johnson rode into Oregon City. "These are plowing and planting days! I should have those mules pulling heavy plows and Hiram should be following with another team to plant all the corn and beans. And all this should have started a few weeks ago," he said. "We missed an entire season."

"There is no way we could have gotten here any sooner, Zeke, so you need to worry about getting your family settled, then build your farm." Travis replied, soothingly.

"You're becoming quite the philosopher, Travis," Zeke laughed, as the three men walked into the main govern-mental offices of the new territory.

"Yes," Zeke said in answer to the 'May I help you?' from a thin man with a pencil moustache, cold dark eyes, and thinning hair, standing behind a bank-like counter, and speaking through a metal grate. "I'm looking for information on filing for farm land in the Willamette Valley of Oregon Territory. My family and I just arrived from Fort Bridger."

"That's just what this territory needs," the man said through clenched teeth, "more damned, poor people arriving with nothing, looking for something free."

"I beg your pardon, sir," Zeke spoke up. *What is this man talking about? How dare he say something like that to me.* Anger flushed Hawthorne's face as he answered the clerk's impudence. "We have much to offer this territory, and yes, this territory has much to offer, as well. Please give me the necessary papers and procedure I need to follow. I am, frankly, astonished that you would speak to me in such a manner!"

"Fill these out," the man snarled, shoving several sheets of paper through the counter grate, "if you know how to write, and be prepared to pay the filing fees when you come back." He turned to speak to several men sitting at desks behind the counter. "So much trash coming west. Oregon will not be better for their coming." He spoke loudly.

"Now just hold on, right there, sir. I take offense to that statement!" Zeke stood as tall as possible, his eyes blazing with fury, and his fists clenched. "I'm well educated, a journeyman cabinetmaker and journeyman blacksmith, and I've operated a fine producing farm in Missouri. You have impugned my character, sir, and I demand an apology. You apologize now, or I will smash an apology from your face."

"You're in no position to demand anything, immigrant, and I'm the one that has what you want. You change your tone of voice to me or you will never see land in Oregon, ever."

"How dare you!" Zeke said, ready to vault the counter and tear the little man's head right off his shoulders. "Your attitude is that of a charlatan, sir." The veins in his neck were pounding, his face was reddened and perspiration was forming on his forehead. Zeke had never backed down from a fight in his life and was not about to take that kind of abuse from anyone. "I'll come across this counter and you will apologize to me or I will throttle you, so help me."

Before he could go any further a large man in a black suit with white shirt and string tie stepped out of an office toward the back of the land office. "What seems to be the problem here?" He walked up to the counter, a stubby fat cigar half chewed off clamped in his teeth. "Farnsworth, are you out of line again?"

"Yes, he was, Mr. Sullivan," one of the men at a desk said. "He said some rather nasty things to the gentleman at the counter. I've spoken to him about this before, sir, but he continues to defy what I ask of him."

"Gather your property, Farnsworth and get out of this office. You're fired, sir, and don't look for a good word from me."

Farnsworth was cursing under his breath, looked Zeke right in the eye, and said, "You'll be sorry for causing this." Then he stormed around the counter and out the door.

"Now, what can the land office do for you?" Sullivan asked, taking Farnsworth's place behind the counter. "We like to think we're here to help people get settled in Oregon Territory."

"Thank you," Zeke said. "I'm looking to file on farm land in the Willamette Valley and was asking what the proper procedure was to do that. I do not appreciate what Mr. Farnsworth said to and about me and my family."

"You won't have that problem again, sir. I see he gave you papers for creating a gravel pit. It seems he was setting you up to fail. Please, come into my office and we'll get you taken care of.

"Are these men with you?" he asked, pointing toward Travis and Johnson.

"Yes, but they are looking to start a couple of businesses here in Oregon City, not start a farm."

"Good," Sullivan said. "Mr. Owens, will you help these gentlemen, please, while I take care of this man? Follow me, sir," Sullivan said walking across the office toward his open door.

Zeke followed him in and the two settled into comfortable chairs on either side of a large oak desk. "I've always found a short bracer makes doing business so much more interesting," Sullivan said, producing a flask and two glasses, pouring each a goodly amount of amber heat. "I believe I heard you say something about farming, but also, cabinet work and blacksmithing. What exactly are your plans?" Then he laughed.

"Well, now," he continued. "Where are my manners?" he chuckled. "I'm Roland Sullivan, Oregon Territory Land Commissioner. We also handle business opportunities in the territory."

"I'm glad to meet you, sir. I'm Ezekiel Hawthorne, recently of Fort Bridger and Missouri before that. My wife and children and I would like to file on some of this fine Willamette Valley land and create a family farm. Yes, you heard right, I am a journeyman cabinetmaker and journeyman blacksmith, but for the time being, I plan to use those crafts to benefit our farm, not to go into business."

Sullivan opened a large cabinet and pulled some maps, spread them out on a conference table, and beckoned

Zeke over. "Here is the valley, you can see the Willamette River, and these parcels marked in red have already been filed on. The parcels in green are not suitable for farming, steep hills and rocks and such, making them difficult to work.

"Now, you see all this area that is bluish in color, is open territory and can be surveyed and claimed. We are currently recommending either one hundred sixty acres or three hundred twenty acre parcels for individuals, and possibly full six hundred forty-acre sections for larger family farm operations."

Sullivan was an outdoorsman, strong and tanned already, this early in the season, and took every opportunity to get out of the office. "You see this area right down here?" and he was pointing to a place where a small stream flowed into the Willamette River. "With three hundred twenty acres on each side of that stream, you would have very good bottom land, good soil, and abundant water for irrigation.

"I would be glad to guide you and your family down river and personally show you that land. The territory charges a flat fee of one hundred dollars for six hundred forty acre sites, and that can be spread over a period of months. There are requirements on building homes, preparing ground, planting, and harvesting, but that's what you're already planning, so we won't even bother going into details."

"You could not have been more helpful, Mr. Sullivan," Zeke said, "but I wonder, will my family be running into more problems such as Mr. Farnsworth? I would not tolerate such."

"Nor should you have to, Mr. Hawthorne, but I'm

afraid there is a small faction of ignorant people in Oregon City that have taken a certain dislike to immigrants. Farnsworth, I'm afraid, is on the extreme edge of that thinking. It's centered in town, and you won't hear much at all once you get in the rural sections of the valley."

IT WAS a full two hours later that Zeke rode back into the camping area with several maps and a folder full of official looking papers. "You look happier than last time I saw you," Travis said, holding Zeke's horse while he dismounted. "Get everything worked out with that little fool in the office?"

"Yes, sir, I sure did. And you? Did you get all the information you needed?"

"Indeed, I did," Travis answered. "Let's have some coffee, maybe just a small touch of rum, and we can tell each other our stories."

Elaine, Sarah, Barbara, Moose, and Hiram had gathered around the campfire by that time. "This is good," Zeke grinned, looking at the group. "With everyone here, we'll only have to tell the story once."

"Where is Johnson? He should be here, too," Travis said.

"He went to look at that property near the river that you were talking about," Moose said. "He's a happy feller, isn't he?"

* * *

THEY SAID their goodbyes around the camp fire that night.

"We made a good deal on the property back about a hundred yards or so from the river. Warehouse is standing, but needs some work, offices need to be built in, and there are two small homes on the property, one for me and Elaine, and one for Barbara," Travis explained. "We'll be in business within the week."

"I have good news, as well," Johnson said. "The transportation company will have an Oregon City office attached to the Travis Mercantile Company, so we are in business at no expense, so far. I'll work with George Felix refitting Travis's two wagons, and he and I can make a trial run to California in them, coming back with merchandise, and then when you no longer have a need of your two, Zeke, we'll get them up here for refitting as well."

"Tell me about this trail from here to California," Zeke said.

"They're calling it the Siskiyou Trail, and it runs from Fort Vancouver, just north of us here," and he pointed across the Columbia River, "south through the Willamette Valley and into California's Central Valley. It's a fair distance but a fine trail. Actually, there's just one high pass over parts of the Cascades. My guess is, the Indians have been using this trail for hundreds of years. It's been widened in the last twenty years or so, and wagons pull through with little trouble."

"I'll let Travis know when you can have my two wagons, Johnson. Whitewater will head north as soon as we get settled on the new place, but we will need him to get things started down there. I'm sure you can use the help, Travis."

"I'll need at least one more teamster," Johnson said,

"but I've already had two or three people asking if there would be work available. Seems that there are many people who showed up in Oregon Territory without plans for their future. Maybe that Farnsworth wasn't all wrong."

"His attitude was all wrong," Zeke snarled. "He ever talks to me like that again, I'll tear his head off." He pulled heavy on his rum laced coffee, calmed himself down a bit, and continued. "Tell me more about what you've heard."

Before Johnson could answer, Hiram said, "Mr. Farnsworth isn't aware that he has made Sharp Knife, scourge of the Crow Nation, an enemy." Laughter sounded around the camp, and Moose punched him lightly in the ribs.

Johnson started up again. "I've found some of the same attitude in California, too. In the towns, not out on the rivers and streams where the gold seekers are. Lots of people have come west and don't have a craft or ability at some type of job. They just hang around and hope somebody will hire them for something, or they become trouble-makers."

"So, men like Farnsworth assume all immigrants are hangers-on or trouble-makers," Zeke said. "Is this something Sarah and I should worry about? Or, you and Elaine, Travis?"

"My store will be open within a week, at which point, we are no longer immigrants," Travis chuckled, "but like you said, Mr.. Sullivan told you that kind of thinking isn't heard much in the farming country. I think it's a town thing."

Moose and Barbara had moved off by themselves a bit, just listening to the conversation. "You two are being awfully quiet," Sarah said. "Have you run into any problems, Barbara?"

"No," she said, smiling at Moose. "Little brother tried to start a riot when he took me to get some lumber to build an addition on the cabin for my store."

"I did not start a riot," Moose said in a very strong voice, coupled with what was probably some Shoshone slang aimed at his big sister. "That man simply did not know how to run a large band saw, and I told him so. That's all."

There was gentle laughter around the fire, more coffee was poured, along with generous helpings of rum, and everyone looked at Moose, all but demanding that he continue. "Well, when everyone quit yelling and the lumber mill owner was standing in front of me, I demonstrated to all of them what I was talking about."

"And that was the end of it?" Sarah asked, knowing better as she said it.

"I start work tomorrow as lead sawyer, at more money than I've ever even heard of. Mr. Donaldson said he wants to talk to me about expanding the operation and taking me on as a junior partner. I signed on to work through next winter, and I will be living at the mill-works, in my own home.

"So, you see, big sister, I did not start a riot."

"I'm glad you're staying with us," Elaine said.

"I am, at least through next winter, Mama, but if there is trouble with The People, I will go back to them. I'm glad I'm staying, too. This has been a wonderful several months, with all of us together, every day. Even Barbara," he laughed, taking a solid punch to the ribs.

"Ouch, they're still sore," he moaned, rolling on the

ground, his big sister laughing and pretending to punch him over and over. "It's gonna be a long year," he laughed.

"He offered you a partnership?" Zeke asked. "That's impressive, Moose. "There's certainly enough timber around here to keep many lumber mills in operation. The forests that cover the coastal range to our west seem immense, and some of the trees are more than huge.

"I think I could build an entire house from the lumber milled from just one of those giants. Sullivan said that I'll see massive trees like that near what is soon to be our property, south of here. Looks like you'll be getting more experience on that buck saw, Hiram, my lad," he laughed. Hiram moaned, rubbing his arm and shoulder muscles.

There was the slightest tinge of sadness to the group as they talked for several more hours, not wanting the evening to end. When tomorrow came, it would be ending enough, with the Hawthorne family moving fifty or more miles south, Moose moving into his own home in the forest to the west, and the Travis family getting their enterprises underway.

"It's been a wonderful several months, as Moose put it," Zeke said, tucking Sarah and the babies into bed. "I'm going to miss hearing Travis howl at every little problem, miss hearing the grinding of those big wagon wheels and the stomping of the mules."

"I will too," Sarah whispered, "but I'm so anxious to find our new home, to watch our children grow, to learn everything there is to learn about this Oregon Territory. We're almost home, Zeke."

"Home," he said softly. He took her in his arms, pulled the heavy buffalo robe around them, and said it again. "Home. What a wonderful word. I promise you, Sarah

"Hummingbird" Hawthorne, I will build you the finest home ever seen in Oregon Territory, and feed you the finest food I can grow, and provide you the best life a woman could ask for."

TRUE TO HIS WORD, Sullivan arrived in camp the next morning riding a fine thoroughbred stud and trailing an equally fine pack mule. "Mr. Hawthorne, good morning," he said, stepping down from the tall horse. "It's a wonderful morning for our journey south."

Zeke was smiling, and introduced Sarah, Hiram, and the babies. "We have beautiful weather for our trip, it seems. Hiram, why don't you drive one team and White-water can drive the other. I'll ride with Mr. Sullivan." They pulled out of camp waving to Travis and his family, and to Mr. Johnson.

"This is a good road, Mr. Sullivan," Zeke said when they had pulled onto the main north-south trail. "We should make good time. You say our new property is about fifty miles south, we might be there in three days if all goes well."

The morning air was filled with late spring, leafy trees still in full bloom, grasses growing tall along the wide pastures and fields. They passed farm after farm, each beautifully laid out with crops beginning to show their color, blaring out their delight in good soil, fresh water, and sunshine.

"After Missouri, my trek across the plains, and the Rocky Mountains, this is heaven." The two men rode about fifty yards in front of the two wagons, both very busy trying to see everything on both sides of the trail at the same time. "From the looks of it, Sullivan, some of these people have been here for awhile, and know how to farm."

"People started moving into the Oregon Country not too long after the Lewis and Clark travels became known," Sullivan said. "Some of these farms date back to the 1820s, Zeke, and some date from last summer." He chuckled a little as he continued. "That Travis family you rode in with will find ready customers when they get that emporium of theirs opened. There's a need for good farm equipment."

"I plan to make most of my own," Zeke said, "and maybe make some extra pieces, like plows, discs, and axes to sell at Travis's. He's big and strong and loud, and will work longer and harder than any man I know. I think those people in Oregon City will be glad he's there."

Sullivan estimated that they made about seventeen or eighteen miles on this first day, as they set up a camp in an open pasture under some large trees. The grass, emerald green in the waning light of the day, stood almost knee high, and waved gently in the afternoon breeze. *Reminds me of walking through the deep grass of the plains,* Zeke was thinking, watching the waves cascading and dancing. *How far I've come. You would like this country, Elizabeth, with so much grass, so many trees, and splashing creeks and big rivers. My God, I have wonderful memories, Liz, and now, I have a big family. Three children and we haven't been married a year.*

Zeke was gently laughing to himself as he helped Hi stake out the teams in the deep grass. "This is so pretty, Papa," Hi said, waving his arm in a great arc, encompassing half a circle. "The Willamette River is right over that little hill there," he pointed, "according to Mr. Sullivan. Can we go see it?"

"Let's do that," Zeke said. "Go get your Mama and the girls, and we'll take a walk before getting supper underway."

It was an hour past noon dinner, on the third day out, when the little wagon train topped a small rise in the trail and Mr. Sullivan called a halt, suggesting they move the wagons into some tall grass on the east side of the trail. With a wave of his hands, he motioned toward a great flat plain with billowing grasses blowing in a gentle wind, toward rolling hills covered in a dense forest, and through the middle, what appeared to be a small river or stream cutting its way toward the Willamette.

"That, my friend, is the Hawthorne Farm. Up the Willamette River another several miles are Salem, the brand-new capitol city of this fine territory, but I'm sure you're far more interested in this country that we're a-looking at. We'll get these wagons parked somewhere and set up for a quick camp, and then tomorrow we'll ride into Salem and file your claim.

"My new offices are still being set up there. Half still in Oregon City and half down here in Salem. This is mill country," he continued. "Mill Creek got its name from the first grist mill and now there's even a good lumber mill being set up. I think it's old man Donaldson adding onto the one he has near Oregon City."

"Let's move the wagons over there near that stand of cottonwoods, Hiram, and get the animals taken care of. We'll just set up a camp that can be moved easily and use

245

it for the next few days until we pick a home-site. This is beautiful country, Mr. Sullivan." Zeke bent down and ran his hand through the grasses, dug his fingers into the soil and came up with a handful.

"Has a good aroma to it, Sarah," he said as she walked up to him, holding the babies. He took one of them, and started pointing around at various landscape features. "You'll be running in those hills next year, little one, and swimming in that creek. We'll have some fruit trees over yonder and you can pick apples and peaches all summer, and climb into the highest branches."

Zeke was laughing, almost dancing with an energy he hadn't felt since leaving his Missouri farm. "It's been a little more than a year, Sarah, and I can feel it in my blood. This is going to be a fine farm."

He and Hi took the mules out for a ride after camp was set up and firewood cut and stacked. "We've got about equal amounts of land on each side of this creek, Hi, so what we want to look at is where we can locate good ground for growing that can be irrigated by way of ditches from that creek. You cut the ditches at the high points on the creek and they can irrigate your crops by gravity alone.

"That's how I had my farm in Missouri, and I'm sure we can do the same thing here. We'll ride along the creek for a bit and give this old place of ours a good look. Plenty of forestland, so there is good wood to build our house, not too many rocks that will have to be hauled out. Rocks will bust up a plow real bad, and it's the one you don't see that'll getcha fast," he laughed.

They were back in about two hours, full of happy talk about timber and water and rocks and good soil to the point that Sarah finally had to shush both Zeke and Hi. "My goodness, you two, you sound like little school girls with a new toy," she teased. "I heard turkeys barking up near those trees, Hiram, if you'd like to go shoot supper for us."

"Yes, Ma'am," he smiled, jumping in the wagon to find his shotgun. "Roast turkey right off my new farm," he said, then caught himself, and said, "I mean, our farm."

"Looks like rain, Zeke," Sullivan said as they saddled up the next morning for the ride into Salem. "That's part of what makes this country so fine. There are some don't much care for rain, and there are times when even I would wish for a little less of this bounty, but you can sit and watch the grass grow, sir."

"Sometimes, Mr. Sullivan, it sounds almost like you're either a salesman working the crowd, or you're running for office. I'll tell you, though, I like what you've led us into. I may not sit and watch grass grow, but you can bet I'll be watching corn, beans, wheat, and a few other things. Will there be any trouble with the filing?"

"No, sir. There should not be trouble of any sort. After all," he laughed, "I am the Oregon Territory Land Commissioner. No sir, the paperwork will take up an hour or so, the recording of the deed and all, and you'll be free to ride back to the Hawthorne Farm."

"You didn't really need to stay with us, did you, Mr. Sullivan?"

"No, I could have just as easily ridden on down to Salem, but I don't have much chance to get out of the office. Spending time with your family, in the outdoors, was a real pleasure for me. I even helped your son clean that turkey we ate last night. Don't get that opportunity much any more."

The ride into Salem, along the banks of the Willamette River, flowing strong with spring runoff, took less than two hours, interrupted by a sight Zeke hadn't seen in a long time. "Will you look at that!" he said, excitement running through his body. "I haven't seen a steamboat since I left Missouri."

"It's the Hoosier," Sullivan said. "She's brand new to us. Started making regular runs between Oregon City and Eugene," he had to think for a moment, "well, sometime in '51. Moves a lot of merchandise at a fair price… and fast."

"I hope Travis knows about this. It could help our transporting business, getting merchandise between the big valley in California and the Willamette Valley here. He needs to have warehouses at each end of that steamboat's run."

"You and Travis are pretty tight, I take it."

"He's my father-in-law, Mr. Sullivan, but he was my friend before that. He says I taught him a lot, and I know he taught me a lot. We've taken on Indian attacks, hunted together, made one long journey together, and now, we're partners in business."

They hadn't ridden twenty yards after spotting the Hoosier making her way down river. Then they sat their horses and watched the grand sight. A few minutes later, they moved off and it wasn't long before they rode into bustling Salem. New buildings were going up along every street, and commerce was active. Zeke saw a busy little town with people dressed in buckskins, in city clothes, and in rough, farm attire.

"Your capitol city seems to be flourishing, Mr. Sullivan," he said.

"Salem's been here since the early forties, Mr. Hawthorne, but only became the territorial capitol last year. Half the capitol hasn't even had a chance to get moved yet, and of course so many new people moving in still think Oregon City is capitol. John Gaines, our illustrious governor... do I sound snide? Well, I mean to," he snuffed, and continued.

"Governor Gaines has been fighting this move since the territory was formed. The people want the capitol to be Salem. It *is* Salem, and that fool is still fighting it. Well, enough of that, let me continue to tell you about this fair city.

"The town got started because of the gristmill and is now a thriving little community. There's even a new lumber mill. You'll find just about everything you need for your farm here.

"One thing we need more of is educated men; men to become leaders. Oregon is going to be a rich state one day, and it will need leaders, well-educated and dedicated. That's why men like Farnsworth are wrong in fermenting their hatred of those moving west."

"Is there an actual movement against immigration?" Zeke asked.

"I wouldn't call it a movement, organized as such, but among the least educated, there is strong sentiment against immigration. Part of it is to do with treaties that have been shoved down our throats dealing with the Willamette Valley Indians. The government is offering up to six hundred forty acres of land to immigrants and in some cases that same government is giving some of the same land to the Indians.

"Things like that just don't make sense. That's our governor for you. As far as the immigrants go, those without a background in farming, or one of the crafts, without an immediate means of employment, are behind the move to keep more immigrants out. Farnsworth is an angry man and got his job with our office only because he lied about his background.

"There is a need for men to run the lumber mills, to run the transportation companies, to build farms and ranches, and they need to be educated. You might be able to learn to run a saw, but you need education to run the company, and that has been lacking in some of those coming to our country."

They tied off their animals and went into Sullivan's land office to complete all the paperwork for the new farm. "Just look at that paneling, sir," Sullivan said. "Wood right off the hillside to your west, Zeke, milled right here in Salem, or just up stream, actually, and my office smells magnificent." The fresh aroma of recently felled trees did indeed permeate the air. "Delicious," Sullivan said.

The walls and floors were done in beautiful hardwood as was the wainscoting, desks, and bannisters throughout the offices. Some of the flooring was parquet inlaid hardwood. "Redwood came from south of us, in California, most of the fir, pine, cedar, and hardwoods from our forests right here."

"Sure gives me some good ideas on what to use when I build our home," Zeke said. "I love that redwood and the cedar is beautiful. Well, Mr. Sullivan, let's get on with the official stuff. I could stand and look at all this fine wood-work for hours."

WITH COPIES of the many transactions safely inside his saddlebags, Zeke decided to ride around Salem for a good look at the capitol before riding back north to the new Hawthorne Homestead. *Feels good having that paperwork done. It's signed and sealed and ours. This has been a long jour-ney, there was considerable danger, lots of pleasure, and I have a wonderful wife and children.* He was wearing a broad smile as he rode out of town late in the day.

22

USING THE PLANS HE'D DRAWN UP WHILE STILL LIVING AT Fort Bridger, Zeke and Sarah started building their farm. "I really like that section of meadow up the creek a-ways for our home, Zeke. It would look out over the whole valley, across that big river, and into the western mountains. Could we have our home there?"

"You have a good eye, Sarah," he smiled. "We'll start work on that today. Hiram, we need to clear that plot then level it, so here is your first day as my number one assistant. Better get down to where we have things stored. The first thing we need to build is a good drag, to clean off the land."

He smiled watching the boy take off at a run. "Don't think he's ever walked a step in his life. Do you need anything before I get started? We'll have those mules dragging that ground for several hours."

She reached up to give him a peck on the cheek. "I think I have everything I'll ever need," she smiled. He gave her a pat on the bottom, kissed his three girls and headed down the slope to find Hiram and the mules.

Zeke and Hi built a solid drag that had enough weight to rip the bushes and weeds right out of the ground. It took about two days to get the home plot dragged clean. Zeke showed Hi what a grader was and how it worked. The forge burned hot for two days while he built one from scratch. Commonly called a Fresno, once the land was cleared, a good operator could make it level and clean with just a few passes.

"It's hard and hot work, Hi, but it's a one-man job, so while I'm putting our grader together, I want you to take the mules up to the home site and drag it one more time. Take it nice and slow, and be aware of the dangers we've talked about."

"I will Papa," he said, about as excited as Zeke had ever seen him. "What do we do with all that brush we've piled up?"

"We'll burn most of it, and hold back some to use when we put in some berms a little later."

It was a pair of tired men that joined Sarah and the babies for supper. "Whitewater Bill said he has a couple of dozen nice trees picked out for you, Zeke, when you're ready to start building." Zeke and Sarah spent hours in the evenings planning the layout of the main ranch house.

"Not much dirt to be moved," Zeke said one night as they sat around the fire. "I'll start grading tomorrow after we set some stakes, Hi. You did a great job clearing that plot, and it's already fairly level.

"Hiram, after we set those stakes, I want you and Whitewater Bill to start bringing logs down to the home site. You know the sizes that I'm looking for, and Whitewater says he has a bunch marked for cutting. Best bet is to use one of the horses. We need to snake those logs out. You'll build some strong muscles when you and Bill get that old buck saw singing its song," he chuckled.

"If you hitch the horse and use the chains we have, you should be able to drag those logs down here without too much trouble. We'll skin 'em and notch 'em as we go. We'll get finished, mill cut lumber for the inside, but that will be down the road a piece."

According to the plans Zeke had drawn, the lower level of the main house would be log style and the upper floor framed and paneled. "I want to get that lower level done just as quickly as possible," he told Hi and Sarah, "so we'll have a home to live in while we do the finish work later."

"I wish it was you and me instead of me and Whitewater," Hiram said. "He's not very easy to work with, Papa. He curses an awful lot, and if things don't go right, he throws things."

"I'm afraid you're going to have to work with him, Son. Neither you nor Whitewater know how to skin and notch, neither one of you know how to level land or build a house. On the other hand," he snickered a little, "both of you know how to use a bucksaw and drive a team of horses.

"He might get a little testy, but he is a good worker and we do need to get that house well started before the seasons change. We still need to get a start on laying out our corn and wheat fields, our orchards, and our pastures for the animals. I'd really like to get winter wheat planted, so we do have to hustle." He wanted to be in the forest with Hiram as well, but knew he couldn't."

"Mama wants that kitchen garden planted this week, too, Hi, so buckle down and remember you can jump in that creek every night after work."

"There's fish in that creek, too," Hi smiled. "I'll catch a couple of fish, then jump in," he laughed.

"We'll take tomorrow off," Zeke said at supper several weeks later. "You boys are bringing me so much timber and we're building so fast, I'm running out of material. I'm going to take the wagon and mules into Salem for supplies. If you need something, jot it down for me. That goes for you too, Sarah. I'm sure you're getting short on food."

The main floor was laid in, outside walls were erected, with the profanity provided by Whitewater Bill, and inside bearing walls were in place. Using block and tackle, the men had the beginnings of a second floor, at least the joices, in place. Openings for windows and doors were set, a grand porch was attached, looking west toward the river, and the kitchen garden was not only planted, some shoots were already showing.

"We'll be warm and dry, and have fresh food for the winter," Sarah smiled, looking at the large farmhouse. "You're an amazing man, Zeke. Don't be going into saloons and getting rowdy tomorrow," she laughed, along with Zeke, Hiram, and Whitewater Bill.

Hiram had the mules hitched to the wagon by sunup and Zeke jumped into the seat for the short ride into town. "Wish I was going with you, Papa," Hi said.

"Not this trip, Son, but you'll go soon enough. Enjoy the day, go swimming, help your mama, shoot a turkey for supper," he smiled, clucking the mules into a nice fast walk toward the main trail. "I like turkey for supper."

Barring some kind of natural disaster, that house will be there for a hundred years or more, he was thinking, driving the team toward the main road. *Hiram is going to be a fine carpenter and cabinetmaker. He's such a fast learner, splits those logs into planks, has them shaved and planed, and I've only had to show him a couple of times.* On his list of materials to bring back from Salem were more blacksmith tools, more carpentry tools, and some scrap iron if he could find it. *I've used up just about everything we picked up in Oregon City, building the drags and grader.*

"You boys will be back pulling plows before long," he said to the mules as they rode along the river road. "I have to build the plows first," he chuckled. He planned to lay out the farm land as soon as the main house was done. *I want to get the fruit trees started late this summer, get that wheat in, and I want to be able to plant the entire farm next spring.*

We need animals too. Sarah needs a milk cow, and I would like a couple of sheep and we'll need some hogs. Well, not this trip. He drove the team down the main street and found the implement store a block off and tied the animals to a hitching rack. It was a warm morning, which would give way to a blistering hot afternoon, and Zeke wanted to get loaded and on the road back to the farm as soon as possible. "Maybe I should have brought Hiram along," he murmured, jumping off the wagon and striding into the emporium.

"The educated immigrant farmer shows up, eh?" the voice called from behind some sacks of beans. "We don't need your kind around here," the man said.

Zeke stood tall, straightened his shoulders and felt his muscles tighten at the taunt. "You man enough to show yourself, or just vermin, hiding. If this is your store, believe me, I can find another one."

"It ain't his store, stranger. Farnsworth, you start trouble in my store, I'll whup your skinny butt clear into the Pacific Ocean."

"Don't need more damn immigrants, Snyder, and you know it. Foul the air, foul the water, take work from honest men, always taking, never giving. This country is worse off because of them."

"I told you in Oregon City that if you ever called me names again, Mr. Farnsworth, I would beat the hell out of you. If you'd care to step outside, if you still have the courage to call me ignorant or dirty or foul, please do so. I won't create trouble in Mr. Snyder's emporium, but I'll sure whup on you outside." Zeke was squared, facing the little man, his fists clenched, hanging loosely at his side, and his eyes had narrowed, glinting in the late morning light.

"Don't waste your time on this foul-mouthed fool, stranger. Farnsworth, you're not welcome in my store. Leave by your own means or I'll pick you up and throw you through the wall," and Snyder took two steps toward the former land clerk. Farnsworth, cussing under his breath, almost ran from the store, Snyder laughing at him all the way out.

"I'm Heck Snyder, proprietor of this fine establishment, stranger. How can I help you today?"

Hector (Heck) Snyder stood about six feet all and carried close to two hundred pounds on a large frame. His hands told Zeke that he was a working man from the day he was old enough to hold a tool, and his chest and the thickness of his legs gave indications that whatever work he used to do, it was heavy. His blue eyes were covered by bushy, thick brows, he wore a full beard, a reddish color to match his long hair, that was held in place by a well used slouch hat.

"It's a pleasure, sir. I'm Ezekiel Hawthorne, recently of Fort Bridger. My family and I have homesteaded a section of land north of here, and I need some supplies. I have a fair list here," Zeke said, shaking hands with the heavy shopkeeper.

"Welcome to Oregon, Hawthorne. Sounded like you've had a run-in with that fool Farnsworth. You the man he claims cost him his job at the Land Office?"

"I do believe I am," Zeke answered. "I hope this isn't something we'll be running into every time we venture off the farm. That man needs a serious lesson in courtesy, and I might just have to offer it."

"He is a fool, and there are a few more like him, but with your size and apparent fearlessness, I don't think you'll have much trouble. Let's see that list of yours and I'll get started on it."

Zeke handed him the list and asked where the lumber mill was. "I need to order up some finished lumber for our house, and need some more tools. Where would I find some blacksmith tools and equipment, as well?" he asked.

"Donaldson's is about three miles up the creek, but I'm not sure they're fully underway. And if you look around my fine little establishment, I think you'll find carpenter and blacksmith equipment. I try to have everything for everyone," he quipped, his bright eyes shining with mirth.

Snyder was similar in build to Sullivan, Zeke was

thinking. *People in the Willamette Valley must eat well.* He spent the next hour looking at everything in the emporium, finding just about everything he needed, while Snyder and a man working for him loaded the wagon with his supplies.

"That just about fills your list, Mr. Hawthorne, and your wagon, too. Those tools you picked out are the kinds I would offer to a journeyman. Do you have that kind of background, sir?"

"Indeed, I do," Zeke smiled. "I was sent off by my father at a young age to learn carpentry and cabinet making, and then again, to learn the art of the blacksmith. My love is the land and farming, but I am a journeyman cabinetmaker and blacksmith."

"You'll surely have visitors to your farm, Mr. Hawthorne, and to buy more than good food. We don't have a shortage of laborers, but we do have a shortage of full fledged journeymen in the arts of woodworking and metal.

"I noticed you don't have smoked salmon on your list. I think you probably should pick up several big slabs for your family. It's the national food of Oregon Territory," he laughed.

Zeke agreed, settled his account, shook hands with the jolly storekeeper and set off for the journey home. *I like that thought,* he mused, easing the mules back onto the trail north. *I'm going home. Yes, sir, I'm going home.*

HE WAS about three miles out from Salem when two riders came out onto the trail from some willows alongside and motioned for Zeke to pull up. Zeke realized his big mistake in not bringing the Hawkins along with him. "Climb down, immigrant," one of the men snarled, waving an old single shot flintlock handgun at him. "We're gonna teach you a lesson."

"No, you're not," Zeke said, and smacked the mules with the reins, giving them full head. Both men had to whip their horses out of the way of the heavy wagon as Zeke urged the mules into a fast run. He heard the gun go off, but where ever the bullet went, it wasn't close to him.

The big wagon, heavy with merchandise from Snyder's, was a hard pull for the mules, and the two men caught up with Zeke within a mile, but Zeke simply wouldn't stop the wagon. One man tried to grab a mule's headstall and Zeke slapped him hard with the buggy whip, while the other man made a move to jump from his horse to the wagon.

"Oh, no you don't," Zeke howled, driving a back handed fist into the man's face. The man tried to cling to the side of the wagon and Zeke stood and drove his boot into the man's face, watching him tumble to the ground. The one working to grab a headstall got another lashing from the whip, a strong, hard, whipping and pulled back, to make a grab for Zeke.

Zeke smashed him in the face with his fist and as he fell away, his lightweight coat snagged on the wagon seat. As the man's weight on the fabric increased, his body was swinging, bouncing off the spokes of the front wheels. The coat finally tore away and the man's body fell, to be run over by the rear wheels.

Zeke let the mules run hard for another mile before pulling them up to a strong walk. "Well, boys, we have made ourselves some enemies, for sure. Time for me to start thinking along the lines that I did at Fort Bridger, only instead of angry Indians, angry fools." He was in a foul mood when he rode onto the farm property an hour later.

Hiram and Sarah met him near their new home when he drove the team in and Zeke spent the next hours unloading the wagon and telling his tale, slowly letting the anger boil away. "Both Sullivan and Snyder say there really isn't much to those that are fighting immigration, but I'm not seeing it that way. I surely do hope those men are right."

It was late the next morning, Zeke and Hiram were splitting some shingles for the roof when Zeke spotted three riders turning off the main road, toward the farm. "Run to the house, Hi, and grab your shotgun. Bring my rifle back with you and tell your mama to stay inside. Hurry now." Hiram was a fast runner and hightailed it to the house while Zeke slowly walked toward the front of the house to await the riders.

When they were about half way between the main road and the porch where Zeke stood, he recognized Sullivan and Heck Snyder, but not the third man. As they rode up, Hi came out of the house with the shotgun, handing the rifle to Zeke. "You won't need that Zeke," Sullivan hollered out. "But it's good thinking on your part."

The three stepped off their horses and Hi took the lead ropes to tie them off at a brand-new hitching rack in front of the house. "Zeke, this is Fred Sharp, Salem town Marshal. Fred, meet Zeke Hawthorne."

Zeke leaned the rifle up next to Hi's shotgun and stuck his hand out to shake with the marshal. "Me and Heck told Fred about the trouble you've had with Farnsworth, and Sharp told us about two men who said you attacked them yesterday. We're here to get all the stories straightened out," Sullivan said, that happy smile still spread across his broad face.

"I'd be willing to bet that Sarah could whip up some hot coffee fast enough," Zeke said. "Let's go inside and talk about my attacking those two ruffians." He picked up the two guns and motioned for Hi to follow along and led the group into the house. "Don't have all the finish work done yet, but I have a fine kitchen table, a good stove, and a beautiful wife."

He introduced Sarah to Heck Snyder and the marshal, along with Hiram. "Mr. Sullivan is already familiar with my family, having spent several days escorting us from Oregon City. Please, sit and we'll have some coffee."

"Looks like you've been a busy man," Sullivan noted. "Nice work, Zeke. Very nice."

The four men gathered around the new kitchen table that Zeke had finished the week before, commenting on the fine woodwork that was done, while Sarah got a pot of coffee underway. "You do beautiful work, sir," Marshal Sharp said, running his hands over the wood. "This is fine work, indeed. You should open a shop in Salem instead of running a farm."

"Thank you for the kind words, Marshal, but we'll stay on the farm. I've wanted this for a long time." He spent the next several minutes telling the story of the two men who tried to stop him the day before. "Their intentions were clear, Marshal. One doesn't make new friends on the highway by waving a pistol at you."

"The man who fell under the wagon wheel is in bad shape but the doc says he'll live. You say he's the one tried to shoot you?"

"Yup. Had an old flintlock pistola. He fired it once and didn't try to reload. Sorry the man's hurt bad but he had no right to try and stop me or try to do me harm."

"No, he didn't," Sharp agreed. "We can do one of two things now. Ignore the whole thing, which I would not suggest, or you, Mr. Hawthorne, file charges against the two. That would be my choice. Farnsworth and his cronies, bunch of damn drunkards," and he stopped dead. "I'm terribly sorry, Ma'am," he said, standing and bowing slightly. "I should never have talked that way in front of you."

Sarah smiled as she brought the coffee pot to the table. "Believe me, Marshal Sharp, having lived at Fort Bridger most of my life, I'm not affected by such language. Those trappers were rather colorful at times."

There was general laughter at the table, and Sharp continued. "Those fools that run with Farnsworth need to be corralled, put in their place, but too many people don't file the necessary charges.

"They're intimidated with threats of beatings, with families put in danger, even with being burned out of their homes. I can't do anything to stop these fools unless people make formal complaints."

"If it had just been Farnsworth's foul mouth and stupidity, I would have let it pass." Zeke said. "Yesterday, though, that was serious. I could have been hurt, my mules could have been hurt, my supplies could have been lost. I'll file whatever complaint you think would do the most good, Marshal. Yes, sir, I will." He took a long drink of his coffee, looking at the three men, and then looking over at Sarah, standing near the hot stove. "There isn't a man big enough to hurt my family, there isn't a threat that would deter me from protecting them. My wife, my children, my farm is all I have in the world, and if you need me to sign a complaint, consider it done."

Sarah walked over and put her hand on his shoulder. "The Crow fear this man, Marshal. "You might pass that on to this Mr. Farnsworth. Sharp Knife will protect our family."

"Sharp Knife, is it?" the marshal said, with a hint of humor crossing his face. Zeke's face darkened just a bit, but the almost embarrassed smile gave him away. He coughed slightly and continued.

"What happens after that?" he asked. "I don't want to have to watch my back every time I come to town. I would rather not have to walk around with a loaded and cocked rifle everywhere I go. I will defend myself, my family to the death, but I would rather the threat not be there in the first place."

"You file the charges, I'll do the rest," Sharp said. "The men will be placed under arrest and brought to trial, and I'll spread the word, forcefully, that I will not tolerate anymore of this harassment of immigrants to the territory."

"Which is one of the reasons that I'm here, Zeke," Sullivan piped up. "We need leaders in this country. There are too many rabble-rousers like Farnsworth mucking up the scenery. Our less-than-adequate governor, John

JOHNNY GUNN

Gaines is probably going to be gone soon, and with him, many of his cronies.

"Snyder, Sharp, and myself, among others, are forming a committee to find people who would sit on city boards, in the legislature, represent the territory in Washington. We've only been a territory for a couple of years, and we haven't had strong leadership.

"We would like you to consider sitting on that committee with us. You're a strong, intelligent man with a lovely family and property. You and men like you will be the backbone of Oregon for years to come."

"There you go, Sully," Snyder said, "giving another fine speech," which brought considerable laughter to the table. "He's a real politician," Snyder said, pouring more coffee for the group. "Now we have a politician and an Indian fighter sitting at the same table. Farnsworth and company should be shaking and quaking about now," he all but guffawed.

"Maybe I do carry on some," Sullivan joked, "but what I'm saying is the gospel, and you know it. Give all this lots of thought, Hawthorne. Oregon needs men like you."

Zeke spent the next couple of hours giving the three men a complete tour of his farm before seeing them off. "Keep me posted on what I have to do, Marshal, and Mr. Sullivan, you keep right on giving speeches. You're good at it."

"I'll send a notice your way when our committee plans to meet next. There are good people in Oregon, Hawthorne, you've just been unlucky enough to meet the bad ones first," he laughed, leading the group back to Salem.

23

SUMMER SEEMED TO BE ON A FAST TRACK TO LEAVE Oregon, according to Zeke. "We've got the house and barn put together and working," he said one morning at breakfast, "and Sarah, you have your milk cow. O'Brien brought those hogs over, and we picked up the sheep from Miles Peterson, but I'm still worried about being ready for next spring."

"You've done an amazing job, Zeke," Sarah said. "We have a beautiful home, the animals are all secure and with food for the winter, my kitchen garden, even as late as I planted, is producing very well. Something's bothering you, more than just winter coming on in the next few months. What is it?"

"Not knowing what to expect, I guess," he said. "Back east, winters were fierce, snow up to the roof line sometimes, spring coming late, floods, and late storms to ruin planting or bringing rain at the wrong time. Heck Snyder says we may not even see any snow, late frosts are something people remember from back east, and rain is a blessing."

"I'm wondering," Sarah said, "if maybe you're still worried about that Farnsworth man and the trouble he tried to cause. Is that part of your worries?"

"I suppose it is," he said. "Snyder and the marshal have pretty much stopped the general harassment of immigrants, and I was pleased with being made a member of the committee to find Oregon leadership."

"Tell me again just how that's going to work," she said. "Is it new laws that are needed, or people, or what?"

"It isn't a lack of laws, but it is definitely a lack of leadership, from the governor right on down. Sullivan is a good man, but he works for the government, half making sure the federal land laws are met, and half establishing Oregon Territory land rules. It's a mess because of the territory people. Heck Snyder is the real kingpin on the committee, and he's going to end up one of the territory's real leaders. I do like that man."

"How is all this going to affect us, Zeke? Are you worried, or are you just maybe a bit anxious about what will happen."

"You know me very well, Sarah, almost reading my mind," he grinned, giving her a little wink. "I'm anxious more than worried, and not that seriously anxious. Snyder and O'Brien have asked me to be the chairman of the farmers and ranchers subcommittee and work with the territorial legislature on how best to make all the land laws and rules work.

"I'm not really sure I'm the man for that," he said. He reached out and grabbed the last piece of toast before Hiram could get it, then giving it to the boy with a little grin. "I've never even sat on a committee of any kind, never belonged to a group, much less been their leader.

"Anxious is a good word for it," he said with a half-hearted smile.

"That's wonderful, Zeke. Of course, you're the man for that. What exactly will it mean to and for us? You're a natural leader, Zeke. You were the leader of our wagons and brought us here," she said.

"Well, because of so much ranch and farm work that has to be done during the summer and fall months, the territorial legislature only meets for a short time during the middle of the winter. Our committee will meet once before the session, and then once during the session, to work for what will be best for the farmers and ranchers in Oregon. Our first session is scheduled for December, the legislature starts meeting in January, and we'll have a second session, probably in February.

"I'll have to spend a few days in Salem during each of our meetings. I think we'll see the last of Governor Gaines during the session."

"I'm very proud of you, Zeke. Just look what you've done. Just look at this beautiful farm, our home, our family." He stood her up and hugged her tight, smoothing back that thick, luxurious hair, so black it was almost blue, and kissed her long and sweet, whispering his love into a willing ear.

He let her go, straightened up, and looked at Hi with a big smile. "I think it's time to send Whitewater Bill back to Oregon City to work for Johnson and Travis. Hiram and I need to plot out the areas for corn, beans, wheat, and grasses, and get the ground turned. I just wish I knew what to expect."

"We won't have snow like at Fort Bridger," Sarah laughed, "and the way the trees and bushes grow around here, I'd say we'll have fairly mild winters compared to what we're used to. You've spent time with Snyder, O'Brien, and Peterson, and they all farm this country. You'll have the best crops of the bunch, Sharp Knife," she teased.

He had to laugh, and knew she was probably right. *She's right, I know. I keep saying it, I'm home, this is home. This is what I've wanted my entire life, a beautiful wife, fine children, and a big farm. Yes, Zeke, accept it, you're home, finally.* He had to smile to himself realizing that they teased back and forth with their Indian names. *I love calling her Hummingbird and she enjoys catching me off guard with the Sharp Knife name every once in a while. I am one lucky man.*

"I'll talk to Whitewater this morning and get him ready to head north. I hate to give up that team and wagon, but it is part of the deal with Johnson. When I go to Salem next, I want you to come with me, Hiram, and we'll pick up another team of mules or good strong plow horses, and you can drive them back with a high-sided wagon, if we can find one."

"Why high-sided, Papa?" Hi asked.

"Gotta have room for all that corn and wheat," Zeke laughed. "Right now, let's go find some good land for corn." He gave Sarah a big hug, patted her on the bottom, kissed the twins, and headed to the equipment shed to find Whitewater Bill and get the day started. "Just look at that sunrise, Hi. My God that's beautiful."

ZEKE AND HI came into the equipment barn late that

evening to put the mules up and clean the plows, and found Michael O'Brien waiting for them. "Sarah said you'd be in soon, Zeke. You sure did build this nice and strong. Plenty of room for everything you'll need on the farm."

"Hello, Mike, good to see you. What drags you away from all those animals of yours?"

"What's that building there?" He was pointing at a shed, half open to the weather, but with sturdy walls and sloping roof. "Too small for animals and heavy equipment, I think."

"That's my new blacksmith shop. Come on, I'll show you. Go tell Mama we're back, Hi, and get washed up. I'll be in shortly."

"I have some bad news, I'm afraid, Zeke. Fred Sharp was beat up pretty bad by a gang of thugs last night. I just got back from Salem. Back several years, when the Cayuga Indians were wiping out Whitman's Mission, a territorial posse of sorts was formed to get revenge. It went by the wayside, but Heck Snyder has formed a group of men in town to round up these bastards that whipped on Sharp."

"Farnsworth's right in the middle, I bet," Zeke said. "I think if you stop Farnsworth, you'll stop most of the problems."

"That's exactly what Heck said. He wanted me to warn you that if Farnsworth hears about them looking for him, he might head north, and that might mean trouble for you. I have to get back to my place, still more than an hour away, Zeke."

The men shook hands, Zeke stood in the doorway of the equipment shed, and watched O'Brien ride off toward his ranch. *Farnsworth, again. Looks like I'll be sleeping with that rifle for the next several nights. Damn that man.*

HECK SNYDER STRODE into Marshal Sharp's bedroom despite Mrs. Sharp's pleading to leave the poor man alone. "Can't do that, Mabel," Heck said. "Morning Fred, hope you're feeling better. Farnsworth's done. Thought you'd like to know. I'm about to ride north and give the good news to Hawthorne."

Two of Sharp's ribs were broken, he had missing and broken teeth, and a knee so bruised and swollen he wouldn't walk for another two or three weeks. He carried a good attempt at a smile at Snyder's words. He nodded his head, still unable to speak, and tried to tell Snyder to tell his story.

"Farnsworth and three of his hooligans were about to whup on old man Walton when we stumbled into them," Snyder said. "They were cornered behind Walton's Funeral Parlor and the stage office. Right now, the two are being looked at by Doc Stone in cell three, the other two are sharing cell one, and nursing some serious bruises.

"Doc says Farnsworth probably won't ever walk again. His own man blew his kneecap to smithereens with a shotgun. Shoulda heard the squallin'," he laughed. "Well, anyway, Ike Walton filed the necessary charges, and coupled with your charges and testimony, those ugly hooligans will find the next many years unpleasant as all get out in Territorial Prison."

Sharp did everything he could to say something, but with lips fat as tomatoes, broken and missing teeth, he couldn't get the words out. His smiling eyes and nodding, however, said what needed to be said. Snyder gave him a gentle pat on the shoulder and headed to his big store. "I'll be heading up north to tell Hawthorne the good news later this morning," he said as he left.

24

"I'M SORRY THE MAN IS INJURED, SORRY HE LOST A LEG, BUT not sorry enough to not feel relieved, knowing we won't be threatened by either him or his outlaw associates," Zeke said, walking from the courtroom following Farnsworth's sentencing. "Being disrespectful to that judge sure didn't help his case any," he snickered.

Heck Snyder and Mike O'Brien chuckled along with him, O'Brien saying something about comments adding years to his term in prison. "Most of my fall work is done now," O'Brien continued. "We need to set a time for our legislative committee to get together. How about you, Hawthorne, you just about caught up?"

"Without a crop to bring in, I guess I would say so. This would be my busiest time if I had been able to get a crop in. Next year, don't expect to see me during these weeks. I can pretty much meet whenever it's convenient for everyone else."

He and Hi had turned the ground they would plant next spring, acres of corn, beans, wheat, and cross-fenced even more acres for pasture. The natural grasses of the Willamette Valley would be augmented by other grasses that he and Hi had planted. Zeke planned on running a few steers and some lambs on the open pastures.

"I'll be spending as much time as possible in the cabinet shop and the blacksmith shop this fall and winter. Hiram will be my apprentice, and he's already learned so much."

"Did I hear right," Snyder asked, "that Sarah was going to offer private schooling for children?"

"She's already working to get a room set up for it. Mike, your wife and some of the other families in the immediate area, are planning on bringing their children in for classes two or three days a week."

"Eva told me about that," O'Brien said. "Little Mike will be a better man for it. Eva said that Sarah ran a school at Fort Bridger; is that right?"

"She was educated in Boston and had as many as twelve students at Bridger's. That's where I met that wonderful girl."

It was on the way back to the farm that everything seemed to come together for Zeke. He and Hiram had come to town for Farnsworth's sentencing and to buy supplies for the fall. "You like those mules, Hiram?" he asked. "They're nice and big. They will be the ones you will be plowing and working with for many years."

"They aren't as well trained as our old ones, Papa," he smiled, hitching them to a new wagon Zeke had picked up from Heck Snyder. "I'll have plenty of time to work them over the winter, and they'll be ready to work the farm come spring."

"We'll give them their first lesson tomorrow, Hi. I

want to get that winter wheat in and this is the perfect time to get that started."

They had both wagons loaded with supplies, mill finished lumber, iron and iron working tools, food, cloth, and what seed was available. Zeke also put in his order for seed for spring. Hiram had fresh apples and half a pound of smoked salmon next to him on the wagon seat, and Zeke had apples and peaches up front for his enjoyment. "Let's get 'em moving," he said, clucking Ruth and Tobias into action.

"Follow along behind my wagon, Son, and we'll be home in just a few hours. Did you grab something to eat on the way?"

"Smoked salmon, Papa," he smiled. "Lots of smoked salmon."

What an amazing boy he is, Zeke thought, putting the mules into a strong walk, leading the wagons out of Salem. "We'll be home before dark," he said to the mules, "and you'll have a chance to determine which of you is the head mule." He chuckled, remembering when he put the horses in with the mules and the rowdy stomping and snorting that took place.

"This has been a year," he said, as much to himself as to his mules. His mind wandered back to the farm in Missouri and so much sadness. "I still miss you, Elizabeth, and I'm sorry that you had to leave us so early." Visions of Sarah, when he first met her at Fort Bridger, how his heart swelled when she said yes, filled his mind as the miles dropped by.

"We've done well," he said with a smile. "I can actually see Hiram grow every day, and those little girls, so full of it." Visions of the farm, fields of corn and wheat dancing in Oregon vistas, blown about by gentle breezes flowing through that verdant valley, filled his mind. "I really am home," he said, again and again. "Thousands of miles from the Ohio Valley, and I have a beautiful family and a good farm. I think Mama would be happy to know that... even Papa might say I've done well.

"He was a cantankerous old man," Zeke laughed, clucking at the mules at the same time. "Hi looks at me sometimes like I'm being too strict with him, when we're doing some serious woodworking. I hope I'm not being as strict as my father was, but maybe it's because he was so strict, that I'm such a good cabinet maker."

These thoughts danced in his head, he entertained his mules with story after story, and the two wagons finally made the turn up the creek to the Hawthorne farm. Sarah, with a girl in each arm, met them when they pulled up near the barns and corrals. Zeke kissed them, one, two, three, and helped Zeke get the animals unhitched and put up for the night.

"I already milked and fed," Sarah said, "so just feed the mules, Hi. Supper will be ready by the time you boys get washed up. My goodness," she said. "You certainly brought in supplies. Let me put the girls in their corrals," she joked, "and I'll help you unload. Does Mr. Snyder have anything left in the store?"

"We'll just unload the foodstuff tonight. Hi and I can get the rest of the material unloaded and put away in the morning. It will take a few hours, I'm thinking." He hefted a couple of boxes and followed Sarah into the house.

"Snyder said there will be thousands of ducks and geese flying through this valley in the next few weeks,

Sarah. I love the venison and turkey that we've been eating, but roast duck and goose is mighty fine."

"I remember Papa bringing home geese, but I don't think I've had any for a long time." Zeke was sitting at the kitchen table, a cup of coffee, laced with some rum in front of him, and Sarah put her hands on his shoulders, gently massaging them with her long fingers.

"We're home, Zeke. You wanted a home, a farm, and a family, and I wanted you. We have three beautiful children, you built us a fine home, and that land out there is starting to look like a farm. What a change this is from my old home at Fort Bridger," she smiled.

"I was told about Oregon country back in Missouri, Sarah, and it's even better than what I heard. I have to be about the happiest man in the world right now. The only thing that would make me happier would be if your mother and father, and your brother and sister could be with us."

"We are close enough that we can visit any time we want, Zeke. Maybe even ride that steamboat north to Oregon City someday." She walked to the stove, pulled a large venison roast from the oven and asked Zeke to call Hiram in for supper.

"Riders coming in, Papa," Hiram said, running into the kitchen. "Looks like at least four men."

"Grab your shotgun, Hi," Zeke said, striding through the living room, grabbing his rifle, and walking onto the large veranda-style front porch. He stood watching five horses trot up the long trail from the main road, finally recognizing one of them.

"Mr. Sullivan, what brings you out here this late in the day?"

"Evening, Zeke," Sullivan said as he and the four riders with him stepped off their horses. Hiram took the leads and tied off for the men. "Heading for Oregon City, got a late start, and hoped that I could persuade you to let us camp here overnight. Besides, there's somebody I want you to meet."

"You'll not be sleeping in the barn, sir," Zeke smiled at his rotund friend. "And, you seemed to time your arrival to exactly when Sarah took that venison roast out of the oven." He laughed, shaking Sullivan's hand and ushering the group into the house.

"Zeke, I want you to meet Joseph Lane," Sullivan said. Lane and Zeke shook hands, and Sullivan also introduced the others with him. "Lane is going to be our Territorial Governor again, once we fully convince John Gaines to leave office. He already has his commission from the president."

"Welcome to our farm, Mr. Governor," Zeke said. "My wife, Sarah, has dinner out, so let's retire to the kitchen." Two of the men with the party excused themselves, saying they would take care of the animals and make sure everything would be ready for them to depart in the morning.

Zeke thought that was a bit strange, but Sullivan and the Governor-to-be seemed to accept their actions, and he let it go. Sarah had potatoes, corn, beans, and bread to go along with the roast venison, and within half an hour there wasn't a morsel left, and the men retired to the living room while Sarah and Hiram cleaned up the kitchen.

"That's a fine boy, you have, Mr. Hawthorne," Lane said, accepting a snifter of brandy from Zeke. "Sullivan tells me you will be part of the committee that's going to help stabilize this territory. He also says that beautiful wife of yours is a schoolteacher and will be running a school here.

"Splendid, I must say. It's leadership and a desire to make life better that has been in short supply in Oregon, recently. We need men and women like you and Sarah. Sullivan has brought me up to date on the problems you had with some of the uneducated fools that want to spread their hate through Oregon. Thank you for your good work."

"I'm glad we were able to at least slow them down, sir." *Just a few weeks ago a man was calling me vile names for moving my family to Oregon and now I have the next governor of Oregon having supper at our table.* Zeke's eyes were wide and bright as the conversation about Oregon Territory continued through one more snifter.

The two camp men brought bedrolls in for those staying in the house, the three were made comfortable, and Sarah and Zeke retired upstairs to their bedroom. "He's the governor?" Sarah asked, snuggling under a down comforter. "I've never met a governor before," she whispered.

"Neither have I," Zeke chuckled. "This is how our new life is going to be, Sarah. We're starting our new life in a new territory of the country. I think I am going to enjoy every minute of every day in this new life."

"You may have to pinch me from time to time, Zeke, so I know I'm not in some kind of dream. This is how our new life is going to be, having the governor stop by for supper, and then having him sleep on the floor of the living room."

They chuckled gently, visualizing what she had just

said, and fell into a deep sleep. Zeke thought he had an idea of what the rest of his life might be like, with a large farm and family, and apparent duties to the governor and the territory. Sarah too had warm thoughts of the future, that might bring another child or two, and teaching the children of the nearby farms and ranches.

Both believed that Oregon Territory would be the best place for them and their family, possibly for generations to come. Morning came early and active, getting the five men fed and on their way north, and Zeke and Hi unloading the wagons filled with equipment and supplies.

They took a break when Sarah called them in for a hot lunch. "I've been thinking about Travis and Elaine all morning, Sarah, and I have an idea. We don't have a harvest of any kind to worry about, only the milk cow, the hogs, a few sheep, and the mules. I'm sure O'Brien would be able to take care of them for a couple of weeks.

"Let's book passage on that steamboat to Oregon City and spend a week with your folks. They can bring us up to date and we can bring them up to date. I miss listening to Travis and all his roistering about."

Sarah was dancing, she was so happy, and they spent the rest of the day making plans for the big visit. "This is the first time I've been away from Mama and Papa since I got back from Boston, and I miss them very much."

Zeke made a ride into Salem and sent a letter to Travis that they would be coming up for a visit and made reservations for the steamboat trip. He also visited with Heck Snyder and told him about his visit with Governor Lane.

"He was governor before," Snyder said, "and there will be many around this country glad to see him back in office. This territory will be a state soon, Zeke, and it ain't gonna happen until we grow up some. Acting like a bunch of back hills fools is what too many of us have been doing. " I guess you heard that old man Donaldson is finally gonna open that new lumber mill here in Salem. Up Mill Creek a few miles.

"Good country up there, good trees, good water. Guess he'll be using the winter months to get things built, and expects to have the mill in full operation come spring. The way Salem is growing, he'll keep those saws humming for sure."

"You were talking about that mill when we moved here," Zeke said. "I thought they were already building it."

"Off and on, Zeke. Get work started, then stop when there weren't any workers, and no real drive to keep it going. Things have changed, I guess, and messages have been posted that hiring would begin again, soon."

Zeke wondered if Moose might be involved in bringing the operation south to Salem. He had that in his mind all the way home and it was the first thing he said to Sarah when he walked in.

"Now wouldn't that be something if Moose ends up running this operation down here. One thing I know, Moose knows how to run a mill." They spent the evening discussing how much things have changed from the time Zeke rode into Fort Bridger with Johnson and his wagon train.

"I made those reservations for two weeks from now, so we have time to put everything together that we'll be bringing and I can get with Mike O'Brien to get the animals taken care of."

ZEKE WAS IN THE BLACKSMITH SHOP ONE AFTERNOON, putting the finishing touches to a set of two-bottom plows he had made when Hiram came running in yelling about wagons coming up the trail. "Slow down, Hi. What are you saying?"

"You gotta come see, Papa," he said, more excited than Zeke had ever seen the boy. "There are four big wagons coming up our road to the house. Come quick, Papa. Four big wagons," and he ran back out, waving his arms.

Zeke put a piece of hot metal down, slipped out of his leather apron, and followed the scampering Hiram up toward the main house. Sure enough, there were four big wagons, each pulled by four horses, lined up for half a mile on the trail from the main road. The first of the wagons was slowly coming to a stop near some cotton-wood trees.

Sarah had the twins in her arms, standing on the porch watching the long procession, hearing the loud voices as the teamsters jockeyed their teams, enjoying the dust being thrown up. Memories of wagon trains pulling into Fort Bridger flooded her vision, and she walked down the steps to join Zeke.

"Have any idea what this is all about?" he asked. "I better go find out, just in case somebody made a wrong turn down there at the main road." He nipped a quick kiss and walked off down the trail, immediately starting into a trot when he recognized the first teamster, pulling his teams up.

"Johnson, you old rascal," he hollered. "Just look at this, will you?" Rutherford Johnson jumped down from the high wagon seat and the two flung their arms around each other.

"It ain't just me, Zeke," he said. "Look who's behind me."

Zeke let go of Johnson and walked back toward the second wagon, got there in time to be accosted by Travis himself. Elaine was still sitting on the wagon seat. "What on earth is going on?" he said, getting a bear hug from the massive old trapper. "Sarah will be so surprised. Let me help you down, Elaine. Who is with you? What's going on?" The questions flowed, one after the other.

Wagon number three was being driven by Barbara, and number four by Moose. "The entire family is here? What a wonderful thing," Zeke said, over and over, walking everyone up to the porch, watching Sarah be engulfed by her family.

"Come on, Mr. Johnson, Hiram, let's get these animals and wagons taken care of, and then we'll join the festivities. Isn't this something?" They took the wagons one at a time and parked them in a neat line, unharnessed the teams and put them into pastures that had been fenced just for this purpose, and finally walked up to the house. The three walked into a madhouse of activity, noise, and a thousand questions. The twins were being handed off, first to one relative, then on to the next.

Sarah, Barbara, and Elaine were in the kitchen with the twins, and the men grabbed a bottle of rum and settled in on the large front veranda. "Well, Mr. Travis, sir, I do believe you have some explaining to do," Zeke smiled as they settled in. "I just sent you a letter saying that we would be in Oregon City in a couple of weeks for a long visit. Looks like we all had the same idea."

"Almost," Travis laughed. "Almost. Mr. Johnson and I are moving our headquarters to the capitol, Zeke. I made a deal with a man down there, and will be joining my mercantile business with his and incorporating our transport business into the operation.

"You might have met him, he's quite a character, smart as a whip, and knows the people in the area well. Name's Hector Snyder. You run into him?"

"You might say that Heck and I are very good friends, Travis. Interesting that he hasn't said anything to me about this."

"He sure did want to, but we wanted this to be a big surprise to you."

"You win this round, Travis. I've never been more surprised in my life." He seemed to be spinning, trying to see everyone at the same time. "What about that big building you have in Oregon City?"

"We're keeping it," Johnson said. "I need it for all the wagons and warehouse space. I've made one round trip to California and it looks like there's more than enough business to keep many wagons on the road. George Felix and Whitewater Bill are on the road right now with two wagons, taking fruit south and they have loads to pick up for the return."

The bottle was passed around and everyone helped themselves, filling their mugs with good rum. "Moose, you're being awfully quiet. Are you feeling alright?" Zeke had a worried look on his face as he spoke, hoping the big man was okay.

"I'm just fine, Zeke. I have too many things on my mind to join the celebration that you all are having."

"Tell me all about it. I understand that Donaldson is finally building that new lumber mill near Salem. Are you going to be involved in that?"

"That's a big part of what's bothering me, Zeke." Moose had always been a man with many responsibilities, to his family, to his tribe, to himself, and all were weighing on him right now. "My village is going to need me, Mr. Donaldson wants me to run the mill in Salem, and I don't want to leave my family. How's that for openers, Zeke? I want to take a long walk with you, like we did at Fort Bridger."

"We did spend a lot of time in the forest working out our problems, Moose. We'll take as much time as necessary, as much time as you want." They looked deep into each other's eyes and knew their friendship was far more than just being brothers-in-law.

Hiram was sitting as close to Moose as he could get. "Hiram, you need to listen in on what Moose and I will be talking about over the next several days. This will be a big part of your growing up. Look how big he's gotten, Moose. You and he would be a force to be reckoned with, I'm thinking."

That broke the gloom and Moose had to chuckle, grabbing Hiram and giving him a bear hug. "Fishing any good around here?" he asked, getting a full nod of approval from Hi.

OVER THE REST of the day and well into the evening, conversations dwelt on who was doing what, on the one hand, and on who would be doing what on the other. "With the capitol now in Salem, it just seemed logical to be there, also," Travis said. "Johnson found out he needed far more space than I could give him, so he will have it all when we get fully moved."

"It sure made sense for me to move, too," Barbara said. "There are families in Salem, and I'm going to have a shop for the latest women's fashions as well as being able to sell my men's stuff in Papa's store. There aren't too many families in Oregon City." She jumped up, almost spilling her coffee. "I almost forgot," and ran over to a trunk that had been brought in, rummaging around for a minute.

"Here, Hiram, these are for you," she said, holding up three beautiful shirts. "That is if you haven't already outgrown them. My, you're getting big," she said, handing him the shirts. She moved a few more things around and came up with two pair of canvas trousers as well. "These are designed for hard work," she laughed.

Hi took them all in hand and scampered upstairs toward his bedroom, stopping at the stairway, coming back with a huge smile on his face. "Thank you, Barbara. Thank you," he said again, desperately wanting to give her a hug and terrified of doing so. He stammered one more thank you and took off at a dead run for the bedroom.

He was back down in a flash wearing new shirt and trousers, and showing them off to everyone. Sarah made him stand still for a couple of minutes while she examined the stitching. "I could not make a stitch that nice by hand, Barbara. You do beautiful work."

It was a late night, and finally everyone turned in, some to the wagons where a camp had been established. Hi gave up his room to Barbara and slept in the camp near his uncle Moose.

ELAINE, Sarah, and Barbara put out a breakfast that threatened the integrity of the new dining room table, and talk of the future continued through several pots of coffee. "Moose, let's take a little walk," Zeke said. "I think you'll like the way Hi and I have this place set up for spring planting."

Hiram, wearing new canvas work pants and one of the new heavy wool work shirts, joined Zeke and Moose as they headed for the fields that had been turned. "Thank you, Zeke, for giving me a chance to get some of this off my mind. All I really want to do is what's right, but I don't know what is right. I'm confused, and I'm not afraid of saying so."

"You are straddling two very different cultures, Moose. You have the world of the Shoshone, and you have the white man's world, and they are as different as day and night. You have a sense of responsibility that is very strong, and the will to do right. What do you see as the big problem?"

"I have an opportunity that not too many men would get," Moose started, "and it scares me. In the short amount of time I've worked for Mr. Donaldson, I have made some big changes to his mill operation. Good changes, and we have increased our production because of them, still offering an exceptional product. The mill is making good money, and he wants me to be the manager of the Salem mill."

"That doesn't really sound like a problem, Moose. It sounds like a wonderful opportunity."

"It is, Zeke, it is," Moose said, but without the big smile. They had reached one of the areas that would be filled with corn come spring. Moose stooped over and grabbed a handful of rich dirt that had been plowed just a few days before. "It even smells good, Zeke," he said. "I guess what bothers me most is my people back in the mountains.

"What if I make this move with Mr. Donaldson and then find that Slow To Fight needs me, that there are big problems at the village?"

"I've found over the years that I can't make my decisions based on "what if" Moose. Every decision you make for the rest of your life will have a "what if" attached to it. I think what you need to look at is more along the lines of what is best for you in the long run. You know you would be well received at the village and you know you're a very good lumber mill operator.

"No one has ever said that making these kinds of decisions are easy, or are even supposed to be easy. You're young, smart, strong, and capable of about anything you choose to do. You will have to decide what is best for you, understanding the consequences of that kind of decision.

"Being half white and half Shoshone adds another

level to that decision and has to be taken into considera-
tion. Are you leaning one way or the other?"

"Yeah, I guess I am," Moose said, a wry smile playing
across his big face. "I really want that mill to be mine. I
want to design it my way, run it my way, and Donaldson
says I can. I'm just worried I might be letting my people
down. Maybe that's what you mean by letting a "what if"
get in the way.

"I understand," he continued. "I do. What if they need
help two years from now, or what if they don't need help
and I give up the mill to be with them." He kicked some
dirt, picked Hiram up as if he was a sack of corn, and
whirled around two or three times.

"Looks like my new name is Moose Travis, Manager,
Donaldson's Mill, Salem, Oregon Territory."

"Your uncle is a very strong, very intelligent man, and
you can learn a lot from him," Zeke said, when Moose put
the boy back to earth.

"He used to scare me, when I was little, but I'm not
afraid of him anymore. I love him, I love you, Moose,
very much."

ZEKE, Travis, and Johnson spent the next week on business plans for the store, the farm, and the transport
company, while Barbara, Elaine, and Sarah designed
clothing and helped Barbara with her planning. "I'm not
really a part of their planning," Moose said to Hiram one
morning as they were feeding all the animals. "I think
maybe you and I need to do some planning of our own,"
he continued with a wink and a grin.

"We could use some fresh meat, since there are so

many people to feed right now," Hi said back to him, with an equal grin. "I know these mountains around here pretty good now, and there are elk and deer. The bears are black bears, so they aren't scary like the big grizzlies."

It took those two less than an hour to pack up one mule with camp supplies, another to help bring back whatever game they shoot, and horses to ride. Hi and Moose took rifles, shotguns, and their bows and arrows and went deep into the nearby mountains. They each rode a mule or horse, and trailed two.

If there had been other eyes, they would have seen two young Shoshone braves, in buckskin shirts and trousers, moccasins with fancy beadwork, and bows and arrows strapped on their backs. Two happy young men setting off on a hunt.

"The plan," Moose said with a grin, "is not to shoot big deer or elk right away. If we do that, we'll have to come back right away. Let's just have some fun, 'cause it might be the last time we can do this for awhile." Moose had already made up his mind that he would take the position offered by Donaldson, and knew that he wouldn't be able to hunt or fish for a long time.

"It will take months of hard work to get that mill built and operating, Hi. I want some time for you and me to wander through the forest, sit by a fire at night, and eat fresh fish and game that we shoot. We're different, you and me, from all the others down there. We're half Shoshone, and we gotta stick together."

"You're my favorite uncle, Moose," Hi said.

"I'm your only uncle," Moose laughed, wrestling Hi down into deep grass, the two rough-housing like little kids. "Better get camp set up before fun and games,"

Moose finally said, brushing grass and leaves from his buckskins.

They found a little meadow deep in the forest with a stream running through it and pitched camp. After the animals were hobbled and their fire ring built, they brought in wood for the fire, and headed to the creek for some serious fishing.

Hi had his bow as did Moose, and they both had large trout on shore in minutes. "We're just too good," Hi laughed, cleaning the fish. "I'm glad you're going to be staying with us," he said.

"I'll have to stay at the mill, Hi, but you can visit anytime you want, anytime you can get away. From the looks of that farm, you and Zeke are going to be very busy. Is Sarah still giving you lessons to do?"

"Oh, yes," he said. "I'm getting pretty good with my numbers, and I love to read. Papa and Mama take turns reading to each other, every night. I'm getting good enough that I can read to them, too. I don't like Shakespeare too much, but I sure do like Homer."

They held off shooting any large animals until the fifth day when Moose dropped a large elk and Hi killed two large buck deer. "We'll have to pack out in the morning, I'm afraid, Hi. Don't want to spoil all this good meat."

"Having you and everyone else as my family, I'm very happy," Hi said the next morning as they rode back toward the farm. "I will always love my real mother and father, but I love Mama and Papa so much. Papa and I have ridden into Salem several times since we got here, and it isn't really that long a ride.

"Maybe I could come and visit you once in a while, and you can show me around the mill. I'm learning an awful lot about wood and how to form it and bend it, how to make it look so pretty. Papa says I'm going to be a good cabinetmaker, like he is. Have you seen the paneling in my bedroom? Papa let me help him make that."

"Zeke is one hell of a man, Hi. You're a very lucky young man to have him as your Papa. I've watched him work with wood and iron, and if you learn only half of what he knows, you will never go hungry."

They stopped several times on the ride back to shoot turkeys, grouse, and even managed to get some shots at geese as they passed over. "This will fill that larder, even if there are so many people at the house," Hi said with a smile.

SARAH, WITH A TWIN IN EACH ARM, STOOD AT THE TOP OF the stairs on the large porch with Zeke and Hiram, and watched the long wagon train move off down the lane toward the main road leading to Salem. "This has been a long ten days, Sarah, my love," Zeke said, giving her a little peck on the cheek. "You must be worn out."

"I sort of let Mama be grandma and take care of the girls, and I let Barbara be little sister again and take care of kitchen duties, and I spent a lot of time watching," she laughed. "I noticed that you, too, Sharp Knife, let Hi and Moose take care of the animals, and Mr. Johnson and Travis see to it that wood and water were in the house."

"We're evil, Sarah, to the bone," he laughed with her, took one of the twins, and they walked back into the house, heading straight for the kitchen. "I want to sit at this table with you and a hot mug of coffee," he said. "And about three hours of quiet."

"I'll put the twins down for a nap. Hi went out with the mules, so it'll just be us and some peace and quiet," she said. The girls were tired just because the adults had been so busy getting packed and moved, and dropped off to sleep as soon as their heads were on the mattresses.

"Blessed quiet," Zeke said when Sarah came back and poured their coffee. He splashed just a bit of rum in his and sat back with a big smile. "It's probably already snowing at Fort Bridger," he said, "and the trees here are still turning into their gaudy colors. Is your kitchen garden still producing?"

"According to Mrs. O'Brien, my garden should produce for several more weeks. It will take some getting used to this weather, I think," she said. "You will have more to learn than I, what with all that acreage to take care of."

"I've been talking to everyone I know about just that," Zeke said, taking a sip of hot coffee. "O'Brien, Snyder, a couple of fellows I met at Snyder's, and they all say the same thing, it's a long growing season and expect more rain than you've probably seen in other places.

"I asked the whole family if they would spend Christmas with us, Sarah. I should have said something to you first, but they will be so busy getting settled in Salem over the next several weeks, that it would be good for them and for us."

"I'm glad you did. It seems years ago that we celebrated Christmas at Fort Bridger, and it hasn't even been eleven months. What an amazing year, Zeke." She laughed as she poured more coffee for the two of them. "At least this time we'll be prepared for them. That was a shock to see all those wagons and horses coming up the road."

"With our family as large as it is and with this farm being close to everyone, I think I'm going to spend time this winter building some guest facilities. I think it's safe to think that we'll have visitors on a regular basis."

"Since you're now a political figure," she joked, "having the governor sleep on the floor and all, I think that would be a good idea. Out near those old cottonwood trees, a little away from the barns and corrals would be a good place for a guesthouse. It would give our guests a little privacy and we'd still have our home for eating and socializing."

OVER THE NEXT SEVERAL WEEKS, Travis and Johnson expanded Snyder's Emporium by at least three-fold and Elaine found a home not too far away for she and Travis. Johnson built an office in one corner of the Emporium and added a sleeping room off to the side. "Don't need much down here since most of our transport business will be headquartered up north."

The amount of merchandise in the large store was impressive and the folks in Salem flocked to the store, finding something new with every visit. "How did you get all this stuff from Fort Bridger to here?" Snyder asked one day.

"We did bring some of it but I've been buying up surplus from all the wagon trains coming into Oregon City, and then, Mr. Johnson has made one run to California and back, so we added more from that trip.

"You keep a big store like this, full to the rafters, and then when people come in, they see things they never knew they needed or wanted. I love watching people find something new," he laughed.

"I always tried to keep my inventory thin," Snyder said,

"and here you come along and triple the stock. I'm not arguing even a little bit, Travis. You're right, people have been coming in and buying everything. It's wonderful."

Barbara wanted her independence, was almost fierce about it, and found a small home just one block off the main street in the capitol, and not two blocks from what is now being called Capitol City Trading Post and Mercantile, dropping the Emporium name and adding Trading Post for a frontier flare.

The sign out front of Barbara's cottage read simply, Barbara Travis, seamstress, and within days it was obvious that she would have a flourishing business. "I think I have shown every woman and most of the men of Salem my sewing machine. I have enough orders for dresses and shirts to keep me busy all winter." Moose helped her get the cottage arranged properly.

"That girl could change her mind twice while she was changing her mind," he snorted one night at supper. "I tell you, Papa, she is a taskmaster." He said all that with a smile because while she was demonstrating how her machine worked, she sewed two new shirts for him. "I won't wear them out for awhile," he said. "Those seams are so tight, I think the shirts might be waterproof."

"How are the plans coming for the new mill?" Travis asked.

"I'll be moving up there next week," he said. "I put together a crew this week to build a cabin and office for me, and we will start work to finish the mill itself in the next day or so. All that talk I heard about how they had been building a mill was just talk. That's what made old man Donaldson so upset. He thought they really were building that thing.

"I'll be out of your hair, too, and won't have to be riding back and forth all the time. Once the equipment is set up and operating, we'll be able to provide our own building lumber, and sell some, too.

"I told Donaldson that I would be selling lumber before Christmas. All I need is three weeks of fair weather. Rain will slow us down, but not like the snow did at Fort Bridger. A few hours of rain isn't the same as a few feet of snow, and with the steam engine Donaldson sent down, we can cut a lot of timber. I need a few more men, though. All that talk that Zeke faced about immigrants taking work from these locals is nonsense. Half of the men I've hired have already quit, and I've fired many others.

"Many just shirk their responsibility and then complain because I work them too hard. Some show up drunk, or wander in late. I pay a good wage and expect a good day's work," he said.

"I put up a sign at the trading post that you're hiring," Travis said. "This isn't the time to get discouraged. You might remember that Mr. Sullivan talked about this in Oregon City. Zeke and Snyder see big changes coming to Salem in the next months, so just keep at it."

"I'm not discouraged, Papa," Moose said. "I'm thinking of asking Barbara to come up and run the crew," he laughed. "She'd get those pikers moving."

"You're lucky she isn't at the table tonight, Moose," Elaine said, gently swatting him across the shoulders. "When I was there, she said you were going to build on to her cottage?"

"She needs a large room to be able to spread out her material and to take measurements from her customers.

I'm going to extend one of the walls in the front of the building. I've got two men who will have it built in just a few days. She'll be supervising, so I'll stay up at the mill this week."

"How can it possibly be Christmas already?" Sarah asked, bringing a platter of pancakes to the kitchen table. "Have you heard from Mama and Papa? Are Moose and Barbara coming? What about the tree? We don't have any decorations done."

Zeke was laughing along with Hiram, listening to her. "Should we answer those questions one at a time, dearly beloved?" he joked. "The whole family is coming, according to a note that was sent by way of O'Brien, and should be here two days before Christmas. Hi and I picked out our tree yesterday and we're going to cut it and get it up tomorrow.

"We were near the pond, looking for a good fir tree and found that the geese are flying through by the hundreds, using our pond as a stopover. I think a couple of geese, roasted up with some of your good Indian cornmeal dressing would be a good Christmas dinner."

"That would be wonderful," Sarah said. "All the vegetables will be fresh right out of my garden, and Hi and I picked several bushels of wild apples this week, so there will be pie, apple sauce, and baked apples. You do remember my apple pie, don't you, Sharp Knife?"

"Oh, I do, indeed," Zeke said, spearing the last pancake before Hiram could get it. "Something to remember, Hi. If a beautiful girl asks you to a picnic and says she makes really good apple pie, plan on spending the rest of your life with her. She's a keeper," he laughed, getting a friendly swat across the shoulders from Sarah.

Two days before Christmas, about two in the afternoon, Travis and Moose rode up in front of the house. "Elaine and Barbara are right behind us," Travis said. "The buggy is loaded with gifts and food. Merry Christmas," he bellowed.

"He's been singing Christmas carols the whole way out," Moose said. "Hiram, let's go fishing before Barbara gets here and puts us to work." Hi and Moose charged to the barn and grabbed fishing gear and were deep in the willows before anyone could say a word, laughing like little ten-year-olds.

It was just minutes later that the buggy arrived, drawn by two horses and carrying two laughing, singing ladies ready for a holiday. The chaos of the greeting finally calmed down and the group, minus Moose and Hi, gathered around the large kitchen table. "Our first Christmas as a family was held at Fort Bridger, and it was us, and Zeke and Sarah," Travis said. "Just one year later, it's us, and Zeke's rather large family. Three children in one year, Zeke, and look where we are."

"Hi and I shot some geese and a swan, so our Christmas dinner will be completely different than the elk and buffalo we had at Bridger, too," Zeke said. They finished off a pot of coffee and Zeke and Travis stepped away from what was developing into a serious girl-talk at the table.

"My next project," Zeke said, as the two walked back toward a stand of cottonwood trees. "This will be three joined two-bedroom cabins surrounding a main kitchen, for our guests. I should have it finished by spring if the weather isn't too wet and cold.

"How do you like Salem? It must be considerably different than Oregon City."

"For sure it is, Zeke. Oregon City is rough and tumble, while Salem is rather more civilized. Expanding is a good word, too. We have many new people moving in, bringing the latest fads from back east, we have people coming north from California as well, disappointed with gold mining.

"Some of the new people are anxious to make new lives, some seem lost and unwilling to learn about a new life. Moose has had trouble keeping workers on the one hand, Barbara can't find enough time to make as many dresses as are being ordered on the other hand.

"We hear a lot of talk about the new governor and about the legislative session coming up. There seems to be a split among the general public on the question of whether Oregon should become a state. What's your call on that?"

Zeke took a sip of coffee, thinking about that question. "It's been discussed at a couple of our committee meetings, but I think statehood for the territory is some years away. Right now, there are many other questions that would seem to be more important than statehood.

"We're still an import territory, Travis, and we don't have a serious economic base yet. I see agriculture, including of course, fishing, and timber as our main economic drivers, and for that to work, we have to develop markets. You and Johnson are certainly helping with that."

Moose and Hi arrived quietly, listening to Travis and

EZEKIEL'S JOURNEY: ONE MAN'S EPIC JOURNEY TOWAR...

Zeke. Moose joined in though when Zeke brought up lumber as an economic driver. "In almost the same words, that's what old man Donaldson said. He said our timber industry will build the territory into a state. Transportation will be the key to make anything work. You can grow all the corn in the world, Zeke, but if you can't get it to a market, it will just rot.

"Donaldson says the same thing about lumber. We will be milling the finest grades of building material in the west, but we need to build a market for that lumber."

The conversation continued off and on for the entire time that the family was together for the holiday, and Zeke could see strong leadership qualities in Moose. *I'm going to make sure that Moose becomes involved in some of our Territorial Commissions and is involved in the legislative process as well.*

CHRISTMAS DINNER COULD HAVE TAKEN place at the large outdoor patio Zeke had built. Rain the day before cleared, the skies were blue and warm all day, but Sarah wanted it inside. The main table, large to begin with, was extended by adding a second table. There were seven people and enough food for fourteen, according to Travis.

Roast swan and roast goose were the centerpieces, with sweet corn, green beans, and baked winter squash, mashed potatoes, and applesauce spread for passing. Great mounds of hot biscuits and fresh butter made the circuit, and for two hours or more the Travis and Hawthorne families celebrated Christmas.

The little girls, old enough to eat solid food, had been fed early and worn out from all the attention given out by a grandmother and an aunt, were sound asleep through dinner. Sarah woke them and had them in her arms as everyone settled in the living room, near a large tree decorated with the combined flamboyance of Hiram and Barbara. Travis pretended to be Santa and handed boxes and packages out to everyone.

The little twins giggled and laughed when Travis sang several songs, demanding that everyone join him, and they finally just gave out. Sarah tucked them back in their little beds and rejoined the party. "Let's make a vow that we will celebrate Christmas as a family every year. Too often in the past, people have been missing."

A huge breakfast was served the next morning, the buggy was filled with more than they had brought, the team hitched, and with Moose and Travis leading the way, mounted on their horses, the Salem branch of the family headed home. "This was wonderful, Sarah. We will do this every year," Elaine said for her goodbye.

"I LEFT my farm in Missouri in 1851, Sarah, and found Fort Bridger, you, and a whole new family by 1852." Zeke said one night, a couple of days after the big party. "Now, here it is almost 1853 and we're settled on six hundred forty acres of good Oregon soil, we have a creek that runs right through the property that I have set up for irrigating, we have three beautiful children, and a vista full of prospects.

"I've never felt better about life, never felt more secure or comfortable." They were in their large bed on the second floor of the new farmhouse, listening to rain pelt the cedar shake roof and drive furiously onto windows.

"They have their type of gold in California," Zeke said, quietly, "and we are listening to our kind of gold right now."

"I overheard you and Hiram talking about crops yesterday. You said you were thinking about making some changes. What kind of changes?"

"I've spent a great deal of time talking with O'Brien and Snyder about weather and crops. They have been in this country for several years, and my thoughts about grains might not work so well. I'm still very much planning on large tracts of corn, but I think we will do better with different varieties of beans to go along with our wheat.

"There's always a market for beans and corn, and Snyder tells me that vine beans thrive in this country. Wheat has been a mainstay for some time, as well.

"Sullivan has purchased some property near the river just south of Salem and he's going to build a brewery, a large one. He will need hops and barley, and they should both grow well here. I've already signed the contract for hops. If he expands his brewery into a distillery, he'll need corn. We've talked about that as well.

"O'Brien is looking to expand his cattle ranch, incorporate a feedlot and slaughter house since he's so close to the river, he'll have transportation for meat into Salem, Eugene, and north into Oregon City. Even across the Columbia into Fort Vancouver. He will be buying a lot of corn from our fields."

"We've come a long way, Sharp Knife," she said, snuggling deep into his arms. "I'm a very happy woman."

The sound of the rain pelting the roof and windows was as a symphony, putting them to a deep and comfortable sleep. The last thing Zeke heard as sleep took over, was Sarah saying, "I want at least one more child." The smile was still on his face when morning light flooded the bedroom.

"I think now would be a good time to start working on that idea of yours," he whispered, snaking an arm around Sarah's neck and pulling her close. "I think your idea is a wonderful way to celebrate the new year, our new life." He pulled her close, kissed her gently and whispered, "I love my little Hummingbird."

A LOOK AT EZEKIEL'S OREGON
(EZEKIEL'S JOURNEY BOOK II)

Ezekiel's Journey continues as he and the family settle on their homestead and begin the hard work of developing a farm. There is a movement afoot to bring Oregon into the union and Zeke is one of those promoting the idea. He discovers his leadership ability and is elected to the Oregon Territorial Legislature.

It's not all roses for the intrepid adventurer as he finds strong opposition to statehood coming from those that want Oregon as a slave state, and those that are dead set against the welcoming of more immigrants.

Rumblings of Indian problems for the thousands that will travelling the Oregon Trail are addressed as well. Oregon Territory stretches from the Pacific Ocean to the Continental Divide. Can such a large area even be governed? Maybe break some off?

AVAILABLE NOW FROM JOHNNY GUNN AND WOLFPACK PUBLISHING

ABOUT THE AUTHOR

Reno, Nevada novelist, Johnny Gunn, is retired from a long career in journalism. He has worked in print, broadcast, and Internet, including a stint as publisher and editor of the Virginia City Legend. These days, Gunn spends most of his time writing novel length fiction, concentrating on the western genre. Or, you can find him down by the Truckee River with a fly rod in hand.

Gunn and his wife, Patty, live on a small hobby farm about twenty miles north of Reno, sharing space with a couple of horses, some meat rabbits, a flock of chickens, and one crazy goat.